What the critics are saying…

"Kelly is back with her usual uplifting erotic romance, this time with a liberal dash of Irish magic tossed in to sweeten the pot." ~ *Ann Leveille, Sensual Romance/The Best Reviews*

"Sahara Kelly has crafted a short story that will delight readers with its magic." ~ *Amanda, Fallen Angel Reviews*

"IRISH ENCHANTMENT is three tales of love, each featuring a wee bit of the paranormal....does fate have a plan for Fay and Aidan? Ms. Kelly has written a delightful paranormal novella in Harpist Bizarre." ~ *Denise Powers, Sensual Romance*

"Strong characters and contemporary concerns play a backdrop in STITCHES IN TIME, [a] tale of unexpected pleasure...With an evocative setting and strong, interesting characters, Hunter starts off this anthology with a bang." ~ *Ann Leveille, Sensual Romance Reviews*

"SECRET SUBMISSION is one of the best … BDSM [novels dealing] with romance. I will be looking for Ms Hunter's other novels." ~ *Patricia McGrew, Sensual Romance Reviews*

"I've got to admit, TABLE FOR FOUR had me from the moment it started.... Diana Hunter has truly out done herself with this book." ~ Cyn Witkus, In The Library Reviews

"Hot, hot, hot best characterizes this friends-turned-lovers story by St. Clare. The chemistry between her characters is intense and the sex scenes smoke." ~ *Ann Leveille Courtesy Sensual Romance Reviews*

"The love scenes between Kit and Jax are breathtaking and scorch the pages. *Tielle St Clare* writes forthright and passionate scenes that are ripe with steamy sex as well as deep emotions." ~ *Amanda at Fallen Angel Reviews*

Irish Enchantment

Diana Hunter

Sahara Kelly

&

Tielle St. Clare

IRISH ENCHANTMENT
An Ellora's Cave Publication, March 2005

Ellora's Cave Publishing, Inc.
1337 Commerce Drive Suite #13
Stow, Ohio 44224

ISBN #1419950762

STITCHES IN TIME Copyright © 2004 Diana Hunter
HARPIST BIZARRE Copyright © 2004 Sahara Kelly
KISSING STONE Copyright © 2004 Tielle St. Clare
Other available formats: ISBN MS Reader (LIT), Adobe (PDF), Rocketbook (RB), Mobipocket (PRC) & HTML

ALL RIGHTS RESERVED. This book may not be reproduced in whole or in part without permission.

This book is a work of fiction and any resemblance to persons, living or dead, or places, events or locales is purely coincidental. They are productions of the authors' imagination and used fictitiously.

Edited by: *Pamela Campbell and Briana St. James*
Cover art by: *Christine Clavel*

Warning:

The following material contains graphic sexual content meant for mature readers. *Irish Enchantment* has been rated *E-rotic* by a minimum of three independent reviewers.

Ellora's Cave Publishing offers three levels of Romantica™ reading entertainment: S (S-ensuous), E (E-rotic), and X (X-treme).

S-*ensuous* love scenes are explicit and leave nothing to the imagination.

E-*rotic* love scenes are explicit, leave nothing to the imagination, and are high in volume per the overall word count. In addition, some E-rated titles might contain fantasy material that some readers find objectionable, such as bondage, submission, same sex encounters, forced seductions, etc. E-rated titles are the most graphic titles we carry; it is common, for instance, for an author to use words such as "fucking", "cock", "pussy", etc., within their work of literature.

X-*treme* titles differ from E-rated titles only in plot premise and storyline execution. Unlike E-rated titles, stories designated with the letter X tend to contain controversial subject matter not for the faint of heart.

Contents

Prologue
~9~

Stitches in Time
By Diana Hunter
~21~

Harpist Bizarre
By Sahara Kelly
~119~

Kissing Stone
By Tielle St. Clare
~241~

Prologue

The early morning mist swirled damply around Bantry Mac Murchadha's knees, adding to his misery. He hated having wet stuff clinging to his solid legs, and he trudged along the narrow path with a frown.

It was all his dratted nephew's fault. If the lad could stay sober more than one night in a row, Bantry's problems would be cleft in two at least, if not removed completely.

He'd already had to offer one of his best sows to Old Naoise, a man who obviously didn't understand the high jinks of youth. Personally, Bantry had thought the blue pig had a certain eye appeal, and the berry-dye would surely fade over time, but Old Naoise wasn't having any of it.

Bantry snorted. Ruined, the man had blustered. Fair ruined. The piglets wouldn't nurse, and what could a man do with twelve squealing hungry mouths?

Then there were the girls. Giggling, simpering, tossing their hair, enough to drive an old man mad, let alone a young one like Aodhgan. All that flesh exposed with a flip of the skirts or a tug of the shifts—what was the world coming to?

And now, the latest problem.

It was jangling and thumping into Bantry's spine.

He shifted the heavy bag on his broad shoulders and muttered an oath. This one was going to take some thinking.

His steps took him to the very edge of the world.

The mist thinned and the first fingers of dawn showed Bantry the roiling sea that curled and smashed itself against the craggy rocks far below. Surprisingly, there was no wind this morning, and Bantry sniffed the air, letting the tang of the salt spray mingle with the scent of the damp earth beneath his feet.

His stomach rumbled, reminding him he'd not yet broken his fast.

He had to do something, but was *this* the right thing to do?

With a grunt, he lowered his burden to the ground. The sacking fell free and Bantry stood staring at the contents it revealed.

Aodhgan had gone and done it now, all right. He'd spent the evening drinking and the nighttime thieving with his cronies, careless of where they went or what they took.

Bantry had known the instant he set eyes on them, that these were not mere trinkets. He thanked the Gods that it had been him to stumble over the sack in the hallway and not his wife. She'd have set up a screech louder than a Banshee.

No, it was on his shoulders. He was responsible for the lad, and it was up to him to fix this mess.

He looked out over the ocean again.

Could he do it? Could he just lace up the sack and toss it over the cliffs, letting Cliodna, Goddess of the Seas, whisk it away to Tuatha? The Land of Promise? Would she tell?

He struggled with the question, and sat down with a thump on the grass next to the untidy burlap.

There were three items reflecting the rays of the rising sun. Cautiously he picked up the first, a piece of rock. Nothing so special to a drunken youth's eyes, he supposed, but here, in the quiet stillness of the dawn, it was easy to see the power shimmering around it, like a soft green film of dew.

Just holding it warmed his hand, and a slight tremor shook him as he fought off some tendrils of magic that swirled into his mind.

Carefully, he wiped a little mud off it and set it aside.

Next to appear was a frayed piece of cloth. The colors were bright and clear, but the edges were ripped...it looked as if it had been torn carelessly from a larger piece.

A tapestry. And a very fine one.

Bantry wished he could see the whole. The piece he held in his hand was striking enough to make him blink.

A little green man had been embroidered in the smallest of stitches, correct in every detail, down to his buckled boots.

Bantry glanced down. Boots very like his own.

But on the tapestry, this little man leaned casually against the bole of an aged tree. A rock rested grandly nearby.

The picture was vivid, the face of the little man alive with interest, and Bantry would very much like to have shaken the hand of the talented woman who'd created it.

'Twould be hard indeed to throw it over the cliff.

The last item was larger than the first two, and Bantry sighed as he pulled it free.

It was a harp. Two strings were broken, and one of the levers didn't work very well, but Bantry allowed himself the privilege of running his fingers cautiously over the remaining strings.

They were finely tuned and the chord they produced charmed the very sun into the morning sky. Once again, Bantry let his hand touch the harp, stilling its song.

The sound died softly into the morning air, and Bantry shivered at the stillness that followed.

Not even the waves so far beneath him could break it.

"Good morrow to you, Bantry Mac Murchadha."

Bantry jumped at least two handlengths into the air, coming down hard on his well-padded bum.

"Great Morrigàn," he swore.

"Not quite."

It was a woman, an older woman by the look of her, swathed in ratty shawls and standing between him and the rising sun.

Somehow he couldn't quite make out her features, though he squinted and held his hand up to shield his eyes.

"You scared the japes out of me, woman."

She ignored his comment and bent her head to study his little cache of goods.

Uncomfortably, Bantry stood, aware that she towered above him. He'd heard of those whose height surpassed his people's, but this was the first time he'd met one.

"Been busy, have you?" She nudged the sacking with her foot. A very elegant and highly arched foot, too, noticed Bantry. A very sensual foot.

In spite of himself, he felt the beginnings of arousal. All for a foot. He blinked, and forced his thoughts away from those shapely toes. He was too old for that kind of thing. At least he'd thought he was.

He squinted at the woman again, trying to see her face more clearly. It was no good. The sun was fully up now, blinding him every time he tried to look her in the eyes.

"Don't worry, little man. I'll not harm you. Tell me of your treasures."

Bantry found his voice. "I...I..." he stuttered.

"Don't lie, Bantry. I'll know it," she warned.

Who was she?

His mouth opened and the truth stumbled out. He told her how his nephew was a trial and wouldn't be listening to Bantry or his wife when they warned him that he'd only end up going bad.

He even told her of the last night's doings, the drinking and the petty thievery.

He finished with a sigh. "This is what I found, lady. And you don't have to tell me they're something special, because I can sense that for myself."

"Bright of you," she murmured, kneeling down next to the sack. "These are indeed powerful morsels. Each has magic in it, Bantry. Can you feel it?"

Bantry gazed at the lock of golden hair that had fallen free of her shawl. "Aye, lady," he whispered.

"'Tis possible they come from the home of Cailleach, Bantry. Know you of whom I speak?"

Bantry's skin turned to ice. Cailleach, the Crone. Not someone to be crossed.

"Oh, please, lady…help me. If it is indeed true that these belong to Cailleach, I fear for my family. And myself too," he added in a burst of honesty.

She stood and turned to the sun, stretching her arms out in a wide embrace and letting the warmth fall on her face.

As she did so, her rough clothing fell away, and Bantry gasped at the beauty it revealed.

Surpassing all others, she was a goddess. Truly a goddess.

He fell to his knees and bowed his head. "Cliodna," he whispered.

"Well done, Bantry. Right first time." She laughed, a joyous sound that made Bantry's heart leap right along with it. Now he understood why so many men would risk death to love this woman in her mortal form.

"'Tis fortunate I happened upon you, Bantry," she smiled. "I will have to leave this world, soon, I know, but it has offered me many pleasures. Ones I will miss when I return to my father's realm."

Her eyes turned briefly to the sea and Bantry caught a look of distress in them.

But then she shrugged her shoulders and threw off her saddening thoughts.

"However, my problems are not yours. Let us think on this for a moment."

Casually she sat down cross-legged on the grass next to the sack and concentrated on the three items spread before her.

Bantry goggled. Then he surreptitiously pinched himself. Just to make sure he really was sitting on a cliff top next to the most beautiful naked woman in the world, who was really the Goddess Cliodna.

Ouch. Yes. He really was.

She snapped her fingers, and Bantry felt his bladder weaken. If she did that again, he'd wet himself for sure.

"I have it, Bantry. Will you undertake a wee journey on my behalf?"

"Um…a wee journey?"

Visions of flying through the clouds on some mythical beast or venturing to the Land of Promise without his breakfast dashed through his mind.

She smiled. "Yes, a wee journey. These artifacts can be put to better use in other places and other times."

Bantry struggled to understand, cursing beneath his breath. Perhaps Goddesses should come with some kind of translation servant, because he sure as sod couldn't understand what she was talking about.

Cliodna sighed. "Listen well, Bantry. There are three people for whom these things can be of use. These items will bring…their heart's desires. Love. Passion. All the things that I…" she paused for moment.

Bantry held his breath.

"…That I will have to leave soon. 'Twould please me to know that I have left a legacy behind me. Will you take these to the right people, no matter where the road leads?"

Bantry nodded. Of course he would. Besides, who was going to say "no" to a Goddess? And a naked one at that.

"Good." She stood and pulled the shawls around her, giving Bantry a chance to recover a portion of his vision. To say her beauty had blinded him was horribly close to the truth.

"You'll have the power to create a little shop for yourself, Bantry. And the knowledge to make it fit wherever it needs to be. My magic will assure you of the skills you'll need. Find the right customer, match them to the right artifact, and your job will be done."

"And Cailleach?" The words came out on a whimper.

So he wasn't brave. He wasn't dead yet, either, and hoped to stay that way.

"I'll take care of her. You do your job, and I'll do mine. Then I can leave knowing that I'll not be forgotten."

"Forgotten? *You*?" Bantry's tone was incredulous.

She smiled at him. "Finish the work I've assigned you, my friend and you shall return here to this very moment. No one will know but you and I. But you'd best keep a closer watch on that damn nephew of yours."

She leaned down towards him and Bantry's senses swam as her fragrance filled his nostrils. He felt her lips brush his cheek and suddenly his loins exploded with fire and his balls ached. Her slightest touch was igniting things he'd prefer remain unlit.

He pulled away on a gasp, fighting the urge to cover the bulge in his breeches with his hands.

Cliodna laughed. "Safe travels, Bantry. And good luck be with you..."

Bantry blinked.
She'd gone.

Stitches in Time

Diana Hunter

Chapter One

"Eight-hundred- eighty-one Euros? Did I hear you right?" Liam Finnerty couldn't quite believe his ears. That tiny scrap of a tapestry—torn from a much larger work, frayed, stained with who knows what, and not much bigger than an oversized postcard—cost how much? "That's over a thousand U.S. dollars!"

"I know. You don't need to make such a big deal of it." Maggie's exasperated sigh could be heard throughout the antique store. "This is all that's left of the castle tapestry. Look, out of the entire picture, only the lucky leprechaun is left. All I said was that was that it wasn't a lot to pay for a piece that old."

Liam Finnerty looked at the petite woman beside him and wondered for the millionth time just why he needed to bring her to Ireland with him on this trip. Liam hadn't exactly been given much say in the matter; Maggie was the boss's daughter and he was expected to teach her his job. But still. The woman had done little but sit in surly silence on the plane all the way across the ocean, and, since their arrival in Dublin, had done little but complain. Sure, she was cute, with deep brown eyes a man could fall into and never want to find his way out again. Sure, the woman had auburn hair that glinted with golden highlights, but she kept it curled tight in that damn knot. How was a man to know whether it was long or short? And sure, she had a figure that looked terrific in the tailored suits she always wore; she even managed to make low-heeled, sensible shoes look sexy. But Maggie Andrew's alabaster skin came wrapped in an invisible shell of professionalism that, so far, Liam Finnerty had been unable to crack.

Maggie Andrews might be the daughter of the company president, but she prided herself on the fact that she had worked her way up through the rungs of corporate life. Her father told her she would take over the company when he retired, but that a good leader knew every single aspect of the business and learning Liam's job had been the next rung she needed to climb. When her father told her she needed to accompany the overbearing man to the Emerald Isles, however, she almost quit right there. Yes, he was incredibly handsome, with broad, muscular shoulders hidden under his custom-made Italian suit. She noticed the jet-black hair that curled around his ears and piercing blue eyes that saw through her every trick, every shortcut she tried to make in doing the job. He was as bad as her father in that way, never letting her get away with doing anything other than her best.

"Maggie, me dear, you get paid a salary—you buy it if you want it so badly." Liam decided he was not about to be pushed around by the boss's daughter—no matter how cute she was. He was not in the habit of buying expensive presents for women he barely knew. And he already knew this one as much as he wanted to.

"You're as American as I am, so you can stop affecting the Irish accent," she shot back at him, her anger building. "I'm not asking you to buy it for me. And for your information, I do not get paid for what I do. My father is old school; believing I should live at home, learn the job, and take over the business when he's good and ready to leave it to me."

She hadn't meant to sound so bitter. Truth was, if her older brother hadn't been killed in that motorcycle accident, she would have already gone on to a career of her own choosing. Forced by her sense of familial obligation to set aside her dreams and instead learn the business, she had mastered every level in the company, while still on an allowance. Yes, it was a generous allowance, but her father insisted that she not receive a paycheck. That was a direct result of Thomas' spending habits—and his death. Tom had lived hard and played hard, and had died as a result. Now his sister paid the price. On an allowance of $1000 per month, Maggie could not afford such an extravagance as this wonderful piece of art.

"Never mind." Maggie turned and stalked away. She didn't want Liam Finnerty to see her frustration and anger with her father—it wasn't professional. Neither were the tears that threatened to fall. In another place and another time, Liam would have been someone she would have wanted to get to know in more than a professional sense. But her commitment to her father and to the company left little room for romantic entanglements. Her jaw in a hard line, she walked to the other end of the store to put as much distance as she could between herself and the man she was forced to work with.

"Now can't ye see the poor girl's hurtin'?"

Liam turned, prepared to blast the wizened old proprietor for sticking his nose in where it didn't belong, except the aisle behind him was empty. Frowning, he turned in a circle, trying to determine who had spoken.

"Sure, an' ye can't see what's in front of yer nose. Lookin' down from that great height, I suppose. Probably miss most of us little folk 'cause ye're always lookin' only at what's right in front of ye, 'stead of bendin' down to see what's hidden in plain sight."

Liam looked toward his shoes, half expecting a fairy he didn't believe in to appear before his eyes. But no dwarf, real or imagined appeared to bedevil him. A loud snort of laughter made him peer at the tapestry again, the colors bright in the dim light of the antique shop. He jumped back when the cloth leprechaun waved at him.

"Fine, strappin' boy ye are!" The little man took Liam's measure even as the American stared at the impossible.

"You're not really talking to me. I only had that one cup of Irish coffee when we got off the plane, but the whiskey in Ireland is known to be strong. That's it, just a wee bit too much whiskey." He rubbed his eyes. "My God, the woman was right, I *am* beginning to talk like one of them and we've only been in the country two hours!"

"That's 'cause Ireland is the country in yer blood, boy-o. I couldn't talk to ye if it weren't."

"I'm going crazy, that's what it is. Stress. Stress and that blasted woman!"

"Ah, yes, and a beauty ye've got there as well. But a bit of a temper, I see." Liam watched in amazement as the leprechaun sighed and crossed his arms, leaning against the bole of a tree. The leaves overhead had been ripped off when the piece was torn away; in fact, all that remained was the outside border on two sides, a rock, the tree—and the saucy-looking leprechaun.

"She's not mine, thank you very much." Of course, that hadn't been for a lack of trying on his part. The woman made his fingers itch to rip off that hard shell of hers, to break the professionalism she hid behind. That little slip of the tongue there—about not being paid? He hadn't known that. 'Course it was easy to see why she'd agree to such an arrangement; the woman stood to be very rich when she inherited the company from Daddy. Still, Liam knew she maintained her own apartment outside the city; that showed an independent spirit. Still, it galled him to find out she was worse off financially than he was, president's daughter or not.

"Ah, I see yer heart has moved a little. That's a good thing, me boy-o, 'cause that's the girl yer goin' to marry!"

Liam's incredulous look was partly because of the absurdity of the leprechaun's statement and partly because he was actually carrying on a conversation with a piece of cloth. The leprechaun grinned and Liam could swear he saw a twinkle in the little man's eyes.

"Oh, face it, man. Ye've undressed that woman so often in yer dreams ye're half-convinced ye already know the sweetness she's covering up."

Liam nodded and then recovered. "Stop it. I am not about to stand here discussing my boss's daughter with a scrap of fabric."

"Ah, the boss's daughter is it? All the better, me boy-o, all the better!" The leprechaun crooked his finger, and before Liam could stop himself he was leaning down to hear what the leprechaun whispered in his ear. "And ye already know I'm more than a scrap of fabric, lad. Ye find the rest of me tapestry, and I'll get you that girl."

"You're serious." Liam stared at the frayed edges; the unique Celtic knot border design would make matching it to its mate easy—if he knew where to look for it. With a start, he shook his head as if coming out of a dream.

"No. I can't believe I'm standing here talking to a leprechaun. Leprechauns don't exist, and neither do talking tapestries. Sorry. This is that Irish coffee talking, that's all. I need to go now."

He turned to leave and took a resolute step forward. Risking a glance backward at the tapestry, his relief was palpable. The small piece of cloth looked just as it had when they had first walked over to it. Quickly he walked away from it, searching for his companion. It was time to leave this place before he fancied the statues talked to him as well.

For several moments he searched the small shop; where could she have gotten? Circling around and weaving through the various items for sale, he stopped short when he finally found her. She was standing before that blasted piece of cloth again, her slender finger brushing along the frayed edges, a faraway look in her deep brown eyes. In an unguarded moment, the mask of the professional woman had slipped, revealing a creature of poetic beauty underneath. Maggie's face had softened, the hard stress lines had disappeared. Sadness emanated from her very soul and Liam recognized her yearning as a longing for something out of her reach.

But even as he watched, she transformed again, her hand dropping to her side and her posture becoming ramrod straight once more. He saw the president's daughter take a deep breath and raise her chin, although he thought he detected a slight hesitation as she did so. With a final wistful little smile at the piece of fabric, the thoroughly professional woman turned away from it, her eyes searching the store for him.

Liam bent down quickly, his heart beating hard. Could he ever hope to break that tough hide of hers that encased such a vulnerable heart? Was it something he even wanted to try? The leprechaun's words came back to him: "You find the rest of me tapestry and I'll get ye that girl." Well, he still thought that coffee had been way too strong for his American system, but if she wanted that scrap of cloth, he'd buy it for her if only to see the woman inside her once more.

Maggie had wandered out of the shop in her search for Liam, obviously getting more and more frustrated with not finding him. That suited him just fine. Grabbing the tapestry from the wall, he ignored the tinkle of laughter that emanated from between his fingers and gave the cloth and his credit card to the proprietor. The sale seemed to make the man very happy; Liam briefly wondered if the old man behind the counter heard the leprechaun's voice as well. Liam was not about to embarrass himself by asking.

Arranging to have the tapestry delivered to the hotel did not take long and then Liam sauntered out of the store, his hands in his pockets and whistling an Irish tune. He knew his nonchalance would bother her and so he took his time to make her wait for him.

Impatient, Maggie stood outside the door tapping her foot. Part of her was curious about what he had found to purchase in that place, but she was not about to ask. She never should have drawn his attention to that tapestry to begin with.

"It's been long enough, our rooms should be ready at the hotel." Not looking to see if he even followed, Maggie turned on her heel and stalked off down the street.

The trip over the ocean had been unusual in that they had landed in Dublin almost an hour ahead of schedule, which, in turn, meant their rooms at the hotel were not ready. After blistering the manager and leaving their luggage, she had resigned herself to spending more time in the company of her traveling companion. Among the single women in the company, she knew Liam was considered a true catch, and she could not deny the man's attractiveness. But she had a job to do and was not about to let her own personal desires get in the way of learning what she was here to learn. Still she had been grateful for Liam's suggestion that they spend their unexpected gift of time exploring the block rather than just sitting in the lobby waiting for their rooms.

Now, however, she just wanted a long soak in a hot bath.

Liam let her lead the way, content to walk a few steps behind her and enjoy the view. Oh, but he would love to get his hands on that fine, firm ass of hers. Even though her jacket always partially covered that delicious fullness, Liam let his mind imagine how those twin cheeks must taper to her waist. Daddy's little girl may or may not be a virgin—she had spent several years away from home while going to college—but he doubted anyone had as yet taken that ass the way it cried out to be taken.

But his was not the only appreciative glance Maggie received. The hotel was only around the corner, yet Liam saw at least three men looking their fill at the swing in her backyard. He grinned. She might choose to ignore the sexpot inside her, but that part of her had ways of making itself known. When one of the men moved up close to Maggie, however, Liam's protective shield locked into place without conscious thought. Lengthening his stride, he closed the distance between the two of them and put his arm around her waist.

She stopped dead in the street and he was hard pressed to push her forward. He did *not* like the look in the predator's eye. "Just come along, dear. The hotel is right here." He almost shoved her through the building's quaint revolving door, turning to eyeball the man who had been about to approach Maggie. The man grinned, nodded, and continued on his way. With a glare, Liam turned and walked his half circle around to meet a very angry Maggie in the lobby.

"Just what do you think you're doing?" Her face red with embarrassment and anger, Maggie had to work to keep her voice from echoing throughout the establishment.

"Now hold on. There was a man who was going to pick your pocket." Liam paused to let his gaze wander along her curves. She had no pockets in the trim suit she wore. "Or steal you purse."

"Liam Finnerty, I can take care of a purse snatcher and I don't need you to protect me. I am perfectly capable of handling myself." Maggie tugged her jacket back into place and smoothed her hair back into its knot. Scowling, she marched up to the registration desk. "Are our rooms ready yet?"

Again, her voice was harsher than she meant it to be. When had she become so uptight? It was that blasted scrap from the old tapestry, that was what it was. It brought to the surface all the dreams she had buried long ago. She was a grown-up now and her family expected her to behave as one. Maggie knew she should rephrase her question to the man behind the counter and she made an effort to still her anger and soften her voice. "Excuse me." Plastering a smile onto her face, she poured sugar into her voice and asked again. "I would like to be shown to my room now. Ms. Andrews." At the man's blank look, she added, "I have a reservation here. Ms. Maggie Andrews?"

A nervous man by nature, the concierge's weak smile did not please Maggie in the least. Her eyes narrowed as the man fussed with the papers on his side of the high desk. Liam sauntered over, deciding that getting into another argument with Miss-High-And-Mighty right now wasn't worth it. They had two weeks in the Emerald Isle and so far, the time felt like it was a lifetime sentence. Still, why wasn't the manager answering her?

"What's the matter, man? Are our rooms ready or aren't they? My secretary made the reservation. One room for Miss Andrews, another for me—check under Liam Finnerty."

"According to our records, Mr. Finnerty, there is a room reserved for you—only." The man's Adam's apple bounced as he swallowed and looked at Maggie as if he expected an eruption. Earlier, he had been on the receiving end of her tongue when the rooms were not prepared for their early arrival. It was only after the couple had gone for their walk that the man discovered only one room had been reserved.

But Maggie did not erupt. She got quiet. Deadly quiet. "Then get on the phone and find me a room in another hotel. Now."

"I'm sorry, Madam, but I have already tried. We pride ourselves on our service and I have called every hotel in the city. There are no rooms in any of the better hotels. Even the motels are filled. It is St. Patrick's Day, day after tomorrow, after all."

"Well, I am not going sleep in the street!" Her voice broke and her pleasant demeanor cracked wide open. Between the stress of the flight over, seeing the tapestry in the little shop, and being forced to accompany a man who hated her, she was tired, cranky and the dam was about to burst.

"How many beds are in the room reserved for me?" Liam could see the floodwaters rising. Let her be mad at him rather than this poor old sot who was obviously scared of the petite woman beside him. Her glare at him was hot enough to melt iron, yet he steadfastly ignored her.

"There is only one bed, sir. It is a queen size bed, but there is only one in the room." The man sidled toward Liam as if for protection.

"I am not going to sleep in your bed, Mr. Finnerty. Try again." She crossed her arms, narrowing her eyes and glowering.

Liam sighed and turned again to the flustered man. "Is there a cot in the place that could be sent up?" He turned to the angry woman. "I'm not much in favor of sharing a room with you either, but you can have the bed and I'll take the cot."

"Sorry, sir, no cot."

"So much for your chivalry." Maggie tossed her head as if daring him to respond to her tart answer.

But Liam just shrugged. "We'll take it. Have the lady's bags sent up along with mine."

"What? We will not...Leave those bags right where they are—"

But the manager had his answer. The shrew was this poor man's problem now. Ignoring her, he signaled to the bellhop to do as he had been told. Maggie was outnumbered.

* * * * *

Considering the amount of money the company was paying for this room, it certainly wasn't very big. The bellhop led them in, depositing the two suitcases and two carry-ons at the foot of a beautiful, four-poster queen-sized bed. It was the old-fashioned kind, with drapes hanging to the sides of the bed, drawn back against the posts. Squeezing himself between the luggage and the wall, the boy opened the drapes, letting the sun in to light up the tiny room. Only then could they see the Celtic dragons carved into the wooden headboard.

Between the far side of the bed and the wall with the window there was just enough room for one person to walk. Sitting on that edge of the bed to put on one's shoes wasn't an option. Not unless that person wanted to sit with his head out the window while doing it.

The near side had quite a bit more room—enough for the ornate dresser that sat beside it and doubled as a nightstand. A small door facing the bed led to the bath, the bellhop explained. The place spoke of a previous era and a certain quaintness—which was the polite way of saying the hotel was old and out of date.

Maggie let Liam tip the bellhop—it was his room, after all. Of course, she would probably find it on his expense account when they returned. All right, maybe she was being unfair. But she was in no mood to think pleasant thoughts about anyone. Unwrapping her scarf and shrugging out of her coat, she dropped both onto the bed and then peeked into the bath.

A wonderfully large, claw-footed, porcelain tub took up most of the room. The bedroom, decorated in nondescript beige, paled in comparison to the dusty rose and burgundy scheme of the bath. A pedestal sink just barely large enough to wash one's face, and a white toilet with a flowered seat cover squeezed into the tiny space that remained. No showerhead poked out of the wall; no curtain enclosed the tub. Maggie checked the door—the sliding bolt would serve to protect her privacy.

Liam closed the door to their tiny boudoir, clicking the lock home as he did so. A small closet behind the door held a few coat hangers, but was otherwise empty. The initial plan called for the two of them to remain in Dublin, meeting with potential clients for two days before moving out to several other Irish cities—that gave them three nights together in the hotel. He sighed and felt the tension gathering in his shoulders.

The water was already running in the bathroom as, in two long strides, he crossed the distance from the door along the short corridor and into the room proper. His jaw set when he saw her coat thrown on the bed and he stepped into the bath to tell her to hang it up. But the words died on his tongue.

Maggie had turned the water on to begin filling the tub; her back was to the bathroom door. As Liam watched, her slender fingers reached up behind her to loosen the tight bun at the crown of her head. She pulled out one, two, three pins and shook her head to loosen her hair. It cascaded down, a river of auburn waves. With her head thrown back, she sighed and ran her fingers from her temples back through her hair, combing out the tension the day had wrought in her psyche. Her arms stretched to either side and as she lowered them and brought her head up a yawn escaped.

How many times had he dreamed of watching that hair fall? Graceful curls fell from her shoulders beyond the middle of her back. He longed to run his fingers through that mass, to feel its silky softness caress his chest, his stomach, his…

She started to turn and Liam quickly backed away. For the second time in a day, he had caught her in an unguarded moment and the sight took his breath away. By the time she reentered the bedroom, he had moved to the tiny closet to hang up his own coat.

Without a word, Maggie picked up her overcoat and waited until he'd cleared the corridor. There wasn't room for two people, at least, not unless they knew each other very well. And she had no intention of getting to know Liam Finnerty any better than she already knew him. As she passed him, she glared at him as if to dare him to say anything about her unbound hair.

Liam knew better than to bite. Instead, he opened his own suitcase and called out to her. "I'll take the bottom two drawers and you can have the top two."

Maggie eyed him with suspicion; he was being nice to her. What was he plotting? She hung her coat beside his, being sure to leave plenty of room between the two. Shaking her head at her own childish foolishness, she took the three steps back to the bedroom proper.

At least the man was efficient. She watched in silence as he took out his carefully folded shirts and set them on the bed. Her suitcase already lay on the bed, ready to be opened. She distinctly remembered the bellhop putting them on the floor. Her eyes narrowed again. Why was he being so nice to her? What was his game?

"Thank you for putting my suitcase in such easy reach, Mr. Finnerty." The sweetness dripped from her voice as she simpered over to the bed and unzipped the case. She gave him a coy smile and batted her lashes at him for good measure to be sure he got the point.

He did. Damn woman. A scowl crossed his features as he sought to regain the upper hand. "Don't let that tub overflow in there or it's you who will be paying the hotel bill."

"I'm paying it anyway," she shot back. "Or did you forget you charged the room to your expense account?"

He had. Damn her again. Slamming the drawer shut, he opened his mouth to blast her. A knock at the door, however, saved her from the blistering he had been about to deliver.

Maggie didn't wait to see who was at the door. She collected her kit from her bag and headed into the bath. Tempted as she was to slam the door on his insufferable attitude, she heard the bellhop's voice and decided discretion was the better course. Closing it gently but firmly, she locked the door and sighed.

The steam from the hot water had already filled the room and Maggie took another deep breath, letting the moist air fill her lungs and cleanse her of the tension she carried. A third breath left her entire body sagging against the door as the 'professional woman' mask fell away.

She felt defeated today. The plane ride over had been a nightmare, having been forced to endure the company of that man. As she tested the water, Maggie tried to determine just why the two of them had taken such a dislike to one another—and why she was so attracted to him in spite of that dislike. The water was perfect. With a deft twist, she turned off the faucets, then opened a small bottle she had brought with her. Pouring in a small amount of liquid soap, she recapped it and took off her no-nonsense business suit before swishing her hand around in the water to make the bubbles foam.

Only a few bubbles today. While submersing herself in a tub filled to the brim with opalescent globes was her favorite way to relax, her practical side had packed only a small bottle of her favorite bubble bath. One thing her father's financial decree had taught her was the value of small luxuries.

Feeling slightly hedonistic, Maggie dropped her clothes on the floor; her frugal nature usually dictated a more careful handing of the few expensive pieces she allowed herself. But the hell with it. She was stuck in a perfectly beautiful country, in a wonderfully quaint little hotel room, with the most rude, obnoxious, and gorgeous man to walk the earth. She might as well enjoy her time in the bath.

A wicked thought made her grin. In here, she would have the privacy denied her by the hotel's mistake. Liam Finnerty might be a cad, but he wouldn't come in here while she was bathing. Stepping into the hot water and sinking down into the bubbles, she moaned in delight with the combined relaxing of her muscles and the realization that, at the moment, she had the upper hand.

For several moments, she let her mind wander as her body adjusted to the temperature of the water. Closing her eyes and letting out a satisfied groan, she let the hot water carry away all the stresses, the tensions, the lost dreams, the realities of life. In bliss, she soaked, letting her arms float on the water as she slid her knees up until the water was at her chin. Childlike, she blew on the bubbles and watched several float up and away to burst like little rainbows on the bathroom mirror.

Voices broke through her reverie although she could not understand the words. Liam must be talking to the bellhop, she decided. Too bad for him. He could deal with any problems that arose while she sat here and got waterlogged.

He certainly could handle the problems her father threw at him. She might be learning his job, but it was not one she would ever be able to perform with the same panache. Being outgoing and polite, cajoling customers and distributors while balancing the demands of the company at the same time made Maggie dizzy. But Liam always knew what was going on; always remembered to ask about a customer's spouse and kids; always made everyone feel welcome.

Except her. Sometimes he treated her like a child and then at other times he looked at her as if she were a sex object. Did he think she wanted his job? Was that why he seemed so demeaning? What for? There was a much better one waiting for her in a few years. In fact, Maggie was hoping to move to vice-president after this trip. Or did Liam want that promotion? Well, if he did, he could wait. Within the next five years, her father planned to retire and turn the reins over to her. Liam could move up then, if she decided he could play nice. Extending a long, slender leg, she admired the shapely curves of her calf as the soap ran down her thigh to the water. Smiling, she knew these legs attracted men's glances — whatever Liam might think of her, men still found her attractive. Someday she would have time for men again.

"What? Are you crazy?" Liam's voice bellowed through the door and Maggie felt a bit of tension creeping back in. No, she was not going to let his problems bother her. She ducked down under the water to wet her hair and block out the discussion going on in the other room.

The still-hot water worked its magic and her face relaxed. She stayed under as long as she could before coming up and wiping the water from her eyes. Eying the sink, Maggie thought about the best way to wash this long mop of hers. That tiny sink was way too small; half her hair would end up being pulled down the drain. A small bottle of hotel shampoo rested on a shelf beside her and she opened it, pouring out a generous amount to use on her hair. What the heck. If they billed the room for additional bottles, let them. He wasn't the only one who might take a small advantage of that expense account.

Gathering her long auburn tresses, she worked the soap into her scalp, piling the long locks on top of her head. The soap would keep her hair out of her face for a while. Waving her hands in the water, she churned up more bubbles to play with as the relatively cool air of the bathroom gave her goose bumps. She grinned at her nipples, now standing straight out. Pinching them a bit to make them hard, her body responded and a different form of relaxation stole over her. Moaning in satisfaction, she leaned against the tub again, letting her head rest on the back while one hand dipped lower in the water.

Pinching her nipple again as her fingers found her clit, her sudden intake of breath, followed by a small moan, echoed in the quiet room. There was no need to remind herself to be quiet—after years of doing this on the sly, silence was ingrained. Maggie was no stranger to creating her own orgasms; creating "le petite mal" at her own hand greatly reduced her daily stress. Although her virginity was lost in college, since coming to work for her father, she had put aside relationships with men to concentrate on her family obligations. But her lack of a sex life was no one's business but hers, and as her fingers slipped along her slit her moans became sighs of contentment.

Slipping one finger into her tight vagina, her other hand slid over her belly to find her clit and tease it. Her body relaxed even further as that tiny organ slipped out from under its hood. Maggie floated in peacefulness; surrounded by bubbles, her eyes closed as her thoughts drifted to her fantasy lover.

For several months now, he had been taking shape in her thoughts. He was tall—over a head taller than her own five-and-a-half foot frame—broad-shouldered and muscular, but not overly so. No bodybuilder for her. Her lips parted as she imagined him walking through the bathroom door to find her naked in the bath. With increasing fervor, her fingers rubbed along the sides of her clit as she slipped two fingers into her pussy. His shirt was open…no, he wore no shirt…and the soft downy hair of his chest shimmered in the diffused light of her imagination.

She watched in fascination as her imaginary lover slowly peeled off his trousers to reveal a magnificent cock nestled between strong thighs of well-toned muscle. A cock already long and hard and pulsing; its glistening head deep purple with desire. Her lover teased her now, turning so she could look her fill. Was there anything more perfect than a man's ass? Especially his. Firm, molded, muscled. She longed to run her hands over and between those magnificent cheeks. In her mind's eye, he turned, drew closer and her body arched, inviting him. His thick cock was at her mouth and she licked her lips in anticipation. Driving her fingers deep into her open hole, she pressed on her clit. Her body gently convulsed as the rolling waves of her orgasm rolled through her. Unable to stop herself, a loud moan escaped even as her fantasy lover faded.

Opening her eyes, Maggie needed a moment to reorient. A satisfied smile spread across her wet lips and she bit the bottom one between her teeth as she stretched and enjoyed the last of the spasms spreading from her clit.

Slowly she became aware that the water had gone cold. With a sigh for her fading fantasy lover, she leaned forward to pull the plug. A hard knocking at the door made her jump and splash water onto the floor.

"That's a shared bathroom, woman. Your hour is up!"

Anger came back with a rush. How dare he? "I'll get out when I'm good and ready to get out!" she shot back.

Defiantly, she leaned back in the tub. But a soapy lock of hair fell down into her face and the water was now uncomfortably cold. Ripping the plug from the drain, she stood, letting the water cascade from her as she shook each shapely leg and stepped out of the tub.

The towels were long and thick with a terrycloth pile and gratefully Maggie wrapped one around her. It was then she saw the rubber hose with a sprinkler head at one end; the other end obviously fit over the faucet to make a makeshift shower. Perfect for rinsing her hair.

Throwing a small towel over the tub's side, Maggie attached the tubing and turned on the water, which immediately sprayed out the nozzle. Grinning, she bent down and let the hot water run over her head, her fingers combing her hair to remove all the soap. It took only a few moments to rinse and twist her hair up into another towel.

It was then she discovered a terrible truth. The only clothes she had in the little room were the soiled ones she had just taken off. They lay in a sodden heap beside the bath where she dropped them in her fit of carelessness, soaked when she splashed at his knock. Maggie had no clothes to wear to get from here to her suitcase.

* * * * *

The bellhop held a shirt-sized box tied with twine in his hands, an expectant look on his face. Liam sighed. The tapestry. And another five Euros out of his pocket. Still, you never knew when a generous tip would pay off. Closing the door, he took the box to the bed and sat, running his fingers through his dark curly hair.

Why had he bought this thing? And what was he going to do with it now? In Maggie's present mood, no way was he going to just hand this to her. She was mad enough just because he had been nice and put her suitcase up on the bed. Damn that woman! A leprechaun torn from an old tapestry catches her fancy and he goes and buys it for her because…he shook his head. Because the leprechaun told him to. No more Irish coffee for Liam Finnerty, that was for darn sure!

The box jumped in his hands. Startled, Liam dropped it on the floor and stared. A not-so-gentle rapping came from inside the lid and Liam stood, putting several feet between himself and the box. In his shock, he spoke out loud. "No, it wasn't real. Leprechauns don't really exist, especially not leprechauns in tapestries that talk. Okay, so I'm in Ireland. Lots of Irishmen like to tell stories about the little people. But they don't exist. I was delivered the wrong box is all. That's it, it's the wrong box."

"Open it up, me boy-o! It's dark in here. I like me light, so be a good boy and open the box, lad."

There was no mistaking that brogue or that voice. "You're a figment of me...of my imagination. Go away." Liam fought to retain his carefully cultured standard American accent.

"Can't. You bought me piece of the tapestry." Even though muffled by the box, the leprechaun's voice came through loud and clear.

"Oh, fine." Liam picked up the box and dropped it on the bed. Scissors and knives were no longer allowed on planes, so he didn't have his trusty pocket-knife. Bending to the task of unknotting the twine, he thought he heard a moan from the bath.

Remaining still, he listened intently, but there was no further sound. "Damn woman," he muttered again, just because he felt like it.

The knot came loose and Liam set the box on the bed, carefully nudging up one corner to peek inside.

"Oh, come on, man! I'm not going to bite you." With that, the leprechaun pushed on the lid and it fell off to one side.

"You...you're standing." Liam stated the obvious.

"Well, now, it would be impolite to carry on a conversation with ye from lying down, now, wouldn't it?

Of course, I'm standing." The little man planted his feet wide and put his fists on his hips.

Liam peered around the leprechaun. Mounted in an oak frame, no glass covered the work of art, a fact that had slipped by him before. The rock was still there, and the bole of the tree, but the space previously occupied by the little elf-like creature had filled in to look like grass. The leprechaun was still clothed in the traditional dark green frockcoat and breeches, the buckles on his shoes tarnished with age. Liam squinted at him. Was he three dimensional now?

Keeping a wary eye on the little man, Liam circled around the box where it lay on the bed. The leprechaun, narrowing his eyes as well, turned with him.

"Stop that!" Liam snapped. "Let me see your back."

"No. Ye don't want to see it. It isn't pretty an' you'll only see me front."

Liam gave up trying. He was getting dizzy. "I suppose your name is Darby O'Gill."

"It isn't. And I'll thank ye kindly for not givin' me the name of that old sot."

The little man crossed his arms and looked decidedly out of sorts. He put his foot up in the air and the rock from the tapestry rose to meet it so the leprechaun could put his foot against it. Liam closed his eyes and rubbed his temples. He didn't want to believe there really was a leprechaun taking his ease in his hotel room. "Well, are you going to tell me your name? Or do I have to guess it like Rumplestiltzkin?"

With a snort, the leprechaun sat on his rock. "Not likely. 'E was a mean old bugger. Got what 'e deserved, 'e did."

"I suppose you knew him."

"Of course. Know all the little people. We're not a very big community, ye know." The leprechaun's tone took on a pedantic tone and Liam hastened to cut him off.

"So what is your name, then, little leprechaun?" Maybe if he patronized the little sucker he could get rid of him.

"Oh, so it's rude yer goin' to be to me! Is that the way of it? Well, then. Perhaps I ought to just go into that there bath and tell the naked little woman that yer madly in love with her and can't wait to jump her bones."

"What!? Are you crazy?" Liam's voice rose and a sudden quiet from the bathroom made him lower his voice. "Besides, no matter how much you might want to be a peeping Tom, you can't leave that tapestry, so don't go making threats, you puny pipsqueak." Liam was rather pleased at his alliteration, although the leprechaun was not.

"Oh, now, me boy-o, now ye done it. Ye've gone and called me honor into question." The little man took a glove out of one of his deep side pockets and waved it in the air as if striking Liam on the cheek.

"Ouch!" Liam's hand flew to his cheek, which most definitely stung from the blow.

"Pull out your sword, man. I'll fight ye fair." From somewhere, the leprechaun produced a tiny silver sword no bigger than a toothpick. Liam was about to protest the absolute ridiculousness of the fight, when a sword appeared in his hand. For several moments, he stared at it, wearing a blank look as his mind wrestled with the inconceivable.

"Well, c'mon, man. Put it up." The leprechaun held his sword to his nose in a salute.

Liam, his brain wrapped in a fog, did the same. Dimly he noted the writing along the flat side of his blade and he turned his head sideways to read it. But his eyes could make no sense of the script that flowed from hilt to tip. As he finally realized the words were from a foreign language, he heard a swish of air and realized the leprechaun had brought his sword to bear. Before he could respond, he felt a pinprick in his belly.

"There! I claim first blood!" The little man put his sword down with a satisfied smile across his face. Liam looked down and saw a small rip in his shirt, the edges stained with red. Pulling aside his shirt with one hand while his sword hand fell to his side, he examined the inch-long scratch in his skin.

"You hurt me!"

"Oh, don't be a baby. 'Tis just a scratch. And me honor is satisfied. No more insulting Seamus O'Brien, understood?"

Liam nodded, still marveling that his belly bled. How had that happened? He glanced at the sword in his hand that he had not even used. Celtic filigree danced along the crosspiece; one of those knot designs that made him dizzy. The hilt was wrapped in dark leather, the blade almost as long as his arm. Yet it was balanced perfectly and felt light in his hand.

"Yes, boy-o. The blade is for ye. My gift."

Liam's eyes narrowed. "Why? What's the catch?"

"No catch." Seamus shrugged his shoulders. "Ye bought me slice of tapestry to give to yon Maggie, now didn't ye?" When Liam nodded, Seamus continued. "Well ye want the shrew for yer wife, even if ye don't know it yet." The leprechaun held up his hands to stave off Liam's protest. "Yes, she's the one ye'll marry, but..." Seamus voice dropped low and, in spite of himself, Liam leaned in to hear him. "But...ye need to tame the shrew in her first."

"Just how am I going to do that?" Liam stood up, shaking his head. "The woman wants no part of me, you saw that. And how do you know I want any part of her?" It was his turn to cross his arms and look defiant.

"Ye bought me tapestry."

Liam's arms fell in defeat. He had bought the old scrap just because she liked it. "I'm not in love with her." Liam's tone was softer, but still just as adamant.

"No, yer not. Yet." Seamus' eyes twinkled. "But we'll see where it goes, boy-o. We'll just see where it goes. Now, she's been in that bath long enough and ye need a cleaning, too. Go tell her to get out and to be quick about it."

Liam's anger at Maggie had long since faded. Now he sought to take her side against the leprechaun's attack. "She's had a long day. Let her soak all she wants."

"Oh, no, lad! That's not the way to win her respect. Being all wishy-washy? Woman like that will only give her heart over to a man who stands up to her. Who can prove he's man enough to handle her. Go! Get her out of there!"

Liam's two strides took him to the door and he knocked harder than he intended. He heard the water splash and knew he'd startled her. Oh, well, the damage was done. "That's a shared bathroom, woman. Your hour is up!"

The leprechaun nodded. "That was a good beginning. Now, leave the top off so as I can breath, and put me down under the bed. Ye bought me out of the kindness of yer heart, but it ain't kindness she'll be wanting from ye. At least, not just yet. Ye can tell her ye bought the sword at the store."

Not quite sure why, Liam did as he was instructed. A bedskirt covered the area, so Maggie wouldn't know he'd stowed a leprechaun under the bed. He shook his head and snorted. Did he really just have a conversation with a little man named Seamus? The late afternoon light shone through the window and glinted off the sword he'd propped against the dresser. Yes, apparently he had.

The water turned on again in the bath and Liam stood, intending to bang on the door again. But the leprechaun's words came back to him. He'd referred to Maggie as a "naked little woman." Liam's mouth curled in a smile. Yes, that pretty, tight-assed, ultra-professional female, was in the next room as naked as the day she was born. His cock nudged against his pants as he imagined those firm breasts in his hands as he wrapped his fingers around her soft flesh. Liam closed his eyes as he fantasized about tasting her nipples. He imagined himself lying beside her, taking a nipple between his lips, licking it to make it hard and hearing her moan.

His cock was rock-hard now and he squirmed, its length uncomfortable in his slacks. But he could find no relief here; not when she might walk out of that bath any moment.

As if he were prescient, the door to the bath cracked open and Maggie stuck her head out.

"Mr. Finnerty, I have forgotten to bring my clothes in here. I am going to come into the room and you will come in here until I have finished dressing."

The blush on her cheeks belied her self-assured commands. The woman was embarrassed! Liam grinned, turning so she would not see the bulge his thoughts had produced. He didn't want her thinking she was responsible for his reaction. Well, she was, but she didn't need to know that.

His grin was no more than she expected. Lout. His mocking bow to her as he acquiesced made her realize her tone had been rather imperious. But she would not apologize for it. If she weren't commanding, he wouldn't respect her. Not that he did anyway.

Liam moved aside and made a show of turning his back so she could enter. But with her body and hair wrapped in two towels, her modesty was assured, so he faced her as he gathered up his own change of clothes and sauntered into the bath.

"Your wish is my command, highness. If you haven't used up all the hot water, I'll take a bath." He paused and poked his head out of the little room. "Oh, and be careful of the sword. It's sharp." The door shut firmly and Maggie was alone again.

Chapter Two

Blast, but what that woman did to him! Liam's thoughts prevented the hot water from relaxing him the way it should have. His brain kept returning to those soft, white shoulders he glimpsed on his way into the shower. Why hadn't he noticed the graceful sweep of her neck or the pearly tint of her skin before?

Liam ran a wet hand through his curly hair and tried to make sense out of the day's events. Stuck on the plane with a partner who barely spoke, landing in Dublin to discover their rooms weren't ready, trying to make the day more pleasant by suggesting a short walk, buying a tapestry scrap that he had no business buying because a leprechaun talked to him, a leprechaun who seemed determined to run his love life, Liam shook his head. Too much for one day.

His thoughts came full circle as he dunked his head under the water and thought about the woman he was traveling with. Maggie Andrews as the girl he would marry? She certainly intrigued him and had since the first day he saw her in her father's office. At that time, she was still several levels below him in position but that tightly wound auburn hair and those intelligent deep brown eyes interested him even then. He had turned on the charm, but her demeanor had been cold and distant and he remembered thinking she had a lot to learn about working with people.

Coming up for air, he shook the water out of his eyes and poured the shampoo generously. Liam considered Maggie's rise up the corporate ladder as he washed his hair. He had kept an eye on her and was pleasantly surprised to see her efficient handling of every project she was given. Her professionalism impressed many of her co-workers even as her lack of interest in their personal lives made them label her with unflattering nicknames. Liam did not get involved. It was her own problem and she would have to deal with it in her own way. But it did make him concerned about what might happen when the old man gave control to his daughter. People worked for Old Man Andrews because they respected him. People would work for his daughter because they got paid.

But they hadn't seen Maggie's momentary vulnerability in the store. Or what she looked like with her hair down. Where Liam reined in his imagination before, now he let it wander. In his mind, her hair was already dry and yet she wore nothing but a towel. He would stand before her and rip that towel from her body, to look his fill at her shapely form. In reality, sensible suits always covered her cleavage, but the glimpse he viewed as she left the bath proved to him that her ample breasts were round and firm; he imagined holding them in his large hands, feeling her soft flesh squeeze out between his fingers. Letting his gaze travel down her body, past her smooth, flat stomach, Liam's imagination viewed the curly patch of auburn hair that would cover her more private area.

But it was the image of that flowing mane of reddish-brown curls that hardened his cock in the water. The way her hair fell from that bun as she shook her head and let herself relax. Grinning, he knew exactly what he would have her do with that hair.

Leading her to the bed, he pictured those long auburn tresses spread out over his chest, their silky softness caressing his skin. The willing woman would move her body sensuously over his, draping her hair to cover his stomach, his waist; dragging her head down to let her curls float over his cock and tickle his balls and the muscles of his thighs.

Leaning back against the porcelain tub, Liam closed his eyes and cupped his thick cock in his hand. Teasing himself with the image of Maggie kneeling over him, he rubbed his thumb along the top, feeling the purple veins ridging along his length. Sliding the bar of soap over his hardened cock, he imagined Maggie leaning forward to blanket his cock with the feathery softness of her hair. Her long and slender fingers would hold him firmly and she would need both hands to massage him since his cock was too long for her to hold in only one.

Liam dwelt on the feel of her hands on him as he slid the soap under and around his balls. While one hand rubbed his cock, the other spread the soap over the twin sacs that hung beneath. And then the little vixen switched positions to use her tongue to torment him. Her face disappeared from view so her little pink tongue could dart around the base of his cock and suckle on the stones hidden in his balls.

And then, her face peering from around his thick cock, she would brush her hair to the side, a naughty grin on her face as she licked her warm, wet tongue from the base of his cock all the way to the very tip. Her mouth surrounded the sensitive, dark tip and Liam's fingers tightened on his cock in response. Her tongue flicked out to lick the small amount of pre-come that gathered in the slit and his hand pumped his cock faster. For many long moments, he hung on the edge as he imagined her ardent lips pressing down just behind the head of his cock while her tongue continued to torment him, sliding around the tip and slithering in and out of that tiny slit. Drawing in her breath, she sucked hard as she kept up the pressure and the exquisite agony.

And then, with her eyes turned up to him in an attitude of servitude and trust, she opened wider and went down on him, taking in his entire length.

His cock hit the back of her throat and she swallowed him down, her throat constricting around his cock as his hand pumped and squeezed tight. She pulled up; his respite was brief before she plunged down again to squeeze his cock with the deep muscles of her throat.

Liam could stand it no longer. Raising his cock so the tip was just above the surface of the water, he groaned as his seed spurted like a geyser to land back in the water near his feet. Over and over the muscles of his body contracted as he pumped his cock until, with an explosive sigh, his body finally emptied and relaxed.

Standing before his semen could cling to him, Liam got out of the tub and let the water drip off his muscled chest. He was proud of his physique and worked hard to maintain the hardened muscles of his youth. Fine, dark hair covered his chest and back and grabbing a towel, he rubbed his tanned skin dry.

He grinned. No doubt he'd lose his job if the boss's daughter ever caught him fantasizing about her that way. The leprechaun had said he would marry her—Liam didn't know about that. But he certainly would not mind bedding the woman—especially if she could really fuck like that.

*****

By the time Liam dressed and entered the bedroom, it was almost eight o'clock, and time for them to meet their first client over dinner. Maggie's professional look firmly in place again, she had dressed in a tailored suit of chocolate brown; an ivory button up blouse peeked from under the buttoned jacket; the straight skirt came demurely to just below her knee. Once again in dark, low heels, she stood as she heard Liam's hand on the doorknob.

Damn, but the man was handsome! In spite of her dislike of his take-charge demeanor, Maggie had to admit he looked incredible. His still-wet dark hair clung to his neck and twisted in little pincurls around his temple. He wore a crisp, white shirt that looked freshly pressed, smoke-gray slacks and, as of yet, no socks. He also wore a satisfied grin. Now she knew for sure what that groan of his had been for.

"We need to get going." Her manner was firm; what he did in the privacy of the bath was his own concern. The fact that she had pleasured herself in the same way was none of his business.

Liam noted that the sword had been moved and her suitcase put away. He couldn't resist as he sat on the edge of the bed to put on his socks. "So, Ms. Andrews, what do you think of the sword?"

She had examined it at length while he had been otherwise occupied. For some reason, it looked vaguely familiar to her. Something about the filigree work tugged at her memory, but since she couldn't quite place it—and certainly she did not read Gaelic—eventually she simply set the long sword on the bed and dressed. Why Liam had bought it was a mystery to her. "It's an interesting piece. Are you a collector?"

"I wasn't." There seemed to be a wryness to his voice and at Maggie's look, he continued. "But one must start sometime."

"You'll have a devil of a time if you try to take that through customs. You'd better mail it back to the States with all the proper paperwork." She was not about to have to spend one extra day with this man because he decided he wanted to collect sharp, pointed objects instead of something safe, like condoms from around the world. She bit her lip to keep from laughing at her suddenly naughty thought.

Where Maggie had brought three pairs of shoes—the navy ones she had worn earlier, the brown ones she wore now and a pair of sneakers she doubted she would need—Liam only brought the one pair of dress loafers. She sighed as he slipped his feet into them and shrugged his broad shoulders into his suit coat. It wasn't fair.

Sliding his wallet into his breast pocket, Liam gestured toward the door. The hotel key lay on the dresser where he had dropped it earlier and Maggie scooped it up, dropping it into her purse with a satisfied smile. Okay, it was only a symbol of control, but right now, she would take every tiny scrap that she could. Looking far more self-assured than she felt, she strode past him and out the door.

* * * * *

Maggie had never seen Liam work a client before; that was why she was on this trip. As the future president of the company, she actually had little to do at the moment but sit back and watch a master at work.

And a master he was. Liam had the facts, the figures, the information all stored in his head. He knew when to push, and he knew when to sit back and let the client lead. After a while, Maggie even found herself enjoying his repartee and the stories he told about the company's success. She was not surprised when the client agreed and Andrew's Unlimited became an international player.

No, the trouble did not start until the two of them returned to the hotel room. Flush with success, Maggie's eyes shone brightly; she would have wonderful news to tell her father when she called him tomorrow. Still conservative, she would not tell him anything until there was a signed piece of paper.

So when she came out of the little bathroom to discover Liam on the phone with her father, already telling him the news, she was furious. Her eyes blazed, then watered with disappointment. It was his right to tell—he made the deal. She turned away to hide the emptiness inside.

But Liam caught a glimpse of her face just as she turned away. What was her problem? He finished his conversation quickly and hung up just as Maggie reached to pull down the covers of the bed.

As she did so, Maggie's foot hit something solid under the bed. She bent down to look as she removed her jacket, but the dust ruffle was in the way and she couldn't see what it was.

"Maggie, no. What are you doing?" He had to stop her. That blasted tapestry was still under the bed, its cover off so the leprechaun could have light. Even to him it sounded absurd.

"There's something under the bed. My foot kicked it." She knelt and pulled up the bedskirt.

"Well, leave it. It's probably something the housekeeper keeps under there. I wouldn't worry about it…" His voice trailed off as she pulled out the box.

For a moment Maggie stared at the tapestry piece, her face a study of confusion. How did this get here? She looked up and saw defeat and guilt plastered all over Liam's face. He had bought it. He had known she really liked it and had bought it just to spite her. She should have known.

He saw the distant coldness spread through her entire being. "Now, Maggie, it isn't what you think…"

"And just what do I think, Mr. Finnerty?" Resolute, she kept her eyes from straying back to the box. It hurt her heart too much.

Liam realized he was trapped. Nothing he could say right now would be right. He ran his fingers through his hair in frustration. He knew she simmered under that icy exterior, but his hopes of thawing the ever-thickening veneer were dimming quickly. Resigned, he shrugged, his shoulders drooping with defeat. "I bought it because you liked it. I was planning to give it to you as a present."

"A thousand-dollar present?" Her eyes darkened. "And just what did you expect me to do for you to deserve a thousand-dollar present, Mr. Finnerty?"

"I expect you to marry me, Maggie Andrews."

Her mouth opened and closed several times. "What?" She shook her head. Surely she had not heard him properly.

Liam couldn't believe what had come out of his mouth. That damn leprechaun. Putting ideas in his head when he wasn't looking. But even as he reconsidered and thought about pulling the words back, Liam realized he didn't want to. Okay, maybe marriage was going a bit too far...but he would no longer deny that he wanted this woman. He let the statement stand.

Maggie shook her head as anger, newly enflamed, built up its heat. "You have a funny way of courting a woman, Mr. Finnerty. Save your money for a woman you can buy."

She flung the box onto the bed where the little leprechaun's jaunty figure gleamed in the light.

"Ah, boy-o, ye've messed this up fer sure."

Liam glared at the leprechaun who stood in the box egging him on. A glance at Maggie made him realize she had not heard the little man's booming voice, nor did she see him standing. Turning his back on her and the box, he strode across the tiny room.

"Yer goin' to have to make it up to her, ye know."

"I know, I know!" Liam forgot himself.

"Well, if you know that, then why did you buy the tapestry?" Maggie's voice was tart.

Now it was Liam's turn to stare blankly. Then he realized he'd spoken out loud the words he meant for the leprechaun. Frustrated, he sketched an exaggerated bow. "Ms. Andrews, I'm sorry. I was presumptuous. I bought the scrap of cloth because I saw that you liked it and for some unknown reason, I decided to do something nice for you." Liam was in no mood to be pleasant. His earlier euphoria at making a deal had evaporated as soon as she kicked the stupid box. And what had made him say he wanted to marry the shrew? He glared again at the leprechaun who merely sighed at him.

"Oh, no, boy-o. Yer not going to win this battle that way."

Maggie's chin shook as Liam's words stung, but she refused to break down and cry in front of him. Pursing her lips, she raised her head and lashed back. "I do not accept it. Take it back in the morning. I cannot be bought, Mr. Finnerty."

"No. I will not take it back. You might reject my present and you might reject me, but you cannot deny your own heart." He held up his hand to stave off her rebuttal. He already had a leprechaun trying to give him orders, he was not about to let this woman tell him what to do. Liam threw down his challenge. "Something about this tapestry spoke to you; I saw it in your eyes. In the shop."

Maggie's shell softened slightly as he spoke of the little tapestry scrap; it *had* spoken to her heart and only she knew the reason why. That tiny little leprechaun, torn from the master tapestry, represented all the years of work and dreams she had invested in life before her brother Tom died. With a Master's in textile art and almost finished with her doctorate in art restoration, Maggie had been well on her way to making a name for herself in a world that did not include her father's business. To find the other piece of this scrap and reunite the two would be the work she had always dreamed of.

He saw her internal struggle. Opening his mouth to urge her to tell him what it was that hurt her so much, he shut it again when Seamus shook his head and held up his hand. There was decidedly less frost in her voice when she spoke again.

"I cannot accept such a present from you, Mr. Finnerty. If you wish to keep it, that is your business. My answer is final." The steady look she gave him convinced him she meant it.

"Get 'er to find the rest of me tapestry, lad. Now, while she's still softened up a bit."

Liam made a face at Seamus and shook his head no. The leprechaun stamped his foot.

"Yes, man! Now! Tell 'er ye've a fancy for wantin' to put the two pieces back together. Tell 'er, or I won't be helpin' ye out of yer troubles no more." The little man crossed his arms and leaned against the bole of the tree once more, a defiant look on his face.

"Fine." Liam's answer was accepted by both of them. Seamus nodded in satisfaction and Maggie simply looked relieved. "I do intend to keep it, Ms. Andrews." Liam ignored the triumphant look on the leprechaun's face. "I intend to find the rest of the tapestry and then have it restored. I will frame the entire piece and hang it in my house as a testament to my folly." He scooped up the box and glared at Seamus as the little man grinned and sat down on his rock.

"You're going...but..." Maggie was torn. She would give her eyeteeth to be a part of this, but how could she tell him that? Assuming an air of indifference, she crossed her arms. "And where are you going to look? Heaven only knows how long ago that scrap was torn off."

Liam looked at the scrap and the leprechaun shrugged his shoulders. "Sorry, boy-o. Ye have got to find it on your own. It's a part of the curse."

"Curse? What curse?" Liam hadn't intended to speak out loud. Maggie's shocked look had him scrambling to cover his mistake. The last thing he wanted was for her to know he was talking to the damn thing. "I mean, what should I do about the curse on it? That's a problem, you know. It can't be reunited with the other piece of cloth until...until..." Liam shook the box to prompt the leprechaun.

"Until me owner finds his one true love."

"Until his owner finds his one true love." The words registered with a vengeance. "What?"

Maggie crossed her arms and narrowed her eyes. She seemed to be doing that a lot lately. If she didn't stop, she was going to end up with crow's feet long before her time. While impressed with Liam's smooth-talking abilities at dinner, the fact that now he seemed bent on giving her a load of baloney did not sit well.

"You're daft, to use a word of the land." Ignoring him, she gathered up her nightclothes and pushed him out of her way so she could change in the bath. "Please try to have your story straight by the time I return." Throwing her hair over her shoulder, she tossed her head and closed the door behind her.

Liam heard the bolt slide home on the bathroom door and threw the box onto the bed. "All right, Seamus O'Brien. Out with it. I want the whole story and I want it fast."

"All right, man, all right. Calm down, it's not that long a story. Sit down and I'll tell ye the whole bloody mess."

Liam sat heavily and propped the tapestry up against one of the hotel pillows. The little man paced two steps one way and two steps the other—all the space he had.

"Well, ye see, it was like this. A long time ago, there were two young lovers. Young William, 'e was a handsome lad, strong and tall. A warrior and leader of his clan. Pretty Margaret was the daughter of the English lord. Yea, ye can see the trouble brewin' already, I see."

Liam nodded his head. The Troubles still raged in parts of Ireland. His family had emigrated over a hundred years ago and still the stories of atrocities—both English and Irish—had been handed down through the generations.

"Well, William and Margaret, they were so much in love...it just broke me heart. So, using a bit o'me magic, I managed to give them a life together. The two eloped."

"Something tells me they didn't live happily ever after."

"Well, they did for quite some time. But then William, he was exiled by Margaret's father for what he done, stealing his daughter an' all. The two lived in hidin' for over five years. Durin' that time, young Margaret worked on a tapestry to immortalize their love. Ah, t'was a beautiful work of art, too. The two of them standing under the trees, looking so lovingly at each other..." Seamus' voice trailed off and Liam scowled.

"Well, come on, tell me what happened. She'll be out of the bathroom in a minute."

The little man shook himself. "Ah, yes. Well, eventually they got caught. The two were brought before her father, who cursed them both."

"By tearing the tapestry?"

"Ach, no, man—that came later. No, his curse was powerless; the man had no power except over the two of them. He sentenced William to the gallows and made Margaret watch as he hanged her true love."

Liam sat unable to speak for several heartbeats. "And did it happen? Did her father really have him hanged?"

"Aye, he did. And she watched her love die a most horrible death. That's when she cursed me, for havin' brought them their heart's desire in the first place."

"And that's when she ripped the tapestry."

"Well, no. Ye see, I wasn't a part of the tapestry, then. I was a free-roamin' leprechaun. But she caught me when I went to console the poor lass and sewed me into the corner in her need for revenge."

"So when did she rip the two pieces apart?"

"She didn't. Her mother did that after they found the girl hanging in the bedroom they'd locked her into after William was dead. It was her mother who found the tapestry and when I spoke to her and tried to get her to let me go, she ripped the piece in two and threw me out the window. I never saw the rest of me cloth again."

"Why do I think there's a lot of this story you aren't telling?"

"Because ye wanted the short version, lad. Here comes yon lass. What are ye goin' to tell her?"

Liam didn't answer, since Maggie opened the door at that precise moment. His reaction was immediate. Dressed in lacy, navy blue baby doll lingerie, Maggie's shapely body was revealed in all her glory. Liam's eye traveled from the graceful curve of her neck over her alabaster shoulders to two beautifully shaped breasts just hidden by the dark, silky material. In the coolness of the room, little buds blossomed at the tips and Liam's cock stirred. His eyes continued downward toward her narrow waist and well-formed thighs—and that was as far as he got.

Blushing to the roots of her hair, Maggie rushed across the room and scrambled into the bed, pulling the blankets up to cover herself. She had paced for several minutes in the bathroom, trying to gather the nerve to make the dash. Now she glared at him from the safety of the bed. "Believe me, Mr. Finnerty, had I known I would be sharing a room with you, I would have packed differently."

He grinned and the devil was in his eyes. "No doubt you would have, Ms. Andrews, no doubt you would have. But now I have visual proof that there's a passionate heart that beats behind those tailored suits." His grin grew wider. "I, however, do not have to worry about what to wear to bed..." Liam stripped off his shirt and tossed it on the floor. His naked chest glimmered just as Maggie always thought it would; a gorgeous, muscular torso faintly covered with soft dark hair that glimmered in the soft light of the hotel room. Her sudden intake of breath was audible in the quiet room.

To cover her reaction, Maggie feigned shock. "Well, you're not sleeping in the nude tonight! I'm tempted to make you sleep in the tub." She had been, too, but had discarded the idea as childish and immature. They were two grown adults stuck in an uncomfortable situation, and she didn't need to get all melodramatic about it. But she had known she wouldn't make it to the bed without some comment from him about her sleepwear. What she hadn't been ready for was his complete appreciation for her appearance. Despite her intent to keep her distance from him, his obvious enjoyment of her teddy gave her a very warm feeling inside. A feeling that resided way too low for her own comfort.

"That's it lad, bed her!"

Through gritted teeth, only the little man heard Liam's murmured, "Shut up." Bending to pull down the covers on his side of the bed, Liam lowered just enough of the blankets to give him a better glimpse of her shapely thighs. But Maggie's hand slammed down and his view was cut off again.

Irritated at the leprechaun and aroused by Maggie's body, Liam straightened to take off his pants. With a tug, he pulled at his snagged belt, making it snap as it came out of the belt loops. The sound cracked through the air and Liam snapped it again, glaring at the little man in the tapestry. His meaning was clear. Seamus shrugged and perched on top of his rock.

At the first snap of his belt, Maggie jumped, but then realized it was unintentional. At the second snap, the warm feeling between her legs gushed with arousal and a sudden fear. Did he intend to use that on her?

Maggie was no virgin, but she hadn't had a lover since she entered the family business. Now she could not deny the excitement she suddenly felt in Liam's presence. Did he intend to have his way with her?

But Liam wasn't looking at her, he was looking at that blasted piece of cloth. She sighed as he dropped the belt on the floor and unzipped his pants.

Liam looked up at the sound of her sigh. Her lips were parted and there was a yearning expression on her face as her eyes rested on his crotch. But then she noticed his glance and turned away fussing with the blankets. Damn the woman, just what did she want from him?

He slid his pants down and kicked them into the corner beside his shirt. Not usually a slob, tonight he just didn't care. Between the long flight, the shopping, the successful business dealings, a talking leprechaun and a woman who didn't know if she wanted to be fire or ice, his head ached. At least he wouldn't be embarrassed by his underwear; plain, old, plaid boxers.

Sliding into the bed, he turned his back to her and pulled the little chain that turned off the light. In the sudden darkness, he squirmed down into the bed and rolled so his back was to Maggie. He could feel the warmth of her body and knew that if he faced her, he would breathe in her sweet scent. Traces of it wafted to his nose and his cock twitched again. He buried his head in his pillow and tried to think about cold things.

Maggie didn't know whether to be relieved or insulted. His look told her he liked what he saw; his body language now indicated he wasn't really interested in her. She knew she should be grateful. Why, then, was she so disappointed? Sliding down under the covers, she was careful not to touch his body with any part of hers. The queen size bed meant it was possible for two to sleep without touching, but only if both slept on the outer rim of the mattress; a place Maggie was not used to sleeping. Still, she pulled the blankets to her ears and lay on her side with her back to the man who didn't want any part of her.

Maggie knew the reputation for cold professionalism she had in the company. But it was important that everyone respect her. She didn't have all the degrees they did; while most in the company studied business and marketing, she spent her time in the arts. Now suddenly thrown in with the wolves, her tough hide was all that got her through some days.

But tonight the cracks in that hide threatened to break open. The long flight, the disappointment in the shop—only to find out Liam had bought the stupid thing just for her, then forced to share a room with him, sitting on the sidelines while he wined and dined the client and made the deal, his obvious appreciation for her body yet lack of desire for her, all piled up on her, pushing her thoughts inward. Inside, where she was lonely and afraid. Her drive to be what her father wanted left her little time for friends or lovers and she spent most of her days afraid the others would discover what a fraud she was in doing her job. A tear trickled from the side of her eye to wet the hotel pillow.

"Ah, the lass is cryin'. Go on, boy, take her in yer arms and tell her it'll be all right."

"You've gotten me in enough trouble tonight. Go away." Liam's quiet whisper could barely be heard.

"But ye need me help, me boy-o. Can't ye see the lass is ripe?"

"I said, go away." Liam reached up and took the box off the dresser. In the dim light that leaked in through the window, Liam saw the little man sitting cross-legged on his rock. "If I wanted to make love to the woman, I wouldn't need your advice."

"What?" Maggie surreptitiously wiped her eyes and peered over her shoulder.

"What?" Liam echoed, trying to sound nonchalant.

"I thought you said something."

"No, not me. Just putting the tapestry away, that's all." Liam set the box on the floor and slid under the covers again.

"Oh."

The word was flat and lifeless and pierced like a dagger through Liam's heart. The leprechaun was right; Maggie was hurting. But the devil take him if he knew why. Rolling onto his back, he tried to make things right between them.

"Maggie, look. I know you don't like me and you're mad because I bought the tapestry when you couldn't afford it. I'm sorry your father's not paying you what you deserve, but I just wanted to do something nice for you. As a friend."

"No, man! As a lover, not a friend! Tell her that her lips are as soft as the budding rose bloom, or that her hair intoxicates you with its satiny shimmer, but don't tell her you only want her as a friend!"

Liam's long arm reached down and shoved the box under the bed.

The strain of keeping the mask in place required too much energy. She sighed as she rolled over onto her back, staring at the ceiling. "Thank you, Liam. I'm sorry I got angry with you. It's just that little scrap of cloth represents so much of what I can't have. It's hard to look at it and know my responsibilities will always keep me from doing what I love."

"And what do you love, Maggie Andrews?" His voice was soft.

In the darkness of the room, Maggie's energy gave out; her mask slid off and the pent-up words tumbled out. "I love finding the piece of art that needs just a touch of restoration to bring it to life once again. Whether it is rare or common, it doesn't matter. To know that I have the skill to restore it to its former glory and give it a new life in our world; to see a piece I've spent hours, days, months uncovering, researching, painstakingly put back together and on display in a museum or gallery for others to see. That's what I love. Knowing that two of us—the talents of the original artist combined with my skills in restoration—produce an entirely recreated piece that shines for a new generation to appreciate."

Liam didn't need a light on to know her eyes shone with passion. This was what the woman had been trained to do; this was what she should be doing. Much as he appreciated her father's business sense, he now doubted the man's parenting skills. The woman's soul wasn't interested in the bottom line; her soul was tied to the glories of ancient art.

"Then why do you work for your father, woman? Why don't you follow your heart?" He knew the answer even as he asked the question, but needed to hear how Maggie saw it.

She was just so tired. Tired of hiding her real personality under a thick wall of professionalism; tired of working for her father's dream instead of her own; tired of not having a friend. Maybe it was the Irish moonlight, maybe it was her own exhaustion, but Maggie found herself answering.

"Because he is my father. He built that company from scratch. He missed so many family gatherings, so many birthdays, because he was working so hard to make a go of it. Thomas…" Her voice cracked and she paused. Swallowing hard, she took a deep breath to steady herself.

The scent of Liam's aftershave filled her nose and desperately she grabbed onto the shreds of her control.

"But Tom died." Liam prompted her. "And you still grieve for him by trying to do his job."

The shreds slipped between her fingers and tears slid from the corners of her eyes. Not trusting her voice, she nodded in the darkness.

"A job you don't really want, do you, Maggie?"

His voice was kind, soft and understanding, gentle. A small sob escaped and she clapped her fingers to her mouth, trying to stuff everything back inside again. But his arm slipped behind her neck and for the first time in her adult life, Maggie cried on another person's shoulder.

She could not hold back the sobs. She cried for her brother's wasted life, and she cried for her lost dreams. She cried for her own inadequacies and for the fact that she couldn't afford the tapestry. Her sobs came from the very depths of her soul and all Liam could do was hold her as her grief and sorrow poured out.

"Ach, the poor lass. She's been shuttin' that in for a long, long time." Seamus' voice floated up and Liam nodded, knowing that somehow, the leprechaun could see him.

"Just hold her, lad. That's all she needs; a good, strong shoulder to cry on."

"Don't suppose you could get me some of those tissues?" Liam's voice was quiet and he pointed in the general direction of the tissue box on the dresser.

"Sure, boy-o. Here ye go."

Liam felt the outline of the box suddenly under his fingers. Deciding this was not the time to worry about the little man's magic, he pulled out several tissues. Maggie's hands lay limply against his chest, and he pushed a tissue between her fingers. As if on automatic, she began to wipe her eyes, taking deep breaths as her tears passed.

"How long have you been holding that in?" Liam brushed a stray lock of auburn hair from her face.

Maggie struggled to sit up. She couldn't breathe lying down after a cry like that. He helped her upright and she looked over at his dim figure and shook her head. "I don't know. I didn't cry like this at his funeral." She sighed. "Look, Liam, I'm sorry. It's been a long day and I didn't mean to impose on you like that."

Liam frowned; she was putting up her barriers again. "It wasn't an imposition, Maggie. If you don't take care of emotions, they tend to blow up on you when you least expect it. It's all right." He knew her eyes would be swollen and red from her tears and he couldn't help himself. He didn't want those walls to go back up. "You are a passionate woman, Maggie, who has denied herself, her real self, for far too long." He leaned in, his cheek brushing along hers to revel in her sweet perfume.

Maggie swayed; her eyes closing as his lips softly caressed her cheek. She turned her face toward him, seeking those lips, wanting to drown her sorrows in his kiss. And when they met, a small whimper sounded from the back of her throat, moved by the gentleness and understanding in his touch.

The salty remains of her tears sank into Liam's consciousness. He shouldn't be doing this. She was vulnerable; it was wrong to take a woman when her defenses had collapsed. But her scent filled his being and when she opened her lips, inviting him deeper into the kiss, he decided to be sorry about it later. His tongue explored her mouth, tasting her deeply, entwining around her tongue as he felt her arms go around his neck.

Maggie knew exactly what she was doing as she threw away her mask. Screw the company, screw her reputation, screw it all. She was tired of carrying the weight of her father's will. Tonight, she wanted only one thing, and she knew Liam would willingly give it to her. The morning was soon enough to pick up her burden and put Liam back in his place. Tonight, she just wanted him to make love to her.

The taste of her tongue ignited the pilot light that had been burning in his belly since the day they met. He took her mouth, possessed it, felt her give it up to him; his cock grew heavy in response. The blood pumped its way through the veins that surrounded it, fed it life as Liam pulled Maggie closer.

His hand traced along her shoulder, pushing the thin strap of the baby doll down her arm. Not letting go of his kiss, she gracefully extricated her elbow from the strap and moaned as his fingers ran over the thin fabric covering her breasts. He cupped her breast through the fabric, his fingers lingering on her nipple, teasing it into hardness. Gently he squeezed the tiny bud until he heard her gasp of pleasure.

Maggie's pussy responded, flooding her panties as he pinched her nipple; her body threatened to turn to jelly at his touch. With one arm still around her, supporting her against him, Liam's hand now brushed the other strap off her shoulder. Shifting position, Maggie leaned into him, nuzzling her kisses under his chin and along his neck as he pushed the garment to her waist. Too long had she gone without a man's touch; far too long had she craved the heat Liam's hands ignited in her body.

The softness of her skin against his chest sent a surge of desire coursing to Liam's cock and it stiffened; his need more intense. Even as he bent to take her nipple between his lips, as her fingers entwined in his hair and her breasts rose to meet him, the forgotten leprechaun spoke up. "Slowly, boy-o. Don't frighten the filly." The leprechaun's voice was soft in his ear, so quiet that Liam might have deemed it his own thought but for the Irish terms.

Liam growled and Maggie grinned. She arched her back to push her breast up, inviting him to play with it. When his lips closed around her hardened nipple, she sighed. And when he used his teeth to gently pull it out toward him, she moaned. "Oh yes, Liam. Please..." another moan cut off the rest of her request.

He lay her back onto the bed, pushing the covers aside to give them both room. Shifting his attention to her nearer breast, he cupped it, rubbing his forefinger over the tightened nipple. With his other hand, he took her arm and raised it up over her head to rest on the pillow. Grinning, she did the same with the other arm, arching her back and letting him play with her body.

"Leave them there until I give you permission to move them." His voice was raspy with his craving for her submission.

Maggie complied with a pleasured sigh. No more control. No more worries. Just Liam's hands on her body, fondling her, carrying her off. She moaned again as his hands ran along her sides, pulling her sexy lingerie down and off her slender legs. Only the navy blue satin panties remained on her otherwise naked body.

For months, Liam had wondered what lay behind Maggie's hard shell. Tonight, her veneer had cracked and for the first time, Liam glimpsed the powerful, sexy tigress that lay at rest behind that professional mask. Controlling such an animal required careful handling — and Liam Finnerty loved a challenge.

"Aye, that's the way, lad. Get yer own knickers off now before ye rip right through 'em. That's a fine twig 'n berry set ye have there — put it to use tonight!"

Liam growled again. "I know how to make love to a woman!"

"Yes, Liam, don't stop." Maggie's voice was breathless, letting herself be carried away.

With another low-throated growl to cover his mistake, he launched himself at Maggie's breasts, kneading one breast while pulling the other into his mouth; gratified by the feel of her body writhing under him. Her hands stayed above her head, her back arching invitingly and Liam let his tongue circle the hard little bud he suckled. He heard her nails on the headboard as her hands sought for purchase on the carved dragons. As long as she didn't bring those hands down to stop him, Liam knew he was on safe ground.

Maggie pushed her breasts up to meet his hungry mouth; he most certainly did know how to make love to a woman. Never had her hunger been greater. It was almost as if her tears released the lock she kept on all her desires and now they flowed out with a vengeance. If he did not let that hand drift lower soon, she knew her need would command her and that she would push his hand down to invade her pussy.

But she held back and kept her hands above her head, as Liam had told her to. There was something deliciously naughty about submitting to him, letting him control her; something that appealed to the tigress that lived entrenched in the deep caverns of her psyche. Not one man had ever been able to let that animal loose. Maggie knew it was there, when she chose to look that deep. But it was too painful to admit that that side of her needed to be locked away, and so she did not look very often. Liam's command of her body threatened to wake the tigress and Maggie squirmed under his touch, both wanting and fearing the animal's release. Breathless, urging him with her body to stroke her even as she feared where his touch would take her, the animal cried out through Maggie's mouth with wordless cries.

Liam needed to get his cock free of his underwear. He was fully extended and much as he didn't want to admit that the leprechaun was right—these boxers needed to come off. Oh, but this breast was so wonderful to torment; it yielded such incredible noises from the woman beneath him. Giving a last small bite to her nipple just to hear her moan, he slid off the bed and pulled down his boxers.

The huskiness in Maggie's voice betrayed how wanton she felt. "I wish there were more light so I could see you, Liam. I want to see all of the man who claims me tonight."

"Yer wish is my command, Lady!"

A thin shaft of moonlight suddenly beamed through the parting in the window curtains to fall directly on Liam's cock. He was vain enough to be pleased by her sudden intake of breath and he rubbed along its length to give her its measure. Two full handspans it stretched from his body and still the purpled tip poked out from his fist.

"I intend to take you, Maggie Andrews. I will bury every inch of this cock inside that hot pussy of yours.

Your body will buck against mine and I will feel your pussy clench around my cock as I force you to come."

Yes! This was what she wanted — to be carried away from the real world by the force of Liam's cock driving into her. Keeping her arms above her head, she squirmed on the bed trying to get relief by the friction of her soaked panties.

"Aye, man, ye've got her right where ye want her now. Take that little scrap of fabric off her and give yerself a clear shot."

Ignoring the leprechaun, Liam did exactly what Seamus told him. With a deep growl, Liam reached forward and roughly yanked down Maggie's panties. Her scent was strong and Liam parted her legs to run his finger down her slit and into her hot, wet pussy.

A dim part of her mind understood that Liam's rough touch was exactly what she needed right now and Maggie's body responded. Another wordless cry escaped her as the tigress clawed at her cage and Maggie threw her head back into the pillows, spreading her legs wider. She was shameless tonight and she reveled in it. Throwing her arms to the sides above her head, one hand curled around the curtains as the fingers of her other hand dug into a pillow. Liam's fingers pumped her pussy and she let her body dance for him.

Oh, but she was tight! While tempted to just plunge his cock into that dark, damp hole, Liam held back; he didn't want to hurt her. While the fingers of one hand worked her pussy, the thumb of the other came up to circle her engorged clit and tease her unmercifully.

"Oh, Liam, please. Please let me come!" Even as the words left her mouth, Maggie couldn't believe she had said them. Never, ever had she begged for release. She always controlled her own orgasms. Always. Until tonight.

"That's it, man! That's yer cue!"

"Stop talking. I know what I'm doing!"

"Yes, Liam…" Another moan as Liam's fingers savagely fucked her pussy cut off anything further Maggie might have said.

"Damn." Liam didn't know whether to be angry at having an audience that found it necessary to give him advice, or pleased. His words, meant for Seamus, had definitely had an effect on Maggie. Her body cried out for release and he controlled it. He dreamt about so much power over a woman and here the little leprechaun had delivered it.

But he was barely controlling his own needs right now. His cock throbbed painfully, the veins bulging with their life-giving blood. Removing his fingers, he put a hand on either side of her. Laying his length between her legs, he eased the tip of his cock into the opening of her waiting pussy.

Eagerly, Maggie raised her hips to make his entrance easier. His movements slow, he groaned as his cock entered her tight, wet, waiting pussy. In and out he pumped, each gentle thrust stretching her; each thrust pushing his thick cock deeper within her willing body. Relaxing into his pace, the last vestiges of her control slid away and she followed his lead as he manipulated her body.

His cock filled the snug space she so eagerly provided. Dutifully, she kept her hands above her head as her body moved to his rhythm. Liam bent down to possess her mouth again as, with a deep thrust, he pushed his entire length into her. Their tempo increasing, he felt her body convulsing under his as his pubic bone crushed her clit on each stroke. Her legs encircled him as her mouth opened to him and the tempo increased again.

Maggie had never felt so stretched. Liam's presence surrounded her; she could not escape him. His cock impaled her pussy; his tongue entwined with hers. There were no choices left. The tingling between her legs grew stronger. She could not take much more.

"Come for me now, Maggie. Come around my cock."

Maggie's body suddenly went stiff as time stood still. She couldn't breathe and didn't want to. Poised on the edge, Liam's cock slammed into her and her body arched as she cried out. Desperately she clung to the cliff's edge, but his cock slammed into her again and she plunged into the abyss. In bliss, the waves of her orgasm swept over her, from the tips of her fingers where she clutched the curtain, to the ends of her feet where they wrapped around Liam's back. Maggie's voice filled the air with wordless cries as she hung onto Liam's body and rode him.

Liam grinned as she screamed and her pussy contracted around his cock. Dimly he hoped the hotel had thick walls otherwise security would be here any second. As the contractions in her pussy squeezed him, he groaned and thrust hard again. And then time stood still for him as well. With loud, satisfied groans, he pumped his seed into her as her muscles milked him dry.

Panting, their movements slowed. Liam remained in her as long as he could, but the tip had become sensitive; pulling out, he shuddered as he collapsed alongside her body. "Maggie…" He wanted to tell her it had never been like that before. He wanted to tell her that he would make love to her like that every time. He wanted to tell her he was falling in love with her.

But she put her finger over his lips. She didn't want him to say words he'd regret in the morning. Long ago she had armed herself against the words of men and even though her heart yearned to hear the soft words he would speak, her already-damaged heart couldn't stand being broken right now. Instead, she snuggled beside him as the coolness of the night made her shiver.

The covers floated up and covered the two of them where they lay entwined in each other's arms, but neither noticed. Contentment and sheer exhaustion had claimed them both.

"Aye, Seamus O'Brien, it is a genius you are."

And under the bed, the little leprechaun doused the magical moonlight and rested in his tapestry.

Chapter Three

Maggie awoke to the sound of a baritone voice singing "When Irish Eyes are Smiling." Blinking against the morning light and stretching, she suddenly remembered where she was and what she had done last night. Peeking under the covers the sight of her naked body was confirmation. Moaning, she put her hands to her head and sat up.

"Maggie Andrews, I can't believe you did that! What were you thinking, girl?" She glanced over to the closed bathroom door as the words of the song dissolved into a very fine humming. The swishing of water followed by a clink on the porcelain sink told her he was shaving.

Rushing to get her clothes before he came out of the bathroom, Maggie found her discarded lingerie flung to the other side of the room. "Flannel. Today I go buy a flannel nightgown. And a robe. I definitely need a robe." Expecting to be in a room all by herself, she hadn't bothered to pack one.

His shirt lay near her discarded nightclothes; it would do. She slipped her arms into it and pulled it together in front of her. At least it covered her rear end. Just as she buttoned the last button, Liam sang the last line of the song and made his entrance.

"...Irish eyes are smiling, Sure 'n, they steal your heart away." He grinned to see her in his shirt. "Mornin', Maggie!"

"Good morning, Mr. Finnerty." She gathered up the clothes she would need for the day while trying to ignore the fact that Liam wore only a towel around his waist.

"Oh, we're back to that, are we?"

His amused smile did nothing to sway her mind. She was determined to put the feelings he stirred in her back into the box where they belonged. She had a job to do.

"Yes, Mr. Finnerty, we are back to that. We never should have left in the first place."

"Oh, lad, she's a handful! Go on, kiss 'er! Let her know who's the boss here."

Liam reached down and scooped up the box from under the bed, giving Seamus a warning glance. For answer the little leprechaun just pointed toward Maggie and made kissing noises.

In disgust, he dropped the box onto the bed and the frame rattled against the cardboard.

"Be careful of that!" Maggie's two steps brought her to the side of the bed. She picked up the frame and turned it over, clucking in dismay as she did so. "Look, it wasn't even mounted properly. There's been a lot of fraying on this piece since it was separated. See? Look here."

Liam bent in close to see where she was pointing. Her formality was still in place, but when she spoke about the little piece of fabric, her tone was softer. His hand slipped around her waist and he felt her stiffen, although she did not move away. She couldn't. He'd left her no room.

The casual familiarity of Liam's hand on her waist threatened to melt her resolve. Frowning, Maggie tried to move around him, but he had her trapped in a tiny space. Pinned between the dresser, the bed and his body, the sudden closeness made her heartbeat race and her cheeks colored to a pretty rose-pink as her flustering attempts to get around him failed.

"Maggie," Liam whispered softly into her ear. She was so sexy wearing his shirt, with her long, slender legs now pinned between his much larger, much stronger thighs. The sight of her — still mussed from sleep, flustered, obviously aroused — stirred his cock beneath the thin hotel towel.

The tapestry frame pressed against his chest where she held it between them; giving it a gentle tug, he pulled it from her fingers and set it on the bed. Face down. Not that he thought that would stop Seamus, but Liam hoped it would at least mute the leprechaun's voice.

Maggie's fingers were nerveless. Liam's eyes did not leave hers. He smelled so clean, of soap and shaving cream and toothpaste; she still wore their combined scents from last night's lovemaking. One of his hands still rested on her waist, with the other, Liam now reached for her top button.

God help her, but she wanted this. All her resolutions to put him in his place dissipated in the heat of his touch. The man was a masterful lover and Maggie found she didn't want to say no.

But she had to. She had already sullied her reputation with Liam — now was the time to repair the damage before things got out of hand. Gritting her teeth, she maneuvered her knee so that it just touched his hardening cock.

"Mr. Finnerty, back away now."

Liam saw the change in her eyes just seconds before he felt her knee in position. He could easily out-maneuver her; by physical strength alone, if necessary. He knew he would lose her forever if he did. Dropping his hands to his side, he stepped back.

"Maggie, you cannot deny what we did last night."

"I do not intend to. It was a mistake. I was vulnerable and you took advantage of that. I will not be so little-girlish as to confide in you again."

"Little-girlish? Maggie, you were no little girl last night. I saw the real you. The one you bury under those tailored suits and that tight bun—just like an old spinster. Is that what you want, Maggie Andrews? Tell me the truth—is that what you want? To be the spinster head of a company you hate?"

"I don't hate my father's company!"

"You hate working there, admit it. Maggie, you have the soul of an artist; I see the way you look at that scrap of fabric. That piece of tapestry means nothing to me but that it touches your heart. When you look at it, I get glimpses of the passionate woman I made love to last night."

She wanted to lie to him, to tell him he was wrong—she loved her work and would be very happy to be married to the company. Unbidden, an image floated in her mind: herself ten years from now, sitting in her father's chair, unsmiling, controlled, professional, alone. A spinster. Spinning on her heel so he would not read the truth in her face, she turned her back to him.

On the bed, face down, lay the tiny tapestry scrap that started it all. That blasted thing had been the catalyst that spiraled her out of control last night and threatened to do so again. What was it about that little leprechaun that moved her heart so? Her heart full, she picked it up and turned it over, once again running her finger along the edges, drinking in its every detail.

Liam knew Maggie could not see the thumbs up sign the little man gave him, but with a frown, he hushed Seamus anyway. Maggie stood on the cusp of a great decision, although Liam doubted she knew it yet. He did not want to disturb the thoughts he had set in motion.

How had the ancient weaver managed to find colors so vibrant? Who was she? Where had this piece come from? Questions swirled around Maggie's brain as she considered the mystery. Liam, of course, was right. For two years she pretended she loved the company, loved the idea of taking over, while fighting the panic that she wasn't good enough. And she wasn't. She never would be. The realization felt like a dagger of betrayal through her heart.

"You remind me of things I left in my past, Mr. Finnerty. My father counts on me; he has always built the company so that he might someday turn it over to his own son. Or daughter. I cannot spend my life wishing Tom back to life. I can only make the best of what I have. To turn my back on my father is not an option."

The words were bitter in her mouth. Setting the tapestry onto the bed, her finger trailed along the edge one last time before she turned away.

"Maggie..." Liam tried to stop her as she stepped toward the bathroom.

"Grab her, man! Don't just stand there like some bloody doormat!"

In desperation, Liam followed Seamus' advice. Taking a step to block the door, he grabbed her shoulders to prevent her from running away.

"Maggie, you have to get rid of your martyr complex. You don't owe this to your father—and he has no right to ask it of you. I remember how surprised he was when you came to him after Tom's funeral and told him you'd like to learn how to lead. He didn't expect it of you, then."

"But he does now."

"Yes, because your act has convinced him you love what you're doing. But a blind man can see you hate it."

"I fooled you. Until that blasted tapestry showed up."

"Well, you have me there. I was convinced you were just a tight-ass with no personality."

Liam knew the words hurt her, but he didn't back down. He had fallen in love with the woman underneath. If being candid was the only way to make her realize she was living a lie, then candid he would be.

"Maggie, you tried so hard to bury the artistic side of you that you went and buried your passion along with it. I've seen how much you love art, and last night I felt your passion." His voice gentled as his fingers traced the line of her jaw. "Maggie, you are a beautiful woman when you aren't hiding from yourself."

Her eyes dropped as she fought back the tears. "Oh, Liam, you don't understand. I can't…I can't let my father down."

She looked like a wounded dove. Sliding his hand under his chin, he tilted her head up and watched a tear escape to slide down her cheek. With his thumb, he brushed it away and bent to kiss her quivering red lips.

Maggie's control hung by a thread. She stood very still as Liam's lips touched hers, desperately trying not to give in. For two years she had been a pillar of steel, denying the life she wanted. Her shoulders slumped as she leaned into him and returned his kiss.

Liam wanted her. God help him, but her pain fanned the embers inside him. His protective nature ignited and he imagined himself with great big wings that he could fold over the two of them, giving her refuge. When he heard Seamus' voice, he dared not look up for fear of seeing those wings in reality.

"Aye, that's the way, man. Gentle her. She's like a hurt wild bird, she is."

Maggie broke the kiss, swallowing hard. Barely able to breathe, she sought his eyes as she faced her truths. "If I don't take the company and keep it in the family, then who would? He would have to sell it or he would be forced to work until he dies. Neither is an option I can allow."

Her eyes searched his and Liam understood she wanted an answer. She only saw the two options; did he have a third?

"Perhaps he can find someone to sell it to he would trust." He took a deep breath and ventured deep, keeping his hands around her waist. "Someone like me."

"You?" Maggie took a step back.

"What's wrong with me? I know the company inside and out; I'm good at what I do—very good. You saw last night. Strange as it may seem, I am not content to stay where I am the rest of my life. I already decided I'd stay for another three years because of the expansion your father is doing—I want to see that through. But then I plan to leave and start my own business."

"And if I weren't there to take over for my father...."

"Then I'd consider staying." He sighed. "No, never mind. It wouldn't work."

"Why not?" The more Maggie considered Liam in her father's position, the more she saw the advantages. She was privy to her father's counsel and knew he thought of Liam as his right hand.

"Because I've set aside enough money to start up a business, not to buy one that's well-established." His eyes narrowed. "Unless…"

He shot a glance at the tapestry.

"Oh, no, boy-o. No pot o' gold here. That's a fairy tale told by them pesky creatures to get us leprechauns in trouble. Sorry, but there's no money to be had from me."

Maggie followed his glance. "How can the tapestry help? Even if we find the other piece and I do restore it, selling it still wouldn't be enough."

Liam's shoulders slumped. "I know."

But Maggie wasn't ready to give up so easily. For the first time since her brother's death, she saw a way out—a way to please both herself and her father. Liam Finnerty was the perfect person to take over the company—and she was going to make sure he did.

She backed away and put her hands on her hips. "Liam…what's your middle name?"

He frowned at her non sequitur. "Patrick, why?"

"Liam Patrick Finnerty, if you don't have more confidence than that, then you'll never get my father's company. If you're really serious, and I mean really, really serious, then I will help you make it happen."

She smiled at his look of astonishment and let her hands drop down. "Liam, you're right. I don't want to work for my father and I don't want to own the company. I want to find a quiet museum or a nice antiquities bureau somewhere, and restore ancient art to my heart's content."

She laughed out loud for the first time in ages. "It may not be glamorous, and I'll never have a position out front, but that's just fine with me."

Liam had never heard her laugh. Like long, deep wind chimes, softly sounding on a warm summer's night, their tones pealing through the darkness, her laughter sang in his heart and he knew his course. With a resolute step, he swept her into his arms and kissed her soundly.

She yielded to him, to the strength in his arms, to the force of his tongue on her lips. Sliding her hands along his forearms, she reveled in the firm muscles bunched under his skin. Her hands slid up and around his neck, feeling freer than she had ever felt before. His tongue slid into her mouth and she tasted him with hunger reawakened.

This time Liam broke the kiss as he stepped back long enough to scoop her up in his arms. "Maggie Andrews, I want to hear you laugh again."

She couldn't hold it in. Her startled exclamation turned into a full-throated laugh; lacing her fingers behind his neck and holding on tightly, she let her head fall back. A river of golden-red hair tumbled over his arm exposing her long, slender neck to his kiss. Twirling her toward the bed, he bent to kiss that vulnerable whiteness. He felt the vibration of her moan through his lips and he kissed her neck again.

Maggie pulled herself up to nuzzle against his ear, but Liam pulled back, raised her up several inches higher—and dropped her on the bed. She shrieked and put her hands out as she bounced, her laughter filling the room again.

The edge of the tapestry frame rested alongside her arm, but before she could pick it up, Liam reached for it.

"Let's just set this little fellow aside for the moment, shall we?" Grinning, he started to set it on the dresser.

"Oh, me boy-o, don't put me upside down again!"

"Sorry, Seamus, my friend. I don't much care for an audience right now." Liam deliberately turned the frame over and set it face down.

Maggie giggled. "You named the leprechaun?"

Liam's mischievous grin answered her. "Well, it just seemed the little guy should have a name, that's all. Ms. Andrews, you are a beautiful woman and I want you very much."

She giggled again and gestured toward the bulge under the towel. "So I can see. Well, Mr. Finnerty, what are you waiting for?"

Liam stripped the towel from his waist in one quick motion. His magnificent cock stood straight out, the dark head pulsing with his arousal. A bit of pre-come already glistened at the tip and Maggie's eyes darkened with desire.

She slithered around on the bed, turning over onto her stomach and lying lengthwise so that she held herself up by her elbows just at the edge of the bed. Her nipples had grown hard under the shirt that now rode up, exposing her rear to his view. She wiggled her ass, enticing him, mischief in her eyes. And when he stepped forward, his long cock right before her face, she complied, wrapping her diminutive hand around his thick shaft and teasing the smooth, velvety tip of his cock with her warm, wet tongue.

His groan gave her a deep feeling of satisfaction. Widening her mouth, she leaned forward to close her soft lips around the entire tip of his cock, permitting him to revel in her tight, wet, warmth. Caressing the head of his cock with her tongue, she tasted her fill of him, her body unable to remain still on the bed as her own need grew.

Damn, but the woman turned him on. Power surged through his body at the sight of her stretched out on the bed, her warm eyes turned up toward him and her sensuous lips wrapped around his cock. "Yes, woman. Suck me."

Maggie grinned around her mouthful of cock. She had always preferred strong men. Not that she had that many lovers in years past, but she was no virgin, despite being chaste for the last several years. Lowering her eyes to appreciate the beauty in front of her, she sucked hard and pulled more of his hard cock into her mouth. The ridges of his throbbing veins rubbed her tongue as she slid it along the underside of his thick shaft.

Liam was tall and broad shouldered, with a cock to match his size. She tried to take it all, but found only about two-thirds of it could fit into her mouth and down her throat in the position she was in. Pulling away, she started to shift position when he stopped her.

"No, not yet. Take off that shirt, Maggie girl."

With a brazen smile, Maggie kneeled on the bed facing him. Her fingers undid the buttons, pulling apart the sides of the shirt to reveal her ample breasts, heavy with arousal. Her nipples, reddened and hard, tingled as the shirt passed over them. Tossing it toward the pile of clothes already on the floor, Maggie sat back on her heels and cupped her breasts, holding them up for his inspection.

His own hand rubbing along his cock, he watched her play with herself. The tigress he had glimpsed last night was now a playful kitten, grinning at him with an abandon he had only dreamed about. She pinched her nipples and he knew he wanted to pinch them harder, just to hear the wonderful noises she would make. But then her hand started to glide down the smooth surface of her stomach and Liam reached out to stop her.

"That's for me to explore. Come here." He knelt on the bed beside her and pushed her backwards, both of them now lay side-by-side across the bed. Her breasts rose and fell with her quickened breathing as he caressed one, squeezing the softness in his hand. Pulling a nipple into his mouth, his tongue flicked over it and felt the little bud swell and become hard.

Taking his time, he teased her nipple, pulling on it with his teeth, then letting it go and smoothing it with his tongue. Glancing up at her face, he saw her eyes were closed; her brow furrowed with pain. But when she arched her back, pushed her breast up to him and used her hands to keep his face where it was, he knew the pain was also pleasure.

Liam shifted his attention to her other breast and Maggie squirmed as he played with her body. He was controlling her and the tigress paced in her cage. Each touch of his hand, his lips, his tongue pushed the bolt further and further back. Last night she had barely controlled the animal. Today, Maggie wondered if she had any control at all. And when his mouth left her breast and his tongue licked its way down her stomach, she knew the animal was in Liam's hands—not hers.

Maggie responded with such incredibly delicious sounds as his tongue traced a path over her smooth skin from her breasts to her navel and over her belly. The hair that covered her mound gathered dark and thick, hiding what he sought. He paused to run his fingers through the fine, silky hair relishing the softness. Another moan made him grin. She made a wonderful instrument for him to play.

Oh, but the man was driving her wild! Her hands groped downward, running along his back, feeling the soft curls of his thick black hair. His breath on her mound made her ache and she tried to arch herself up to him, to hurry him along.

Liam grinned at her attempts to take control and looked up at her. "Maggie, my dear, your body is mine. Now if you can't behave, I'll just have to tie you down so I can play in peace."

"You wouldn't!" In spite of her words, the thought actually excited her and she knew more of her juices had joined the pool gathering at the entrance of her pussy.

His eyes narrowed. "Is that a dare?"

After a moment's hesitation, she replied. "No." She pulled her hands from his shoulders and raised them over her head. Immediately she felt vulnerable and open to his every whim—and it excited her even as it raised her curiosity.

"Good. Now keep them there."

Liam turned back to her mound, where he had continuously been running his fingers. Hiding his grin, he couldn't believe that she had done what he asked. That hardened, professional, always-in-control woman really was a front, just as he always suspected. Underneath was a passionate, sexy, submissive woman. Changing positions, he knelt on the bed and decided to test his theory.

"Spread your legs."

The command was demeaning and Maggie kept her legs shut tight, even though she wanted his touch. She was no whore to be ordered about.

He stroked his cock and raised an eyebrow at her. "You need to let me in, Maggie. Now spread your legs for me."

Liam knew he could just as easily part her thighs himself and that in the normal course of lovemaking, he probably would have. But he wanted to see just how far her submissiveness extended.

"Make me."

She threw the challenge at him with a glint of laughter in her eyes. He wanted to dominate her? He needed to tame the tigress first. Did he have it in him? Fervently, Maggie hoped Liam would accept the challenge.

A slow smile spread over his face as Liam understood. "Very well." He stood and bent down beside the bed to pull out the bottom drawer with a hard tug. Taking out something from the inside, he palmed it and stood up. "I warned you."

Liam reached forward, ostensibly to caress her calf. But when his hand reached her ankle, he pulled on it, turning her on the bed while sliding his tie under her limb. Before she could pull away, her ankle was caught in a noose. Grinning, he tied the other end of his good silk tie to the post at the corner of the bed.

"What! Liam! I can't believe..." Maggie sat up quickly, her voice trailing off as he bent to get another tie. Even as her fingers tried to undo the first knot, Liam pulled her other leg and spread her wide open. Off balance, she leaned to the side, still trying to work the first knot.

But Liam had picked up two ties this time. Once her leg was firmly anchored to the post, he took his last tie and grabbed her hands. Not stopping to let her catch her breath, he looped the tie around her wrists and tied her hands together. Then, forcing her to lie down, he pulled her hands up over her head.

But now he was stuck. The carved wooden headboard gave him no place to anchor the last tie. And he had only brought three with him. Hanging onto the end of her tether, he stood beside the bed and flipped over the tapestry.

"Oh, now ye need me help, ye'll let me watch ye."

Maggie was giggling on the bed at Liam's predicament. Clearly he would not be able to tie her up quite as much as he wanted to. Part of her triumphed and pulled on the tie he held; part of her was disappointed and she turned her head.

And so she did not see Liam's urgent look at the little leprechaun. Nor did she see a small opening appear in the headboard right at mattress level. All she felt was Liam's tug on her bindings as he straightened out her arms and fastened them to the headboard.

Only then did he pause and look her in the eye, gauging her reaction.

Her face was snarled with frustration. How had he done that? She struggled against her bindings and Liam checked to see that they did not tighten. They didn't. He knew how to tie a knot that wouldn't move and cut off her circulation. Maggie was held fast.

"Liam Finnerty, you let me go right now!"

"Is that what you want, Maggie? Do you really want me to let you go?" His fingers caressed her skin, running along her chin and brushing over her neck.

She almost spit out the word "yes," but found it stuck in her throat. She was helpless, at his mercy. His hand slid back to her breast and his fingers rolled her nipple, squeezing it tightly. She moaned instead.

"I'll take that as permission to continue." His smile was soft and gentle as his hand drifted down her body, making her writhe again.

She knew where he was going. He would touch her pussy and find out how wet she was. He had mastered her at her own game and her juices flowed freely. Never had anyone tied her down and as she pulled against her bindings, Maggie was surprised at how freeing they were. For the first time in her life, she could not control the situation in any matter whatsoever. Totally at Liam's mercy, she only had to relax and enjoy what he did to her. Still, nervousness kept her on edge.

Reaching up, Liam pulled a pillow down and slid it under Maggie's hips. He hid his delight when she raised her body to give him room. The little tigress enjoyed this! Satisfied she was in easy reach, he slid onto the bed and lay between her spread knees, his face inches from her pussy.

The smell of her arousal was potent. With her legs spread wide, she could not stop him from touching her and that, in turn, made him hard again. But he would play just a little more before he entered her. He wanted to see how far she would let him go before begging him for release.

Maggie could feel his warm breath on her pussy lips. No one had ever tasted her before. No one. She held her breath in anticipation. Would he? Or would Liam turn away as other lovers had? Swallowing down a whimper, she waited.

Liam sensed her stillness and glanced up at her face. Her breathing was steady and deep and after a moment, she looked down at him with longing in her eyes. He smiled and inched himself forward, turning his attention to those two luscious lips that hid a treasure he wished to sample.

With his fingers, he parted those twin gates that leaked their precious fluid and gazed at her exquisite sex. Her vagina gaped open, her creamy whiteness pooled just inside, a testament to her arousal. Just above, her clit peeked out from under its hood and Liam knew his tongue would engorge it further.

Using his fingers to spread her labia, he leaned forward to take her clit between his lips. Sucking gently, he slowly rolled his tongue over and around the hard little bud. She moaned and he glanced up to see her head thrown back and her breasts pointed to the ceiling as she arched her back.

Maggie didn't know if it was pleasure or pain, but she didn't want it to stop. She cried out as his tongue moved faster. His teeth closed on her sensitive bud and her mind went numb. She heard the cars and trucks in the street outside, but they ceased to have meaning. Over and over, his tongue flicked her clit without mercy and she thrashed in her bindings.

"What do you want, Maggie? I control your body, but I will give you back that control if you want it. Tell me, Maggie, shall I untie you?"

Liam's voice compelled an answer, but her ragged breath could only gasp out her answer. "No! Liam, please. Please don't stop."

Her juices caused his fingers to slip on her labia so he adjusted his position, pulling back those swollen lips. Again Maggie's inner lips opened of their own volition, inviting him in; this time he accepted the invitation. His hot tongue scooped up a large swallow of her juices, savoring her salty taste and her musky scent before he swallowed her essence, making her a part of him. Plunging his tongue into her pussy, he pushed on her clit with his nose, overwhelming himself with her scent and taste. Grinding his face into her, he drove her body fiercely. Bucking against her bindings, she begged him for release.

Maggie was past thinking. Her pleas and wordless cries turned raspy as he enjoyed her clit and Liam knew she could not take much more. Withdrawing, he knelt, much as he had last night. She lay spread before him; helpless, spread-eagled for his pleasure and Liam prepared to ram his cock home where it belonged.

"I am going to take you hard, Maggie Andrews. And you will come only when I say so. Do you hear me?"

Through the agony of her need, Liam's words resonated in her soul and her body replied to his domination with increased fervor. "Yes, Liam, please. Oh, please, take me now. Please!"

She had begged. It was all he asked for. With a forceful thrust, Liam's cock entered her, stretching her wide. She screamed and he thrust again.

"Yes, Liam! Oh, please, yes." Maggie's muscles grabbed his thick cock, hungry to have him deeper into her body.

Liam's groans joined hers as he pounded into her again and again. Suddenly she lay very still, every muscle tightened, poised; breathing in tiny spurts; whimpering. One second. Two. She lost count. The tigress pounced and, with a cry wrenched from her soul, Maggie's body wracked her passion upon his cock. Again and again, Liam felt her muscles milk him until, with a cry to match hers, his body shuddered as his seed shot deep into her body.

How long she stayed, balanced on the edge of her orgasm, Maggie had no idea. Only that when she exploded, she felt it deep into her soul. She let go and her body writhed as each wave convulsed through her being. Every thrust Liam made carried her higher. For long minutes she floated as spasms wracked her body; dimly she was aware of them slowing, then stopping.

Spent, Liam collapsed beside her. For several moments, he could not think, but simply floated in his own haze of sated exhaustion. He lay his head on her breast, listening to her heartbeat slow to a more normal pace and when he had the strength, he raised his head to look at her.

Maggie's eyes were still closed, but as he watched, she took in a deep breath, letting it out in a long, slow, contented sigh. Opening her eyes, she smiled a lazy smile and shivered.

"Let me get you untied." Liam stretched as he stood, his now limp cock shrunken, yet still impressive. In a few moments, Maggie was free and she stretched along the bed, not really wanting to get up. Liam humored her, pulling the covers up over her and sliding in beside her.

She nestled into his arms and looked up at him.

"Do I dare believe I might really not have to run the company?"

"Dare to believe it, Maggie. I don't know how I can get enough money to buy it from your father, but I'm sure something will turn up." He leaned over and winked at the tapestry. "Right, Seamus?"

"Ah, me boy-o, I do believe yer right. In fact…"

Seamus' comment was cut off by Maggie's cry. "Liam! The time! You have an appointment in fifteen minutes!"

"Damn!"

In a flash, Liam was out of the bed and on his way into the bath to wash up after their escapade. "Damn and damn again." Returning, he took the boxers Maggie held out for him. "You're not going?"

Maggie laughed out loud at the absurd thought. "No, Liam, my savior. I am not going. I'm staying here and taking a long, leisurely bath to wash off not one, but two sexual rendezvous!"

He grinned. "Give me a little while and I'll cover you again, Maggie Andrews. And make you beg me for it."

She wrinkled her nose as he pulled up his pants. "Fat chance, Liam Finnerty. You may have pushed my buttons this time, but we'll see who the boss is next time."

Maggie buttoned his sleeves as he buttoned his shirt. All his ties were still tied around the bedposts and she chose one while he finished up. Smoothing it out as best she could, she handed it to him.

"Ye can always blame the wrinkles on yer suitcase, lad."

Liam grinned into the mirror over the dresser and tightened the knot. Perhaps he'd stop and buy another tie on his way back to the hotel. He turned and Maggie handed him his briefcase. Still nude, she had forgotten her nakedness in the rush to get him out the door. Leaning over, he tweaked a nipple as he stole a goodbye kiss.

She squealed and pushed him toward the door, ducking into the bath so she couldn't be seen from the hallway. Waiting until she heard the door click shut, she emerged, rummaging around the drawers until she found the clothes she wanted. Humming to herself, she went off to take her bath.

And on the little scrap of cloth, sitting face up on the dresser top, a little man dressed all in green clapped his hands and kicked his heels.

"Ah, yes, Seamus O'Brien. Ye are a genius indeed!"

Chapter Four

After her bath, dressed in jeans and sweater, Maggie felt truly relaxed for the first time in two years. Telling her father she would no longer accept responsibility for the company would be difficult; but already the wheels were turning in her brain, determining just how she would broach the subject and tell him her plans.

There was no denying her emotions were running high. Liam's dominance of her this morning had no right to thrill her as much as it did. She was an independent, modern woman, damn it. So why was she so excited when he tied her up? He certainly hadn't raped her — Maggie knew she consented to every part of what he did to her. And boy, what he did to her!

A knock at the door disrupted her reverie; the bellboy stood there with the morning paper in his hand. "Mr. Finnerty said to bring this up to you, Ma'am. He said you might want something to read."

And Mr. Finnerty must've already tipped him well, Maggie surmised as the young man simply delivered the paper and left without holding out his hand. Shutting the door, she threw the paper on the bed and opened the curtains

Sunlight streamed in, but Maggie could see the day was a chilly one. Everyone who hurried below had their collars turned up and bent their bodies into the wind. Glad she didn't need to go out into the cold, she decided a morning spent with the paper wasn't such a bad idea.

Tucking her legs under her, she curled up on the bed with the tapestry on the dresser beside her and the paper spread on her lap.

"Well, Seamus, looks like it's just the two of us for the rest of the morning."

Out of the corner of her eye, she thought she saw the leprechaun wink. Looking again, it looked no different than before and she just shook her head.

The front pages of the paper were dedicated to world and national news; Maggie skimmed the headlines—the world was still turning. Another section, devoted to local affairs, seemed more promising. Sightseeing was not why they were in Ireland, but still, she had hopes that they might get around to see a few of the landmarks before they had to fly home.

Scanning the articles, she was just about to turn the page when a rather striking photograph of an old castle tower caught her eye. Ireland was filled with old ruins, but for some reason, this structure looked familiar. "Glenquin Castle...south of Limerick. Pretty country. Wonder what's going on there?"

Her gaze skimmed the article under the picture—apparently the castle was undergoing restoration and some items of interest had been found. A hidden vault under the structure had been opened and the archeologists had discovered a treasure trove of antiquities. Several pieces of common jewelry, dozens of casks and crocks of all sizes, clothing, and a few old, rusted swords. A price hadn't yet been put on the value of the find.

She read the article all the way to the last paragraph, where she stopped, reading out loud in her shock. "The most curious find was that of a torn tapestry, according to the curator of Glenquin Castle. Faded and worn, the figures of a man and woman embracing are still visible. What makes it so unique is the Celtic pattern of the border around the outside of the tapestry. This interwoven knot is unlike most others in early Irish design. It is thought to be, perhaps, a family motif."

For several moments, Maggie stared at the paragraph, reading over the words, her heart thumping in her chest. With wide eyes, she reached for the tapestry scrap and examined it again. Unlike the tapestry mentioned in the paper, her leprechaun's colors were still bright and vibrant. And the knot design that niggled at her brain in the store...she grabbed the paper and read the last line again. "It is thought to be, perhaps, a family design."

"A family design...blast it! I know I've seen that pattern somewhere before! But it looks like we may have found your greater half, little leprechaun." She snorted. "Seamus. Leave it to Liam to name a figure in a picture."

*****

Liam returned just after lunch, but Maggie wasn't in the room. The tapestry lay on the pillow with a note on top:

"Gone to rent a car. Be back soon."

"Seamus, what is she up to?"

The little leprechaun popped up out of the fabric. "Ah, me boy-o, I'm not spilling the lass's secrets! But she's a fine woman and I'm almost home."

"What do you mean—almost home?"

Seamus danced around the tree bole, which had also popped up, and clicked his heels again. "Not tellin' ye. The lass will be back any minute and she'll tell ye, she will. Just do as she asks, mind ye. It'll sound preposterous, but do it anyway. Promise me."

"Her note says she's gone to rent a car."

"Aye. Now give me yer promise that ye'll do as she asks. Don't make me get out me sword again."

Liam remembered all to well how the little leprechaun drew first blood the last time they had 'dueled' and he held up his hands in surrender. "Fine, fine! I promise I'll do as she asks."

The key turned in the lock and Maggie entered, looking a bit flustered. "I did it! I rented a car and got directions to Limerick. From there we go to Newcastlewest and then sort of south to Killeedy." She waved a piece of paper as she entered.

"Why do we want to kill Edie?" Seamus was right, this was a preposterous request.

Maggie stopped mid-stride and gave him a puzzled look, then laughed. "We're not going to kill anyone. We're going to a place called Killeedy. See?" She showed him the map she had picked up downstairs at the desk. A line highlighted a route from Dublin toward Limerick, then veered south to pass through another large town before stopping at a vague point between North and South Killeedy.

"Do I get to ask why?"

"I'll tell you in the car. Go ahead and change into comfortable clothes—did you bring boots?" When Liam shook his head, she continued. "Neither did I. Well, with any luck, it won't be too wet. Go on, change your clothes."

Liam stepped up to her and kissed her soundly instead.

The crush of his lips on hers took her breath away and for a moment, she forgot their mission. Her head swimming, she swayed and Liam caught her shoulders to steady her. Opening her eyes, Maggie needed to blink several times before his broad chest came back into focus. "What was that for?"

"Because I have never seen you so beautiful. The uptight, unhappy woman I walked into this hotel with yesterday is certainly not the excited, vibrant woman who's ordering me about today. I like you better this way."

His compliment made her blush and smile. So intent was she on solving the mystery of the tapestry that she had forgotten to put on the mask that would keep him at a distance. A distance she no longer wanted. "Maybe I should just give you some privacy and let you get dressed…" Feeling suddenly shy and awkward, she escaped into the bath.

"So what's in Killeedy, Seamus?" Liam pulled out a pair of jeans and quickly changed.

"True love," was the only answer the little man would give him.

Collecting the tapestry, Liam knocked on the bathroom door. In only a few more moments, they were out the door and on their way.

* * * * *

Driving on the left side of the road through the city would have given Liam nightmares, but Maggie handled the car as if she'd been driving 'backwards' all her life.

Confident and self-assured, she wove in and out of the traffic while filling in the story for Liam.

"I don't know any more about that tapestry other than what the newspaper said, but the border patterns have to match! I just wish I could remember where I've seen that pattern before."

"What, the border pattern? Why? What's so special about it?" They were out of Dublin now and moving quickly down the motorway, bound for Limerick.

"I know I've seen it somewhere before. The paper said the experts thought it might be a family knot design, although that's not traditionally how they were used."

Liam frowned. "How else might they have been used?"

"Mostly borders of that sort were just decoration. The Book of Kells has lots of them; practically every page is bordered by some sort of design. Animals, knots, flowers or vines." Maggie shrugged. "The tapestry has a rare pattern, however."

"Well, it can't be that rare. It's the same pattern as on my ring."

"What?" In shock, Maggie looked over at Liam, who held up his hand. *That* was where she'd seen the pattern before! All this time it had been right in front of her! "Why didn't you say something?"

"I didn't think it was important. This ring has been in the family for eons. But there's nothing fancy about it; just silver twisted into a bunch of knots. Always thought it a bit plain, myself."

"The simplicity is what makes it beautiful. If you follow the pattern, you'll see it's all one line interwoven on itself."

"I know. It used to keep me occupied when sitting through boring meetings." He grinned and Maggie laughed.

"I thought you loved the company and all that went with it."

"Doesn't mean I didn't find some of those meetings deadly boring. Especially early on when I wasn't leading them."

She chose to ignore his comment, although it didn't surprise her. He liked the limelight as much as she hated it. "You said that ring has been in the family for generations. Are there any stories connected with it?"

"If there were, they've all been lost. My grandfather used to wear it and when he died, he bequeathed it to me. All he ever told me was that his grandfather gave it to him with the instruction that he was to pass it on to his own grandson. I wear it more in his honor than anything else."

Maggie had never considered Liam's family. To know he honored his grandfather's memory touched her; in spite of his earlier words, he valued family as well.

The scenery was beautiful and although tempted to stop several times, the two continued driving. While the hundred and thirty or so miles would take only a little over two hours on US highways, traveling in Ireland took a little longer. While they were on the main motorway, they made good time, but as the roads became smaller and smaller, the amount of money spent on their upkeep dwindled. Soon Maggie was dodging potholes and swerving around corners not designed for cars. Again, Liam was impressed with Maggie's driving abilities.

When she wasn't putting on a show for the employees, her natural confidence beamed.

She also wasn't afraid to stop and ask directions. Since neither of them knew exactly where Glenquin Castle was, they were dependent on the locals to get them the final few miles. Finally they saw the tower looming in the distance and it was simply a matter of getting to it.

Three stories of almost solid grey stone climbed into the sky. The cylindrical tower was the tallest structure within eyesight and they found it with ease.

Parking the car, Liam picked up the tapestry and held his ring to the side. The knot designs were identical. Maggie shook her head, still amazed. "If the curator here is right and that design is a family one, then perhaps your ancestors lived here at one time."

"My ancestors did come from County Limerick, but that was a hundred and fifty years ago. I'm afraid what part of the county is lost information."

"Ah, me home! I haven't seen me castle in hundreds of years. Nice to see the people doing some work to keep it up."

Liam chanced a glance at the leprechaun. Seamus was standing on his rock, peering out toward the building they approached. With a loud sniff, the little man pulled out a huge green handkerchief, noisily blew his nose and wiped his eyes. Liam sighed. Soon the leprechaun would be reunited with the lovers he'd been torn from and Liam would never see him again. Just as he was getting used to having the little guy around.

This was Maggie's show and Liam stepped back as they approached the castle entrance. Her no-nonsense business attitude stood her in good stead when she asked to meet with the curator. At first the attendant tried to put Maggie off as just another American tourist, but Maggie politely put the woman in her place and insisted on an interview with the man in charge.

A short, balding, bespectacled man, looking rather like an Irish leprechaun, came out of an office at the attendant's bidding. Perhaps it was his forest green waistcoat, trimmed with gold buttons, or perhaps it was his round face, lit up with a jovial smile. But for Liam it was the twinkle in his eye as he winked at him when the two introduced themselves. He couldn't help but glance down at the tapestry piece in his hands to be sure that Seamus was still in place. The tapestry leprechaun was only cloth.

Before Liam could say anything, however, the curator was ushering them into his office and bidding them to have a seat in the large leather chairs that sat before his desk.

"Please call me Ian. I've lived in these parts all me life and I can't say we've ever had such a find as the treasure we found in the storeroom. We'll be years researchin' and restorin'. A curator's dream!" Sitting up on the edge of the chair, he leaned over the desk with excitement in his eye. "Now, ye say ye have the matching piece to our tapestry that was hidden all these long years?"

"Yes, we think we do. Liam?" Maggie gestured to Liam, who still held the scrap of fabric in its frame. Almost reluctantly, he set it on the desk before the curator, eyeing him suspiciously. Seamus-the-leprechaun remained just a picture while the curator picked up the frame to examine the cloth. They might have different names, and their features might only be similar, but Liam was becoming more and more convinced the leprechaun was playing tricks somehow.

"The colors here are much more vibrant than the colors of the tapestry we found."

"Yes, but that could be due to several reasons." Maggie prepared to list them, but the curator held up his hand. She paused.

"I cannot be sure without checking the two pieces together. Why don't the two of you take a walk around the grounds while I get the other piece?"

Maggie hesitated, looking to Liam for support. While she was sure the curator would be careful with their little piece, she didn't just want to give it to the man, especially when it wasn't really hers.

Liam stood. "That will be fine. Maggie?" Gesturing to the door, Liam's intent was clear. She stood and started toward the door with Liam right behind her. Just about to leave, she turned and looked at the curator, who stood behind his desk, a bemused expression on his face. His spectacles were pushed up on his head and he held the piece close to his eyes. Without a word, Maggie turned and left the office.

Once more outside the building, she took Liam's arm, a look of consternation on her face.

"What's the matter?" He squeezed her hand where it rested in the crook of his arm. Leading her around the tower, he steered her toward a hedgerow. The late afternoon sun hung low in the clear sky. If the sailor's adage was true, there would be fair weather for the parade on the morrow.

Maggie's sigh came from her toes. "I don't know, Liam. Didn't you think there was something odd about that man?"

Chancing an askance look at the woman beside him, Liam feigned an air of nonchalance. "Odd? No, I didn't think so."

She shook her head. "I can't quite put my finger on it, but it's almost like I've met him before."

Liam steered her further away from the tower and toward a more private area of the grounds. "I don't know where you would have met him." He needed to get her off the topic. A low rock just ahead provided a diversion. "Here, let's have a seat."

With a gentleman-like flourish, Liam brushed off the stone and made an elaborate bow to his lady. Giggling, Maggie curtsied to him and flounced out imaginary skirts as she turned and sat on the rock. Liam put his foot next to her and leaned down to kiss her.

Except that the rock was slippery with moss and his foot slipped. Maggie squealed and only her hands catching his shoulders saved his head from banging on the tree behind them. He righted himself and the two burst into laughter.

"So much for my romantic side." Liam brushed the dirt from his jeans.

"You are very romantic, Liam." Maggie stood and put her hands out to him. He took them and swung her around in a circle until they were dizzy and out of breath. She wobbled over to lean against a tree to catch her breath, laughing at him, swaying and regaining his balance where he stood.

His grin was decidedly lopsided as he gazed at her. "Do you realize that's the first time you've ever called me 'Liam'?"

She blushed. It was. Her heart lodged in her throat at the sight of him striding toward her, the breeze lifting the curls of his hair. With new eyes she saw him, as if he were clad in armor, a sword strapped to his side, a horse waiting behind him. With a sudden clarity, Maggie saw him for what he was—her knight in shining armor and she loved him.

In two strides, Liam covered the distance between them to bury his fingers in her hair and turn her face toward his. A face so incredibly beautiful in the soft, dying light of the day. The sun's rays glimmered in her auburn tresses, forming a halo of fire around her face. In his mind's eye, she wore a garland woven of wildflowers and a flowing gown the color of pure ivory. Her eyes radiated love and trust and Liam admitted what the leprechaun knew all along: he loved Maggie Andrews.

So intent on one another, they did not hear the approach of quiet footsteps. Ian, the curator, carried two pieces of cloth in his hands, one large and faded, one small and vibrant. The two lovers embraced and he held the larger piece up, a mirror image of the couple before him; William of Killeedy dressed in armor for battle and Margaret of Glenquin, the Englishman's daughter, in her billowing dress.

"Aye, just the way it was meant to be, eh, Seamus, me brother?"

"Would ye just put the two pieces together? I've been stuck here long enough! Besides which these two are the rightful owners of me tapestry and old Bantry will be wantin' to get home."

"Ah, don't go gettin' yer knickers in a twist. Here."

Ian held up the smaller piece, now released from the frame. As Liam leaned in to kiss Maggie, the two pieces touched, their edges melding as the threads rewove themselves. Color flowed from Seamus through the mend and flowers faded with time suddenly sprang to new life. The leaves on the tree turned green as life spread up the bole of the tree, now rejoined with its branches. And a pair of lovers, pale and grey, now glowed with renewal as their love blossomed again.

And beneath a real tree, only a little ways away, another pair of lovers embraced one another in the fading light.

"Kiss her, me boy-o. Kiss her and me spell is broken."

If Liam heard the little leprechaun, he gave him no heed; his attention too intent upon the woman whose face looked up at him, so trusting, so beautiful. Leaning forward, he brushed his lips against hers, savoring their softness. In the darkness, his voice was a whisper. "I love you, Maggie Andrews."

Maggie stood on tiptoe to meet him; a soft kiss at first, before pressing closer. His hands encircled her waist and she slid her palms along the muscles of his arms to embrace his shoulders. With a small, satisfied sigh, the last vestiges of her hard, professional shell slipped away. "I love you, Liam Finnerty."

Unnoticed by the lovers, Seamus O'Brien, at last freed from his spell, popped out of the tapestry and landed with a spring next to Ian, his brother leprechaun.

"Ian, I do believe ye've grown since last I stood next to ye!"

"Seamus, lad. That's what ye get for gettin' yerself stuck in a piece o' cloth all these years. Ahh, don't they look good together?"

"Aye, that they do." For several moments, the magical men watched Liam and Maggie fall more deeply in love. As the moon rose and the last of the sunlight faded from the sky, Seamus chuckled as he spread the tapestry upon the rock. Turning to his brother, they left the lovers.

"Ah, yes, Ian-lad, I tell ye, 'tis a genius I am."

About the author:

For many years, Diana Hunter confined herself to mainstream writings. Her interest in the world of dominance and submission, dormant for years, bloomed when she met a man who was willing to let her explore the submissive side of her personality. In her academic approach to learning about the lifestyle, she discovered hundreds of short stories that existed on the topic, but none of them seemed to express her view of a d/s relationship. Challenged by a friend to write a better one, she wrote her first BDSM novel, *Secret Submission*, published by Ellora's Cave Publishing.

Diana welcomes mail from readers. You can write to her c/o Ellora's Cave Publishing at 1337 Commerce Drive, Suite 13, Stow OH 44224.

Also by Diana Hunter:
Learning Curve
Secret Submission
Table For Four
Writers Unblocked
(*Ellora's Cavemen: Tales from the Temple III anthology*)

HARPIST BIZARRE

Sahara Kelly

Chapter One

"Dear Carly,

I'm here! Yes, after endless hours of trying to sleep and not beating the crap out of the kid who kicked the back of my seat halfway across the Atlantic, I'm finally on the 'Emerald Isle'! I have to tell you it's very 'emerald', too. Of course the fact that it's rained for the last few hours since I got here probably contributes to the greenness, but hell, right now I don't care.

I'm glad I followed your advice and got away from the orchestra AND dumb-shit idiot Steven. It was like leaving all that junk behind me when the plane lifted off from Logan, and I don't mind telling you that I was glad to see the back of that damned endless New England winter.

No rehearsals, no concerts, and most of all, no whining bassoon-players haunting my dressing room and trying to make nice-nice with me.

How he thought I was about to forgive him after finding him practicing his fingering on Dorothy's cleavage, I haven't a clue.

And you know something? She's welcome to him.

Sure I was hurt. After all, he was supposed to be MY boyfriend. But I guess it was more in his mind (and other places) than in mine. Because, frankly, my dear Carly, I don't give a damn! (Giggle) I'm relieved. Dorothy and her big boobs can have him. He can stick his bassoon anywhere he wants for all I care. And she can stick her flute...well, let's just leave it to the imagination. And yeah, I know what you're imagining. I spent most of the flight imagining the same thing!

Anyway, that's all behind me now. Tomorrow I'm going to play tourist and shop 'til I drop. I'll try and find you something very 'Irish', but I'm not sure the budget will run to that Waterford vase you asked for. I don't even know if there's a shop that carries it here in Ballyreath. It really is the absolutely typical little Irish village, and it has the usual assortment of small stores, (plenty of pubs of course), but I haven't really had time to explore yet.

Do you know I even saw a cottage with a thatched roof from the taxi on the way here? It was like something out of those fairy tales Mom used to read. No dwarfs or leprechauns though, just a normal looking pair of little rubber boots on the doorstep.

Well, I'm getting really tired so I'm going to close this letter and grab some downtime. My inner clock is way off base, and although it's early evening here, my body is telling me its midnight or something. I don't know if I can sleep, but I'm going to try. Luckily it's very quiet, not much traffic outside, so here's hoping!

Love ya sis, take care...

Fay"

* * * * *

Her pillow must have been filled with chunks of the Blarney Stone.

Fay Krakowski punched it for the fourteenth time, and attempted to find a spot that didn't crush her ear to numbness.

She sighed as she settled once more, knowing that it was probably her exhaustion that kept her from sleep, not the poor unfortunate pillow.

She'd lost track of the hours since she'd left Boston, and trying to figure out how long she'd been traveling simply gave her a headache.

Thinking about what she'd left behind gave her a headache too.

As guest pianist for the season with the Yankee Symphony Orchestra, her days had been filled with rehearsals, practice and more practice, and her nights had been spent doing what she loved best—making music.

And making out with Steven Greeley.

She turned over and snuggled under the puffy quilt, pulling it up around her ears to blot out his image.

It didn't work. He was tall, very good looking in an aesthetic sort of way, and had amazingly good hands. Well, it stood to reason that a bassoonist would be adept with his fingers, and he'd certainly proved the point.

Unfortunately he'd also proved the point with his mouth. On the second flautist's breasts.

Okay. So they were bigger than Fay's. A *lot* bigger. And Steven had made no secret of the fact that he was a breast man at heart.

Fay frowned. So why had he decided to target *her* for an affair? She never had been able to figure that one out. She knew she was pretty much the textbook definition of "average", with curly brown hair to her shoulders and her only distinguishing feature a pair of sea-blue eyes, ringed by long lashes.

They were a throwback to some of her Irish ancestors, her mother proudly told her. Blue eyes "put in with dirty fingers" she used to say. Which was also why a nice Polish girl was blessed with the unlikely name of Fay.

Sadly, she bore absolutely no resemblance to any kind of "fey" creature. Of average height, average build, and nondescript assets, Fay knew she'd probably be more of a brown worker-fairy, than a flitting little Victorian flower sprite.

Or a leprechaun, come to think of it.

After all, she was in Ireland now. Perhaps if she got up early enough she'd catch one of those little buggers and make him part with his pot of gold. Or was that wishes? Three of 'em?

Sleepily, she tried to remember if it was Aladdin who got the three wishes or the one who caught a leprechaun. And did you have to do it by his ear or his toe? Something about rainbows maybe.

Her thoughts tumbled over each other and she finally drifted off to sleep.

Sometime during the night, the dream came.

* * * * *

Fay stood in a field, high up, surrounded by green and rolling hills. A soft mist brushed their peaks and the light of sunrise turned the sky to shades of pink and gold.

Her heart beat fast, and she waited for something—someone. She had no idea who, but she knew he would come.

And there he was.

She saw his head, long black hair flying, as he climbed the slope of the field towards her.

Then his body, clad in an old fashioned shirt with laces untied and sleeves billowing. Tight breeches covered his legs, and his boots clung to his calves, flexing with his muscles as his long stride brought him closer.

He was gorgeous.

Fay blinked at the sight of him. Bright green eyes blinked back at her as his mouth curved into a welcoming smile.

"Ye're here at last, mavourneen," he whispered.

Fay's voice seemed to have deserted her. She didn't know this man, and yet she'd been waiting for him.

"It's been a long lonely time without ye." His arms slipped around her and she felt his heat through their thin clothes.

Good God. He was going to kiss her.

And she was going to let him.

His gaze lowered to her lips, and a thrill shuddered through her, making her nipples harden against his chest.

She slid her hands up to the back of his neck, tangling them in the long dark hair that fell wildly past his shoulders.

The silky texture was familiar, wonderful, and she couldn't wait for the touch of his mouth on hers. She raised herself on tiptoe and pressed herself close to him, letting the feel of his body spread into hers.

He was so solid and real. The scent of rain and fresh air clung to him and she felt the roughness of his cheek as it grazed hers.

His lips were full and firm and parting now as he lowered his head to claim her.

His presence surrounded her, enveloping her in a sensual heat that drowned her and swept away her inhibitions.

She wanted this man. Wanted his mouth, his hands, and above all wanted that rigid length that pressed into her belly and turned her thighs to mush.

She could feel the moisture between her legs and the electric tingles of a major sexual meltdown beginning deep inside her belly.

Her need for him peaked as their lips met…

* * * * *

And Fay woke up.

Sweating, aching, nightgown rucked up around her armpits, Fay gasped in agony.

God-fucking-*damn*!

Her nipples were beaded into marbles and she couldn't help herself. Slipping her hand between her parted thighs, she found her clit and brushed it lightly.

It was enough.

A shuddering orgasm rocked her, sending bolts of bliss up and down her spine and curling her toes with pleasure. It was shattering, extended, and the most incredible climax she could remember having for a long time. Even with her best vibrator.

There was only one thing missing.

Him.

* * * * *

Music filled Fay's mind as she struggled to wakefulness the following morning.

A Liszt concerto and cowbells.

The concerto was running through her subconscious, especially the passage that continually challenged her to get the phrasing right.

But as far as she could remember, Liszt hadn't written anything that included cowbells. Not in his piano concertos anyway.

She opened her eyes and spent a few moments trying to remember where she was.

Oh yes. Ireland.

Morning sunshine streamed in through the delicate lacy curtains covering the window, and the sound of cowbells mixed with the song of birds.

Fay smiled.

Good. Sunshine and Ireland. It was going to be a wonderful day.

The sweet-faced redhead at the desk gave her a wide grin as she came downstairs, showered and dressed and ready to get her first good look at her home for the next couple of weeks.

"Top o' the morning to you, Miss Krak...Krakooff...um..." The girl blushed. "'Tis sorry I am, but how *do* you pronounce yer last name?"

Fay laughed. "Call me Fay. Everyone has the same problem. I blame my father for it all the time."

"I'm Maureen. And anything we can do to make yer stay a pleasant one, just let us know, yes?"

Now *this* was Irish hospitality.

"Thanks, Maureen, I'll do that." She passed over her room key. "Would you hold onto this for me? I'm going exploring and I'd hate to lose it somewhere."

No need to tell Maureen that Fay had a bad habit of misplacing things. Of course that was usually when her mind flooded with music and began practicing intricate passages instead of focusing on her surroundings.

"Be happy to, Miss Fay. There's a wee breakfast buffet in the dining room, if you'd care for a spot of tea before yer walk. I can recommend the scones."

Maureen grinned proudly and waved her hand to the large room opening off the foyer.

"Thanks, sounds great."

Fortified with tea and mouthwateringly delicious scones, Fay took a deep breath as she stepped outside her small hotel. The sunlight was dazzling, the sky a crystal clear blue, and the world around her sparkled in more shades of green than she could put a name to.

She'd made it at last. Look out Ballyreath.

Fay Krakowski was in town.

Chapter Two

Three hours later, Fay's credit card seethed with frustration. It appeared that just about everything, in its owner's opinion, was "priceless", since she hadn't bought a damn thing.

Fay, however, had enjoyed herself more than she'd done in years.

The small shops were populated with warmly chatty folks, all talking with the most musical Irish accents, and they'd greeted Fay like a long-lost relative.

She'd been charmed to discover that there were actually separate shops for things like meat, and vegetables, and had enjoyed a good twenty minutes listening to the greengrocer as he'd told her about his new granddaughter.

Whether his daughter would have liked the details of her childbirth experiences discussed with a total stranger was another matter.

Fay simply listened with a smile on her face.

It was a new experience—this sharing of pleasures. She couldn't imagine the manager of the designer salon at Saks taking the time to fill Fay in on her family, let alone how long it took to deliver a "grand wee lass".

Nor would such an exalted person have offered to buy her a Guinness at the "Rolling Pig" later on.

She'd deflected that invitation, since the thought of the thick bitter stuff was enough to send her digestive tract into spasms.

It figured she'd be the one tourist who couldn't stomach the special brew that made Ireland famous. She'd have to settle for something else if she stopped by the "Rolling Pig".

Now *there* was a name for a pub.

She made a mental note to get a photo of the sign. Carly would adore it.

Fay strolled on through the sunshine, her heart light and her eyes darting everywhere, taking snapshots in her mind of the delightful village. Her camera was tucked away in her baggage for another day, since today was supposed to be for serious shopping.

But as yet, nothing had shouted "Yoo hoo, buy *ME*" at her.

Her meandering steps took her towards the small thatched cottage that lay at the end of the main street.

Without its mask of rain, Fay could see a small sign in front of it stating that it was called, appropriately enough, "The Thatched Cottage" and that it was open for business.

What that business was, however, was not stated.

Well hell. Fay responded to a challenge as well as anybody.

She pushed open the gate and glanced around at the neat garden.

Perhaps it was a tea shop. Or a real estate agency. Who cared? It was damn cute, and Fay was going to explore.

The boots had vanished from the worn doorstep, and Fay grinned at the small iron gryphon decorated with a glaze of mud. It was a bootscraper, and was resting contentedly, having done its duty rather well by the look of it.

She lifted her hand to the aged door and cautiously turned the knob, peeking through the crack into the darkness.

"Hello?"

The door opened wide, and Fay's eyes did the same thing as sunlight flooded the interior and revealed a gift shop.

Of sorts.

Besides the glass fronted counter, and the inevitable rack of scenic postcards, there was a jumble of delightful clutter.

Heavy knitted scarves hung in profusion over the back of an ancient and worn easy chair, and baskets were stuffed full with skeins of soft yarn.

Pots of honey stacked themselves neatly on a shelf and grinned warmly at her.

There was even a kilt or two, and fragrant sachets of lavender and pine tumbled over each other, scenting the air and making her breathe deeply with pleasure.

Small glass figurines glittered on another shelf—little dragons and warriors, and of course, lots of shamrocks.

It was entrancing, and Fay figured that at last she'd found someplace where she could do some serious damage to her credit card balance.

Oh God. That assumed they took credit cards here.

With the growing terror that possesses all tourists when the thought that their plastic might not work when they needed it most, Fay looked around her for some help.

And that was when she saw it.

The harp.

* * * * *

"Dia dhuit ar mhaidin."

As soon as the words dropped from his lips, Bantry cursed himself. He kept forgetting that he was no longer Bantry Mac Murchadha, but was now Bantry Murphy, proprietor of a twenty-first century gift shop. Complete with website and on-line ordering.

Not that anyone did, since the whole site was created for one specific purpose. Not to work.

Only to lure the "right" person. Which it looked like it had done.

He cursed at himself silently again as the young woman in front of him blinked.

"Good morning, Miss. I'm sorry about the Gaelic. Sometimes the old tongue just slips out."

He put on his best "I hope you're going to spend a fortune" smile, and she relaxed into a grin.

"Please don't apologize. It sounded lovely. What did it mean?"

Bantry grinned back. "'Tis just a morning greeting, and one which suits such a fine day, and a lovely lady like yourself."

She blushed. Yes, she definitely blushed. The day was getting better all the time.

Bantry's hair stood up on the back of his neck, and his toes were itching inside his boots. These were all good signs. Unlike some who would have sought medical attention immediately, Bantry relished the irritating sensations.

They were his senses telling him that he was about to accomplish something very important. Something he'd been hoping to do a long time before this.

Here at last could be the woman he'd been waiting for.

Or rather the harp had been waiting for.

She could barely keep her eyes off it.

And very pretty eyes they were too, mused Bantry. Stormy blue, with the longest of lashes, they added a great deal of character to an otherwise straightforwardly pretty face.

Surreptitiously sliding his gaze downwards, Bantry appreciated her feminine curves, the nicely rounded breasts, and especially the firm bottom that filled out those blue jeans to perfection.

She tossed her hair back over her shoulder as she strolled around the store, always keeping the harp in view, but trying to appear casual as she browsed his eclectic assortment of merchandise.

Most of it was crap, in his private opinion, but to his surprise he'd actually done quite a bit of profitable business in the last couple of weeks.

The fact that he'd only materialized in this very spot a little more than a fortnight ago was irrelevant.

The residents of Ballyreath were convinced he'd been there forever. As well they should.

After all, Goddesses were only as good as their spells and Cliodna was a damn fine Goddess.

"And would you be Miss Fay from America, then?"

The woman glanced up from a tray of shamrock necklaces. "My goodness. Word travels fast around here, doesn't it?"

Bantry smiled again. "We love visitors, Miss Fay. We welcome the chance to chat and learn from them, and of course relieve them of some of those lovely dollars they bring with them."

Fay laughed. "I'll bet you do."

"See anything you fancy then?"

Fay stroked a dark plaid kilt and let her eyes roam once more. They landed right where they should.

On the harp.

* * * * *

Fay battled with herself.

Something about that old harp hanging quietly on the wall lured her like the scent of chocolate on a spring breeze.

She could have sworn that when she first saw it there was a glow around it, a little tongue of green fire flickering over its worn surface.

And the sound. For one microsecond, a sound had rung deep in her heart. Something was still echoing deep inside her in response.

It was too weird for words, and she wanted it so badly she could taste it.

Her Yankee thriftiness shouldered its way forward through her mystical thoughts.

"Do you accept credit cards, Mr...er..."

"Call me Bantry, love. Everyone round here does. My name's Bantry Murphy, but there's so darned many Murphys it gets a wee bit confusing. And yes, we accept Mastercard, Lady Visa and American Express."

Fay's brow wrinkled. "Lady Visa?"

"A little old Gaelic humor, lass. Master Card? Lady Visa?"

"Oh. Got it." She chuckled. "Well, Bantry, you have some lovely things. I could spend all day just browsing."

"Glad you like the selection," answered Bantry. He moved behind his counter and straightened the display of delicate lace handkerchiefs.

"So what do you do, Miss Fay, when you're not holidaying here in Ireland?"

"Me? Oh I play piano," said Fay absently.

"You might like a closer look at yon harp, perhaps. You being musically inclined and all?"

Bantry's words tightened the excitement around Fay's heart, but she fought down the urge to hurry over and touch the thing.

"Harp? Oh you mean that old one over there?"

She was coolness personified. The ultimate bargain hunter, not revealing herself to her prey by so much as the flicker of an eyelash.

Bantry's chuckle echoed through the quiet shop. "Yep. That would be the one. The old harp you've been eyeing for the last five minutes."

Shit. This little old fellow's eyes were a lot sharper than she'd thought.

Ruefully, she smiled at him. "Not much gets past you, does it? Yes, I'll admit it. I'm fascinated by the darn thing. Can I take a look at it?"

Bantry tugged a three-legged footstool over to the wall and gently lifted the harp off its display hook.

A small puff of dust and a couple of cobwebs came with it, and Bantry brushed them away with a snort.

"Don't mind the Irish lace, Miss Fay. This thing's been hanging up here for a while."

Irish lace? What the heck was he babbling about?

"The cobwebs, lass."

Fay shook her head. She'd been thinking that they spoke the same language in Ireland. She was clearly mistaken.

Her eyes widened as Bantry stood the harp on the counter with a little grunt.

It was bigger than she'd originally thought, and her fingers itched to touch it.

"Go ahead, lass. You can touch it."

Mindreading must be among this little fellow's talents too.

"It looks very old." Fay stood in front of the counter, letting her eyes roam over the simple carving and delightful lines of the instrument.

"It is that. Created by one of our ancient Goddesses, it was. Back in the mists of our past. 'Tis said that this particular harp belonged to Cailleach…"

"Bantry?"

"Yes Miss Fay?"

"Cut out the sales pitch."

Bantry sighed gustily, making Fay smile.

The smile grew as she let her fingers brush the smooth surface, barely touching it, but in a caress that was as gentle as a kiss.

"Well would ye care to know that it's made from bog oak?" asked Bantry.

"Bog oak?"

Bantry leaned on the counter and crossed his arms comfortably. "Aye, bog oak. Harps this old were meant to be used. And carried from place to place. That meant they'd get wet from all our lovely Irish dew."

"Ah. They got rained on a lot did they?"

Bantry grimaced. "You're a hard-headed lass, aren't you?"

"Just practical. Most of the time."

"Anyway," continued Bantry with a slight frown. "As I was saying, the craftsmen used wood that withstood the weather. See the bow in the front here and how smooth it is?"

His gnarled hand pointed to the elegant curve in the front of the harp. "This here would swell and contract according to the weather, but never make a change in the tuning of its sweet voice."

Fay raised an eyebrow. In her experience, climatic conditions had some pretty major effects on just about any stringed instrument.

"Riiight..." she drawled.

"But you'd know about that, now, wouldn't you? You being a musician and all."

Fay nodded. "Yup."

She was entranced with this piece of Irish magic. It could have come right off the cover of a beer label, yet it was so simple, so unadorned, that she had no problem believing it was damn near as old as Bantry claimed.

The Goddess thing was a bit much to swallow, but the fine woodwork and complete lack of any modern additions, like steel tuning levers or metal strings, told their own story. The joints were clearly hand-tooled, and mortise fit tenon without a breath between them.

It was, indeed, very very old.

"Well go ahead, Miss Fay. Try it," encouraged Bantry.

"Uh…I'm a pianist, not a harpist you know," said Fay, raising her hands in spite of herself.

"The left goes on top, lass." Bantry pointed to the positioning of the hands.

"It does?"

Fay's eyebrows rose. This was quite the reverse of the usual positions she'd seen in her concert performances.

"Aye. And the strings are to be tapped with the fingernails rather than plucked like a chicken. This…" Bantry's chest swelled with pride. "*This* is no chicken."

"You're right about that," breathed Fay.

The wide sound box was rubbed smooth as silk and Fay let it lean against her shoulder as she raised her hands to the strings.

A couple of them were missing, but that was a minor defect compared to the beauty of the piece. Strong, simple and elegant, the harp nestled against her as if it had found a home.

Raising her hands in the reverse position suggested by Bantry, Fay let her fingernails tap the strings, using her right hand as a damper to soften the chord.

The sound she produced made her shudder all the way down to her toes.

It was god-awful.

Chapter Three

"You'll be needing a place to practice, I reckon." Bantry grinned at her as he passed over her copy of the charge slip.

Fay chuckled. "You got an old barn about five miles away from anyone?"

"No. Sorry. Besides the cows mightn't like it. Daren't sour the milk, now, do we?"

"That bad?"

Bantry's mouth twisted. "Well, I'm sure you play the piano beautifully, Miss Fay...but—"

"Yeah. Point taken."

"Don't give up on it, lass. 'Tis a special piece for a special lady. I'm thinking it was waiting up there for you."

"I'm thinking it probably should have waited some more."

"Nope. You're the one, all right."

Fay smiled at him. "You're a fabulous salesman, Bantry. Here I am, the proud owner of an instrument I don't even know if I can carry, let alone play, and I've just paid you a king's ransom for the darn thing."

Bantry looked hurt. "'Twas a fair price, Miss Fay. I'd not charge you more than it's worth."

Fay grinned. "Oh Bantry. You've kissed the Blarney Stone, haven't you?"

Bantry's expression changed, and he glanced around at a small basket behind him.

Uneasily he turned back to Fay. "I've done a deal more than kiss it, lass. But that's another story for another time."

Unsure of his meaning, Fay just nodded and reached for the harp.

Her harp, as of two minutes ago when her credit card had happily given up a respectable portion of its current balance.

"But I wasn't joking about finding a nice place to enjoy yourself." Bantry's mood softened. "No more than a mile or so down yon lane you'll find a quiet spot, nice and private. Maybe you'd find your fingers work better there."

"Walk a mile? With this?" Fay's urban nature stood up and screamed at her. No taxis? Not even a bus? *Walk?*

Bantry smiled. "'Tis a beautiful day. The sun is bright and warm, and you're in the most magical place in the world. You'd be surprised what you can do, Miss Fay."

With a raised eyebrow, Fay glanced at Bantry and picked up the harp.

Surprisingly light for something its size, it settled in her arm quite comfortably, and Fay found herself toying with the idea of finding that 'quiet place' Bantry mentioned.

"Down the lane, you said?"

"Aye. You can't miss it."

"Well, perhaps. If you get sour milk tomorrow, it'll be my fault." Fay grimaced at him.

"Enjoy it, lass. 'Twas made for you."

"Thanks, Bantry. For everything. I'll let you know how I make out." She paused at the door as the little man politely opened it for her. "Oh, and I might just come back for that kilt over there, too. Love the colors."

"Hold that thought," said Bantry quietly. "Things change quite suddenly here in Ireland, you know. 'Twas a pleasure meeting you, Miss Fay. Have a happy life, m'dear."

Fay blinked. That sounded awfully final.

She shrugged and smiled as she left the shop and walked into the sunshine with her harp tucked against her.

* * * * *

Aodhan Mac Murchadha fidgeted.

Time had ceased to hold any meaning for him since the day Cailleach the Crone had wrought her vengeance on him.

"Yer days of thievery are over, poxy slime," she'd bellowed. "Ye've stolen ma music. 'Tis nothing ye'll be until ma songs are played once more."

And "nothing" pretty much summed up what he was.

Trapped inside some vague cavern, Aodhan had been allowed to survive, yet not to live.

Snippets of voices had disturbed him from time to time, and he'd awoken occasionally to learn of the world beyond his prison, and how it was changing.

There was little else to do.

He'd heard battles and storms, the weeping of women and the laughter of children.

He'd heard mighty roars from machines that flew across the skies and the steady thuds of mechanical engines that now carried folks wherever they wanted to go without the need for a stout horse.

Yes, the world he knew had gone. Changed beyond recognition.

One thing had remained constant...his uncle Bantry.

That unmistakable voice had been there, sometimes soft, sometimes harsh, but always there, anchoring him, consoling him, and helping him as his quick mind absorbed the knowledge that filtered in to his isolated existence.

Sometimes he'd even caught his own name, Aodhan, although now it was simply Aidan, Aidan Murphy.

It was fitting. The old Aodhan Mac Murchadha had long since evolved into a new person.

Aidan Murphy.

A man who had aged little since his imprisonment, but who had grown in wisdom and intelligence enough to realize just what an ass he'd been.

And to wonder if he'd ever be free again.

Then the dreams had started.

At first she'd been a faceless, nebulous presence, brushing against his sleeping mind with a light caress and bringing a smile to his lips.

But lately, she'd become more detailed, her face lighting up in a welcoming smile as she raised her arms to hold him close.

And now he could see her in his mind's eye even when awake.

Eyes blue as a stormy sea, warm brown hair blowing free around her face, her body was meant for him and her heart called him with a song that he knew intimately.

The last dream had been the most vivid, and Aidan could recall the feel of her warmth as she pressed herself against him.

He'd come alive in those moments, cock upstanding and ready to claim what was his, and lips closer than a breath to tasting hers.

She was near, this mystery woman, and she was the key to his release.

Aidan fidgeted again as his cock pressed against his pants. She was the key, all right. In more ways than one.

He glanced down at himself, noticing that his clothing had changed yet again.

It happened occasionally, and more often these days, that he would awaken to find himself wearing strange new garments. Ones he could only assume reflected the current fashions.

At least he was keeping up with the times.

When he finally attained his freedom, he'd be able to blend in with the rest of the world.

If that rare event ever came to pass.

Until then, he was condemned to this restless existence neither in nor out of time, a spirit locked in enchantment, awaiting the right moment—the right woman—to set him free.

His heart quickened as he settled himself to sleep once more. Perhaps his dreams would bring her to him once again.

Perhaps this time he'd get to kiss her.

Perhaps...

* * * * *

Fay strolled along the country lane, surprised at how light the harp was in her arms.

It was a little awkward at first, but once she'd nestled it against her body and gotten the balance just right, it seemed to fit her curves and make itself right at home.

The musician in her was piqued.

She was a concert pianist, for chrissake. She knew her theory and her notation—the fundamentals that applied to all music. She had a good ear. She should *not* have produced a sound that very much resembled a pissed-off cat.

A little bolt of determination traveled up her spine.

Dammit, she'd get a chord out of it if she had to practice until her fingers bled.

And *that* looked a likely place to get some peace and quiet.

A low jumble of rotting logs barred a hole in the high hedge, and through it Fay could see rolling fields sloping off into the distance.

She peeked through, checking for wildlife. Nope. No cows.

She wasn't sure if Bantry had been kidding about the sour milk thing, but she didn't want to take any chances.

Besides, these were very expensive sneakers, and slogging through cow patties while wearing them wasn't on her list of things to do today.

Carefully she clambered over the logs and trudged across the soft hillocks, admiring the occasional flower and breathing in the delightfully fresh air that swirled around her.

Towards the far side of the field, the ground dropped away, affording Fay an exquisite view of the surrounding countryside.

Some outcroppings of whitish rock were conveniently placed nearby, and with a grin, Fay dropped her bag and placed the harp on the flattest one.

Mother Nature had provided a natural scenic view—no redwood picnic tables or benches, or a sign saying "look to your right to see hills". Just a natural seating arrangement that was a bit on the hard side.

And of course she didn't have her camera.

Easing out of her fleece jacket, Fay folded it and put it on a smoothly indented rock.

The sun was warm, the spot sheltered, and as she settled into her makeshift recliner, Fay found herself wondering how many other bottoms had rested just where she was at this moment.

Thousands, probably, since the rock seemed to have been ground out to perfect human-bottom dimensions.

She sighed with pleasure and opened several buttons on her shirt, letting the rays of the sun brush her chest.

Now *this* was what Fay called a vacation.

Surrounded by the songs of birds whose names she didn't know, and bathed by the warmth of an Irish sun shining high in a clear blue sky, Fay let her mind rest for once and empty itself of worries, demanding concert schedules and the thousand-and-one other things that had plagued her.

It was a rare moment of relaxation for someone who'd driven herself to succeed since she was old enough to sit on the piano bench and plink out the first notes to the "Itsy Bitsy Spider".

Her purchase sat beside her, challenging her, encouraging her, egging her on. *"Come on Fay, you can do it. Make me sing."*

"Piss off," said Fay tranquilly. "I'm not going to risk this gorgeous day by making you twang again."

"Oh Faaaaayyyy…I'm waiting…"

Fay closed her eyes and ignored the harp.

Being a trained musician didn't necessarily mean she could play any instrument she put her hands on, of course. There had been that embarrassing incident with a tuba many years ago. Followed closely by the trombone episode, which had nearly decapitated the kid standing in front of her.

Thus proving conclusively that wind instruments were certainly not her forté.

Stringed instruments, however, were something else again.

The harp seemed to thrum gently in the breeze.

Fay considered it, wondering if old Bantry had been right and it was the product of some long ago artisan, working at the command of an ancient Goddess.

It didn't take a vivid imagination to picture the scene—a day like this, a field like this, and gossamer silks flying around the perfect body of a gorgeous woman. She would be smiling as she stood over a craftsman carving the smooth wood into the belly and sounding box of the harp.

Fay could almost hear the Goddess laugh with pleasure as the strings were threaded and tightened and the first notes flew from the heart of the thing. A sound full of joy and mischief and the music of the magical isle that surrounded them.

Fay's feet moved restlessly as the tempo of the song increased and became a delightful dance.

A gurgle of enjoyment escaped her own throat as she listened, and the urge to move became too great.

"Dance for me, mavourneen."

The words whispered through Fay's mind as she stood and let the sun beat down on her shoulders.

To her surprise, she found she was naked.

But instead of being shocked and horrified, she was thrilled. Instead of reaching for her clothes, she widened her arms and welcomed the touch of the air.

Instead of covering herself with her hands, she tossed her head back.

And danced.

Chapter Four

"Dance for me, mavourneen."

Aidan awoke to find the words trembling on his lips and music in his ears.

It was the first music he'd heard in a thousand lifetimes, and for a moment he thought he was finally dead.

But no—his heart still beat, and strongly too, and he had a definite cramp in one calf muscle.

Rubbing it, he sat up and listened, wondering what brought the soft humming sounds into the darkness that surrounded him.

He recognized the song from some long-ago memory, a jig if he wasn't mistaken, and one the farmers had loved dancing to at the end of a long week's labor.

His feet itched to follow the rhythm and he closed his eyes, luxuriating in the sounds that stirred his soul.

A whoosh of air brushed his cheek and he found himself standing in a field, dazzled for a moment by bright sunshine.

He looked down, astounded to find himself naked as the day he was born. Another dream?

He thought not, since there was a sharp pebble cutting into his foot, and he could feel himself beginning to harden as the music throbbed and swirled around him.

He hardened even more as he raised his eyes and saw her.

His mavourneen. His darling.

Standing in a patch of sunlight and moving to the same lilting sounds he heard, she was everything he'd ever wished for and created in his mind during his age-long imprisonment.

Her hips were rounded and full, and just meant for his hands to cup them as he pulled her close.

Her breasts were soft and tipped with dusky nipples, and her hair flew loose as she twirled and dipped to the music.

There was no shadow of curls between her thighs, but she was definitely all-woman. Soft pinkness gleamed at him as her legs parted and closed again, and he gasped with the need that flooded through him.

He wanted to touch her. To taste her, to lick those daringly revealed folds and suck her juices. To sink himself deep inside her and feel those thighs close around him as she pulled him close.

He groaned.

Was this yet another torture devised by Cailleach? To show him what he could not have?

There was only one way to find out.

Aidan Murphy swallowed down his fear and took a step towards his fantasy, expecting to wake again in his dark chamber with nothing in his hands but his hard cock.

This time, however, was different. Aidan sucked in a breath to his starving lungs.

She was no dream.

She was real.

* * * * *

Fay threw back her head and laughed, amazed at herself, but unable to prevent the pleasure that rocked her as she danced naked on an Irish hillside.

She should have been horrified, embarrassed, and a thousand other proper things. She felt none of them.

She felt *right*.

The music pounded into her brain, and urged her on, pushing all other thoughts aside.

Sunlight glittered on the grass around her, and a mist had risen in the distance, obscuring everything but the field in which she danced.

The mood of the music changed, slowing from its rapid four-four timing down to a more leisurely pace. The chords became softer, more sensual, and Fay found herself at a loss, needing to move again but not sure how.

And then she saw him.

Standing not six feet away from her, he watched her, green eyes alight with—something.

She could see through him.

Misty and insubstantial, he seemed more like a wraith of green fog than a real person, but his eyes were bright and passionate as they flickered over her naked body.

They left a heated trail of arousal as they caressed her thighs and her breasts, returning again and again to her pussy.

He licked his lips and she felt the answering rush of moisture between her legs.

Her nipples hardened and she stood still as he took a step towards her.

And another.

He was on her before she realized it.

Tumbling to the soft grass, she rolled, over and over, entwined with him—with something—pressed against her, around her, touching every part of her.

Like hot breath his hands roved over her skin, caressing and heating it as they moved.

Fay moaned aloud as he brushed her nipples and slid between her legs, settling himself on top of her.

"*Mavourneen*," he whispered.

"F...F...Fay," she stuttered. "My name is Fay."

Although how she could remember it with an armful of hefty handsome ghost hovering over her was a miracle.

"Fay. A good name for a faery queen."

His laugh was rough, husky, as if he'd not laughed in some time, and it sent a bolt of need to her pussy. She was wet and hot and she parted her thighs even wider in welcome .

This was *so* not like her.

He pushed against her with his hips, letting her feel the hard length of his cock as he rubbed it over her mound.

It was wonderful.

His head dipped to her lips and her breasts and all those sensitive places in between, making her writhe with pleasure.

"I'm Aidan." He nipped at that special place where her neck muscles joined her shoulder and sent a shiver down her spine.

"Aidan," she mouthed, scarcely aware she'd spoken. "Oh Aidan…"

Her hands reached for him, finding a moist softness where his shoulders should be.

She sobbed with impatience, wanting to run her fingers through the dark silkiness of his hair, but was unable to get a firm grasp on it. Like one of those frustrating dreams, he was real but not real. Touching her but not touching her.

I'm losing my mind.

"No you're not, my Fay," he said, in answer to her unspoken cry. "Relax, and let me pleasure you."

If she'd had the strength she would have snorted. Sure. *Relax*, he said. Flat on her back, naked and being petted and caressed by a green misty naked dream hunk. Named Aidan.

All things guaranteed to make a girl relax. *Not*.

Then he touched his lips to hers and her muddled thoughts vanished.

Just a brush at first, he was warm and firm, and their skin rested together for a second or two.

Then he opened his mouth and stroked his tongue across her sensitive flesh, encouraging her to part her lips and welcome him inside.

And welcome him she did.

Her body was crushed by his, yet she felt lightweight and buoyant as his tongue swept inside her mouth.

His taste was unique, like honey and heather and spice, all mixed up into an entrancing flavor that seduced Fay into blissful surrender.

His tongue plunged into her, learning her, teasing her and urging her to answer his kiss with an exploration of her own.

His mouth certainly seemed real enough. Hot to her touch and demanding, she let her own tongue thrust back, twining around his and tugging it in a sensual duel that swept her breath away and made her toes curl.

She moaned as he pulled back, missing his kiss already.

"My Fay, my *mavourneen*," he said huskily.

"What does that mean?"

His head dropped to her breasts and he suckled hard on one taut nipple, bringing Fay's spine arching up towards him.

"It means my darling," he answered. "My darling."

His head moved to her other breast and Fay cried out in pleasure. "Aidan…oh God."

"You like this, Fay?"

She nodded, not trusting her voice.

"There's more, *mavourneen*. Much more."

"There can't be. You're killing me here…" She groaned, hips jerking up towards his, and her hands scrabbling in the grass beside her.

He laughed again, a sound not unlike the chords of the harp. Rich and musical it resounded through Fay's body and made her shudder beneath him.

"Let me show you."

His hands slid from her waist down the outside of her thighs and she felt his weight shift as he kissed a trail from her breasts to her belly and lower.

Oh *God*.

His lips brushed her inner thighs and traced their way down to her knees and back up again.

Fay trembled, knowing that he had one goal in mind. One target. The one that she presented to him in delicious naked abandon. The one that she'd painstakingly and daringly shaved that very morning in an act of defiance against the strictures of her past.

Fay Krakowski, concert pianist, would never have shaved her pussy.

Fay, the wild and uninhibited naked girl lying in an Irish field being pleasured by a green spirit man, was proud of her naked pussy.

She sincerely hoped her pride was not misplaced, and that he'd like it too.

Apparently he did.

* * * * *

Aidan's senses were alive for the first time in more years than he could remember.

The honeyed fragrance of Fay's arousal was like food to a starving man, and Aidan recognized himself as being just that.

Starving. Desperate for a taste of her, a mouthful of those luscious pussy lips turning redder and redder as her arousal grew.

He slid his hands between her legs and parted her folds, watching as her moisture pooled and dripped from them, weeping just for him.

He sucked in a deep breath, scenting her, letting her unique aroma swirl up his nose and into his soul.

She was beautiful. All shiny and swollen and ready for his mouth.

The sudden thought flashed through him that this was what he'd been waiting for through so many long lifetimes.

This pussy, these lips, this woman...and her clit, which protruded hungrily from its covering, begging for him to run his tongue around it.

He did.

Fay's cry was echoed by the strings of the harp that lay next to them.

He suckled and licked and stroked her with every flick and caress he could remember, and a few he invented right there on the spot.

He buried his nose in her sweetness and tickled her cunt with his tongue, holding tight to her hips as she struggled to push her body into his face.

Her thighs hardened and her breathing became harsh, little pants of pleasure that mimicked his movements.

She was coming.

He returned to her clit, sliding his face over her and suckling it gently into his mouth.

It was enough to tip her over the edge.

With a scream that would have deafened a banshee, Fay orgasmed against his mouth, clamping her thighs to his head as if she wanted to hold him there forever.

Her pussy spasmed, her cunt contracted and a flood of her juices soaked him.

It was incredible, and Aidan buried his face in her as deeply as he could just for the joy of feeling her body as it rode out the waves of pleasure.

His cock was harder than the rocks behind them, and as her orgasm faded, Aidan rose, ready to join their flesh and make himself one with Fay.

He eased himself up over her limp body, and watched her sea-blue eyes as they opened, staring deep into his.

He settled his hips between hers and slid the head of his cock through her moisture.

His heart pounded and the veins that marked his length throbbed as he eased himself into position—and thrust.

At that precise moment, he woke, and found himself back in his dark cavern, holding his cock and crying out in anger and frustration.

Fuuuuuuck.

Chapter Five

Fay's cry of agony woke her.

She blinked, choking down hot snarls of frustration, and found herself sitting on her jacket, legs wide apart and the harp resting against her mound.

The crotch of her jeans was soaked and her muscles were still shuddering from the force of the orgasm Aidan's mouth had given her.

Aidan.

She clutched the harp tight to her chest as tears welled up in her eyes and tumbled down her hot cheeks.

They'd been so *close*. His cock had been hard and ready and she'd wanted him inside her so badly she could still taste it.

And him.

The sweet spicy tang of his kiss lingered on her lips and the bright gleam of passion in his eyes had burned itself into her brain.

Oh *God*. It wasn't fair.

He'd seemed so real to her. So loving and so hot, and doing such wonderful things to her naked body…

Well, that was a dead giveaway right there. She wasn't naked. She was alone, dozing in the Irish sunshine, and probably suffering the worst case of jet lag known to mankind.

Why else would she be having these vividly sexual dreams that left her panting and wet and wanting?

With hands that still shook a little, Fay gathered her belongings, strangely reluctant to remove the harp from between her legs.

Hesitantly, she pressed the wood against herself, bringing a shudder of pleasure to her still-aroused pussy.

Sheeeeiiiitt. This would never do.

Concert pianists didn't give themselves orgasms in fields. No matter what instruments they held.

A flush of embarrassment heated her cheeks, and Fay rose rather self-consciously, aware of a distinct unsteadiness in her legs.

Legs that he'd kissed so tenderly.

Damn. Her jeans were bloody uncomfortable, and she had booked a bus tour for this afternoon.

With the harp in her arms and her jacket tucked over her bag, Fay turned her back on the field.

And Aidan.

He was a figment of her tired brain, an invention she'd created to fill the void left by Steven Greeley.

That was it.

If she hurried, she'd make the tour on time and perhaps have a chance to change her jeans. And her underwear too. She couldn't remember the last time she'd been this wet.

Certainly not for Mr. "I-like-big-breasts" Greeley.

Fay snorted as she walked back down the lane to Ballyreath. Dream, or ghost, or Irish pixie—whatever Aidan was, he could certainly teach that bassoonist a thing or two.

Humming a vaguely familiar Irish jig, Fay made her way back to the village.

* * * * *

Aidan's cry of frustration was heard by no one but himself.

It took but one quick stroke of his hand and he came, gushing freely in spurts from the cock that refused to stop aching for that hot sweet cunt it had been about to claim.

Fay.

Her scent was all around him, on his face, his lips and his hands. His balls tightened even more and his hot come spewed out onto his belly as he lay on his lonely bed.

He closed his eyes and saw her again, naked and lovely, staring into his heart with her sea-blue gaze. She had been so ready for his possession.

Damn Cailleach to the darkest recesses of hell.

Fay was *his*!

Panting, he rested, letting his cock soften and his thoughts whirl.

Through the anger and the sexual drive that still flooded his veins, Aidan dared to feel the one thing he'd denied himself all this time.

Hope.

Perhaps now was the time, and Fay was the woman.

Maybe after long-forgotten ages of existing in another place where none but he held domain, there was finally a woman who could free him from his prison.

His uncle Bantry must have known, or at least guessed that Fay might hold the key. Otherwise, why would he have sold her the harp? Oh certainly there had been others who had expressed an interest, but this was the first time Aidan could remember the harp leaving Bantry's side.

Sighing, Aidan struggled to sort out his memories. They were blurred as always, yet now, after Fay, some things were becoming clearer.

Aidan remembered a small cottage, and the sound of his uncle yelling at him for something or other. He smiled. He'd been a right bastard, that was for sure, and bless Bantry's old heart for putting up with his antics without killing him.

He remembered women too, soft thighs and welcoming smiles. And he remembered one night...

He and his friends were out for a lark, a bit of naughtiness to lighten their days of hard work in the fields. They'd stolen into a large and somber mansion, just to take a look around.

Truly, that was all it had been. They'd not known it was Cailleach the Crone's house, nor that their "souvenirs" would cause such trouble.

Bantry had vanished the next morning, and Aidan had found himself on his knees before the old woman, trembling at her vicious tone.

His memories faded as the last thing he recalled was her yelling something about her music.

How he'd stolen her music.

And now here he was. In a vague cavern, with few openings to let in the light. Feeling neither hunger nor thirst, sleeping away lifetimes, waking to others, and unable to make his way back out. Nor, it seemed, did he want to.

Until now. Until Fay had entered his dreams and he'd nearly entered her body.

He rose from his bed and paced the worn floor, forcing himself to the walls and touching them for the first time he could remember. They were rough, yet carefully hewn. Gently, he tapped on them with his knuckles and the hollow sound resounded throughout the small space.

Now he knew where he was.

Inside the bloody *harp*!

* * * * *

Fay tried hard to concentrate on the beautiful Irish scenery that flew past the window of the tour bus.

She also tried to listen to the knowledgeable and charming voice of the guide as he told his passengers all about the mystical heritage of the land through which they were driving.

But it was a futile effort, the facts and stories wasted on the woman in the third row who stared blankly off into space.

All Fay could think about was Aidan.

His gorgeous green eyes, the taste of his lips and the feel of his body against her. How she could recall this so precisely was a puzzle, since he'd seemed to be made of some dream-like mist that refused to become solid beneath her hands.

And yet she'd held his head between her thighs as he'd tongued her into the most shattering orgasm of her life.

She shivered, and then realized the bus was pulling to a stop.

They'd reached the end of the world.

Or at least it looked that way to Fay when she followed her fellow-tourists and stepped off the bus and onto a cliff overlooking the ocean.

Fay listened with half an ear as their guide told them that this was where the Irish Sea met the Atlantic, and to her untrained eyes it really did look like the two seas were busily duking it out. Wild and churning, the waters clashed and roared in a seething blend of colors and foam.

Here, according to the guide, the giant Finn McCool had made his home. The stuff of legends, Finn McCool was said to have fallen in love with a lady giant who lived on the island of Staffa in the Hebrides.

In an effort to make their love affair easier, Finn had built a highway between them, and it was the remains of this highway that had Fay's eyes widening as she looked across the incredible landscape.

The "Giant's Causeway".

While the conversation drifted off onto topics of volcanic eruptions, basalt, lava cooling patterns and stress relief, Fay just gazed at the awe-inspiring sight of thousands of columns thrusting up from the ground in an odd kind of jumbled order.

Her mind struggled to absorb the images, and she automatically reached for her camera to preserve this fantastic view.

Half a roll of film later, she sighed.

They would cause a lot of sensational comments when she got home, but basically her photos were empty.

The Giant's Causeway had been created by a man in love. The heck with the geologists, that was the theory Fay was going to hang on to. Sadly, her photos wouldn't contain anything that told of the depth of that love.

Not the gut-churning feeling of wanting someone desperately, or needing their touch so badly that the very heart in one's body ached with it.

And none of the feelings that were wreaking havoc on Fay's concentration, making her hands shake as she tried to focus her camera, and bringing the glisten of tears to her eyes as she recalled their final moments together.

There was no photo of the spirit that haunted her, the man she'd found in her dreams and who had brought a part of her to life. A part that she'd not even known she possessed.

There would be no photographs of him, just the images imprinted in Fay's mind. The ones that would stay with her, even if she never saw him again.

Aidan.

* * * * *

"There's a nice fire going for you in your room, Miss Fay," said Maureen. "Just the thing for a cool night like this."

Fay wearily smiled her thanks, accepting her room key from the receptionist.

"And we've put a wee bottle of Irish Mist on yer dresser, in case you'd like to try a little. 'Tis our finest liqueur, some say, and just the thing to settle you down for the night."

"Thanks, that's lovely."

Fay knew she should probably have been a bit more effusive. The idea of a crackling fire and a drink sounded like heaven, but her heart was aching, her thoughts were confused, and she simply nodded goodnight to Maureen.

It had been a very long day, and Fay sighed with relief as her door closed firmly behind her.

The lure of her own fireplace had tempted Fay to this hotel, and now, seeing the bright flames crackling merrily behind the screen, she was very glad she'd followed her instincts.

It seemed like coming home.

With a groan, she slipped from her clothes and snuggled into her nightgown. The soft bed beckoned, but the fire enticed her even more, so she sat cross-legged on the rug in front of it, and watched the flickering shadows as they lit the room.

She held her tumbler of Irish Mist to her eye and peeked at the flames through the crystal. Deformed and twisted by the glass, they leaped like wild things, encouraging Fay to lose herself in them. Such heat. And such brilliance.

Sighing, she took a sip of the amber liquid.

Strong and sweet, it burned a little as she swallowed, but left the tang of honey and heather dancing around her taste buds.

It was like…like Aidan.

Like the taste of him as he'd swirled his tongue over hers.

She fidgeted against the arousal she felt blooming all over again between her legs.

Damn. She was in some serious trouble here.

Fay reached for her writing pad and pen. She'd promised Carly a day-by-day account of her trip, and she was going to stick to it. Even if it meant telling her own sister that Fay was probably losing her mind and needed some heavy medication.

"Dear Carly."

Fay nibbled the end of her pen and then took another sip of her drink. It was really good stuff, and took some of the edge off her shattered nerves.

"I think I'm going insane."

Nope. Fay crossed out the words. Why scare the crap out of her sister?

"I think the jet-lag has hit me harder than I expected."

There, much better.

"I love this country, and its people, and of course the darling Irish accents. Ballyreath is just perfect, and you can make friends just by crossing the street. It's soooo not like home at all, and yet it's easy to feel at home here right away.

Helping things along are these crazy dreams I'm having.

Yes, dreams. Your practical, responsible sister, who has spent most of her life at the piano, is having incredibly erotic dreams.

(You're laughing aren't you? I can hear you from here.)"

Fay smiled to herself. Carly would really yak up a storm when she read this. They'd spent much of their youth arguing about boys and dating, with Fay always being the sensible one, and Carly the incurable romantic.

My, how things were changing.

"I'm dreaming a lot, Carly. And those dreams are taking me places and showing me things about myself I never would have guessed at. Actually, it's not so much the dreams, as the person in them. A man. His name is Aidan."

Seeing his name written down on paper brought a shiver to Fay's skin. It made him more real, more like someone she'd really met, not just dreamed about.

She settled the paper more comfortably on her lap and continued.

"He's Irish, of course, and has a lovely lilt to his voice. His eyes are so green I can't describe them, and his hair is like long black silk. He has a body that's just meant for passion, and he looks fabulous naked.

Yes, that's right. It's my dream, my fantasy, so damn it—he's naked.

After all, if I'm going to indulge in a major erotic experience with a dream-hunk that looks like a cover model, why the hell should I keep him clothed?"

Fay chuckled to herself, as she remembered Aidan naked. She doubted even the finest writer could find the words to do justice to him. The expression "droolingly fabulous" came to mind.

"But it's not so much what he looks like…" Yeah, right.

"It's what he does to me and with me, and how he touches me and looks at me and—oh hell, he turns me on like a furnace." A very wet and soggy furnace, but a furnace nevertheless.

Fay determinedly continued.

"It's as if we've been waiting for each other. There's a sense of familiarity, some kind of 'knowing' that I experience every time I dream of him. I wish I could explain it better, but you're the one with the paranormal romance obsession. Perhaps you can explain it to me!"

The room was silent now, and dark, lit only by the fire and a small lamp on the bedside table. Fay had to angle her knees to see the words she'd scrawled on her writing paper.

It was true. This dream "presence" had stirred her like no other man ever had. How on earth could she have created such a lover for herself? Had she been seriously repressed or something?

A log crackled and popped out an ember that fell through the wrought iron fire screen towards the harp.

Fay gasped and quickly flicked it back into the stone hearth.

The harp sat there, soaking up the warmth of the fire, much like Fay herself.

Putting her paper aside, Fay reached for it and tucked it against her body where it fit like a long-lost friend.

The Irish Mist had mellowed her nerves, and the comforting feel of the smooth wood against her chest seemed right.

She raised her hands to the strings.

Chapter Six

Aidan felt the sounds before he heard them.

Fay.

She was near. The chamber hummed with soft notes, shuddering through the walls and into Aidan's soul.

He could almost feel her, smell her, taste her—sense her with everything that he was and then some.

He could remember her as clear as day, with her blue eyes darkening as he aroused her, and her soft skin glowing against the grass on which they'd lain.

These weren't the blurry memories of past dreams. These were fresh, vibrant images that lit up his brain and brought fire to his loins.

Her breasts had been firm, yielding to his caresses and their nipples hardened as he'd suckled her into his mouth.

She'd tossed and writhed beneath him, a wanton and wanting creature he'd awoken with his lips and his tongue and his...

Oh shit. Yes, *that*. His cock. Which was now hardening rapidly at the memories and the music and was going to bring him another long night if he didn't do something about it. And fast.

Aidan moved from the bed, cursing these tight trousers he now wore. Damn, why couldn't this world have kept those breeches that gave a man room to grow inside them?

And this blue stuff was hard, stiff as his cock, and seamed in all the wrong places.

Absently he ran a hand over his chest, meeting a much softer fabric and a shirt that left a good portion of his arms bare.

There were no fasteners or laces, just the ease of movement that came from a fine cotton.

Aidan dismissed thoughts of his clothing from his mind as the melody continued to vibrate through his domain.

It was a lonely song, one of love and loss and sadness, yet touched by that magic that whispered of rolling green hills and the magic of the land that was now called Ireland.

It was an old song, and one Aidan recognized from some dim memory of a long ago time.

In fact, he could vaguely recall dancing to it with a girl in his arms.

The skin at the back of his neck prickled.

If the song was *that* old, perhaps it might serve to fulfill Cailleach's prophecy. The one that said he'd be nothing until her music was returned to her.

He chilled at the thought and stifled the flare of hope that had burst to life within him. Too many times during his imprisonment he'd permitted himself the pleasure of expecting one particular day to be his last inside this spell.

He didn't want to face such disappointment yet again.

The sound continued, growing louder now, as the fingers on the strings seemed to gain in confidence and strength.

The tune became clear, distinct, and blended into a waterfall of chords and sounds that cascaded over Aidan.

He moved restlessly, pacing the space between the walls yet afraid to touch them. The music might stop. But it didn't.

It continued on, finding a rhythm all its own and a melody that could have been wrenched from the heart of the Emerald Isle.

Finally, he could stand it no more.

Taking a deep breath, Aidan marched to the wall of his prison and boldly stepped into it, praying that it would give way and not bar him from the paradise that awaited him on the other side.

His head swam as his vision blurred, and for an instant the sound of girlish laughter rang in his ears.

Then something soft met the soles of his feet and his darkness was lit by the flames of a fire.

He was through.

He was free.

Miracle of miracles.

He was with Fay.

* * * * *

Her fingers flew across the strings as if possessed.

Fay's eyes were closed, and she let some other force, some *power*, guide her movements.

For the first time, the hand positions felt comfortable, and the knack of flicking the strings with her fingertips came naturally, bringing the light and effervescent sounds from the harp like water over a dam.

Chords and notes poured into the quiet room, melodies she'd never heard, rhythms she'd never played, and all coming with a speed and accuracy that amazed her.

Something in her pianist's soul responded to this music.

She wanted to write it down, transpose it, score it for a full orchestra and unleash it on the world.

She wanted to see people dancing wildly to it, laughing as they did so. She wanted to share these songs, these magical tunes, and share the joy she felt bubbling up inside her as her fingers flew.

It was unconstrained and free of the limitations imposed by sheet music or a metronome.

No boundaries were set by time signatures, treble clefs or a conductor controlling her performance.

And yet it was still perfect.

Each note, each chord, each arpeggio followed naturally and led from one merry song into another, telling a musical tale of Ireland, its past and its pleasures.

Even the missing strings were no impediment, since her hands bypassed the gaps and filled in with improvisations that simply enhanced the melody.

Fay gave herself up to the moment.

She asked no questions, cleared her mind of troublesome thoughts, and just let the music take her.

She rediscovered the thrill of playing.

The rush of adrenaline that hits a performer when things go just *right*.

The knowledge that her hands, her skill and her fingers were all combining to produce something pleasurable—something magical.

It was a feeling she'd lost somewhere in the organized chaos of life as a concert pianist. The joy had given way to a need for improved technique. The pleasure had been surrendered to a desire to be technically perfect.

Until this moment, Fay hadn't realized what she'd missed, or how much a part of her soul had been subdued by the rigorous and demanding schedule of rehearsals and concerts.

This—*this* was what music was truly all about.

Her playing slowed, the song a sad one now, sensual and seductive, mourning lost loves and days passed alone. The minor key emphasized the loneliness, and in her mind Fay could see empty fields and the darkness of night as it crept over the Irish countryside

Tears started to her eyes as the melody wound to a close, and she breathed in deeply, resting her tired hands on the strings as they shivered with echoes of the last notes.

She leaned her head on the harp.

Her heart awoke, and in that one moment, she seemed to see her life clearly for the first time.

Devoid of anything but music, Fay realized she'd existed within a structured shell, living a life that was superficially complete, but spiritually empty.

It had taken the song of an old Irish harp to make her realize that something was missing.

She opened her eyes and gazed into the fire, trying to come to terms with the revelation.

A movement in the shadows made her heart jump into her throat.

A man stood quietly, leaning against the old wooden mantelpiece and watching her.

Not just any man.

Aidan.

* * * * *

He told himself he was dead.

And he didn't care one whit.

His Fay was sitting in the firelight, holding a harp like every good angel should, and playing songs that could only be described as heavenly.

He'd be quite content to stay right where he was for the rest of eternity, just looking at her. Seeing how the flames flickered over her hair, sparking red glints from its tumbled darkness, and how her eyes were closed as the music poured from her talented hands.

Then she stopped, and rested her head on the harp.

Aidan held his breath.

Well damn. If he could hold his breath, he must be still breathing, and as a consequence of that thought, he must still be alive.

And if he was alive…

Fay opened her eyes and saw him.

A sea-blue gaze swept over him, an expression of disbelief and joy mingling with a healthy dash of fear.

"Aidan?"

She breathed the word on a sigh, as if afraid to acknowledge his presence.

"Yes, Fay."

His answer was hoarse, choked by some emotion that clogged his throat and sent his heart pounding into his ears.

"You're...you're *here*?"

Aidan blinked. He wasn't sure how to answer her.

Was he here? Where was "here"? He could feel the heat of the fire through his trouser-clad legs, and the softness of the rug beneath his bare feet. He could hear Fay's indrawn breath and smell the fragrance of her light perfume.

Did that mean he was "here" or was he still dreaming, buried in his cavern of darkness?

There was only one way to find out.

Slowly he straightened and moved towards Fay. Bending down he took the harp from her hands and set it aside, drawing her up to her feet so that she stood in front of him.

With infinite care he raised a hand and cradled her cheek. It was warm, and soft, and alive.

"I'm here, Fay. I'm really here."

His body filled with little tingles of pleasure as he caressed her skin, and he could have spent years just watching the changing colors of her eyes as she leaned in to his touch.

"I can't believe it," she murmured.

"Neither can I, *mavourneen*."

Slowly, Fay raised her own hand and cradled his cheek in return, running her fingers down the side of his face and back up again. A look of wonder spread over her face as she rasped the stubble on his chin and swept a lock of his hair back behind his ear.

"You *are* here," she breathed "Real, in the flesh, honest-to-God here."

"That I am, love."

Her lips trembled and parted, and Aidan went from shock to arousal in the blink of an eye.

"How?"

Her mouth formed the word, but Aidan's ears scarcely registered it. All he could see was the beckon of those rosy lips, and the welcome that flooded her eyes.

He lowered his head towards her. "I don't know, love. And right now, I don't care."

She raised herself on tiptoe and Aidan felt her hands slip to his shoulders and around his neck. His arms encircled her and he pulled her body against his with a groan.

"My mavourneen," he sighed.

And kissed her.

Chapter Seven

The second their lips met, Fay's carefully ordered world ceased to exist.

Still astounded that he was warm, living flesh beneath her fingers, she opened her mouth and welcomed his tongue, his unique flavor blending with the traces of her Irish Mist.

She dug her nails into his shoulders and pressed herself against him, letting his heat reassure her that he was truly holding her tight, kissing her for all he was worth and sending thrills of arousal through every nerve ending she possessed.

For what seemed like hours they explored each other's mouths, turning their heads and seeking that perfect spot that would blend them into one loving unit.

Finally, Fay drew back a little.

"I still can't believe it," she whispered. "You're real. You're here. I can touch you. Taste you." She blushed. "You taste good."

As she watched, Aidan's handsome face crinkled into a grin that was so full of devilry and passion it took her breath away.

"You taste even better, love. Do I detect a wee drop of our local liquor on your tongue?"

She nodded at the small decanter. "It's Irish Mist. The hotel left me some to try."

Fay eased from his arms, fighting to calm herself and not leap on Aidan like a starving coyote on fresh kill.

But *damn*. He looked good enough to eat. And God was she hungry. "Would you like some?"

So perhaps she was a little late with the good-hostess bit. She probably should have offered him a drink before plastering her lips all over his. *Shit.*

She grinned. It had been worth it. That had been some kiss. And she hoped there'd be more to come. There would be if she had any say in the matter.

"I'd love some," he answered. "It's been a long while since I've had a chance to savor a wee drink."

Fay did her best not to crack the damn crystal as she poured a healthy shot of Irish Mist into one of the delicate liqueur glasses. It would help if she wasn't shaking like the proverbial leaf. In a very high wind.

Aidan's hand covered hers as she offered him the glass, and he raised them both to his lips, sipping from the liquid and then brushing her fingers with a light kiss.

Oooh. Nice touch.

Fay's nipples agreed, giving this charming man their version of a standing ovation.

His smile of pleasure as he swallowed merited another standing ovation, but this time it was her crotch that was declaring its pleasure by doing some serious dampening.

Damn. He was hot. And he made her hotter still.

"I wish I understood all this," she breathed.

"So do I, love. But I'm here now. With you. And I think this is where I'm supposed to be."

"You think? You're not sure?" Fay did her very best not to whine. Or whimper.

The fact that the hunk-from-her-dreams had just materialized in the darkness of a small hotel room in Ireland should have sent her screaming for Valium. And some serious psychological counseling.

It didn't. It simply made her ache with longing. It made her breasts swell, her pussy weep, and her heart pound at the thought that she might finally get a nice piece of that hardness he'd nearly plunged into her the last time she'd dreamed of him.

And this time, the weather forecast didn't include fog. Or mist, or anything other than a nice solid piece of flesh.

She licked her lips.

Aidan tossed back the rest of his drink with a sigh of pleasure and put the glass on the night table, stretching himself out on the bed. It squeaked a little as his weight crushed the quilt.

Okay. Another convincing argument for the fact that he was real. Ghosts didn't make bedsprings squeak.

He patted the covers next to him, and Fay's heart jumped at the look of invitation he scorched her with. *Ooooh mama.*

"Fay, love, I wish I could answer your questions, and mine too. But it's all hazy in my mind until I—I sort of—awoke, just now, and saw you playing the harp." Aidan's brow crinkled as he struggled for words.

"But I saw you in my dreams," said Fay, sitting on the bed next to him. The urge to launch herself into a flying triple-gainer and land on his hard chest was very strong, but she suppressed it. For the time being, anyway.

"And I saw you in mine," answered Aidan. "Dancing, you were. And very nicely too."

His eyes roamed her body hotly, and she felt herself color up as she recalled that dance very well indeed. She'd been stark naked at the time.

Of course, so had he.

She did a bit of her own hot gazing.

Yup. Everything was still where she remembered it. Covered by a T-shirt and jeans, dammit, but still there.

Aidan's eyes turned dark as she glanced back up at his face, realizing that she'd been caught staring at the bulge distorting his fly.

Ooops.

"Why don't you come here, next to me, Fay? I want to feel you lying beside me. I want to warm my soul with your heat. I want...I want *you*."

Well, all right. That was more like it.

With a smile on her lips and a little imp of pleasure dancing through her belly, Fay slithered up onto the soft bed and cuddled into Aidan.

* * * * *

She fit into his body like water on the shoreline, rippling along his side and filling all his hollows with her curves.

Aidan caught his breath on a hiss of pleasure as her breasts nestled into his chest and her head found the ideal spot on his shoulder.

"Aidan, this is so weird," she breathed. "And yet so right."

He shifted his legs, sliding one between hers and tugging her even closer. "It is indeed, love. But as you say, so right."

"Where did you come from?" Her breath was warm against his shirt. "Why are you here? What was in that Irish Mist?"

Aidan smiled. "It wasn't anything in the drink, Fay. I'm thinking it was something here…" He gently brushed the area over her heart. And yes, her breast was in the way, but who was he to complain? "Something inside you that called me. Some song you've been hiding that lured me to your side."

"Wow. I don't think I've ever lured anyone before. Especially not anyone like *you*." Her hands slid around him, trailing hot tingles as she let them rove over his body. "I'm pretty certain I would have remembered any 'luring' like this."

He could hear the pleasure in her voice and his smile widened. "Well, perhaps it's something in the magical Irish air."

"It's the harp. There's something in that harp that just called me. I had to have it, to try it out." Fay pulled herself up a little. "That's it, isn't it? You're some kind of spirit and I played the harp and you arrived."

Aidan swallowed. Now how was he supposed to handle *that*?

Without realizing it, the right words popped from his mouth. "Fay, love, you've been reading too many crazy books. Do I look like a spirit to you?" He ran his hand down her soft nightdress. "Do I *feel* like a spirit to you?"

She giggled and let her hand drift to his groin. "Well, I have to admit I never thought spirits could manage such a respectable…er…dimension." She curled her fingers around his cock through the fabric of his pants.

Oh lord. His shamrocks were jumping and his balls rivaled the Blarney Stone. He toyed with the idea of asking her if she'd like to kiss the Blarney Stone.

"There's just one problem, though, Aidan."

"What's that, love?"

"We're wearing *far* too many clothes."

With a smile that rocked him to his toenails, Fay slithered to her knees and reached for the hem of her nightgown.

Aidan gulped. This was happening too fast. He wanted to savor this moment—these moments—since the Goddess knew if he'd be allowed to hold onto these memories. Damned if he was going to waste them.

"Slowly, Fay, slowly. Don't hurry. Tease me, love."

Licking her lips, Fay obliged.

With deliberate care, she eased the flowery stuff over her knees and thighs, pausing for a moment and looking at him with eyes that burned hotly.

Shit. Don't stop. Not there.

Her arms moved again, just raising the hem a little more, teasing him with a glimpse of pink folds and then hiding them again.

He groaned. He couldn't help it. He'd asked her to go slow, but hadn't realized the implications. Aidan had often wondered if he'd go insane stuck inside his prison for so many long and lonely eons.

Now he wondered if he'd go insane within the next minute.

He fought the urge to rip that damn nightgown off her and let her continue with her delightful disrobing, biting back a sigh of relief as she finally lifted her skirts to her waist.

"Oh Goddess, you're lovely, Fay."

His words brought the color flying to her cheeks, and she stifled a giggle, trembling a little as she pulled her gown up even further. "Do you really think so?"

It was more of a breath than a question, and Aidan's hand fell to his cock, shifting it slightly as it jumped in response to her breasts. The rosy nipples were just peeking out from beneath the lacy stuff that she gathered in her hands.

"Oh yes, love, I do." He glanced down at himself. "*We* do."

Fay's smile lit up the room. "I'm glad. I..." She paused, and pulled the gown over her head, kneeling before him, finally naked. "I think you're lovely too."

Aidan barely heard her.

The firelight danced over her creamy skin and cast shadows over her body where it flickered across her breasts. Her nipples were beading, puckering even as he stared at them, and he could almost see her pulse pounding as her heart thudded behind them.

Paralyzed by his need for her, Aidan licked his lips and waited. He had no clue what to do next. His mind was blank, all conscious thought evaporating under the heat of her gaze.

He'd never imagined a tide of desire like the one that flooded through him at this moment. It stripped him of his brains, rendered his body useless, and centered itself in his cock.

He wasn't sure if loving Fay would mean his death or his return to life. It could be either. And at that moment, he didn't care.

He just knew he had to have her beneath him, on top of him, around him or over him. Any way at all. It didn't matter.

Whatever way it happened, it would be more than his cock she'd be taking.

It would be his heart.

Chapter Eight

Fay burned.

A combination of embarrassment, self-consciousness and desire roiled through her from her toenails to her ears.

Never had she ever imagined stripping for a man, slowly, wantonly, and enjoying every single moment, every flutter of his eyelashes and indrawn breath that her slightest move produced.

Aidan's eyes were heavy lidded now, and the growing length beneath his fly told her all kinds of nice things.

Not that she believed too many of them.

"Such beautiful breasts you have, Fay love," he whispered.

Fay blinked. "Uh...me?"

Didn't he notice that they were rather ordinary? Perhaps he'd been deprived of any female companionship for too long. Maybe whatever magical spell had brought him to her had forgotten to send a copy of Playboy along, or the latest Victoria's Secret catalog.

"Oh yes. You. Those..." He nodded at her chest. *Her* breasts. Well, *damn*. Her inhibitions slithered away along with the last of her self-doubts.

She raised her hands and cupped her breasts. "You mean *these*?"

Best to make sure. In case Pamela Anderson had materialized behind her or something.

Aidan groaned as she held herself. Her inner slut developed a huge and rather naughty grin on its face.

She smoothed her hands over her breasts, and let her fingers linger on her own nipples.

Aidan fidgeted and darned if she didn't see a little bead of sweat break out on his forehead. *Cooooool.*

"Aaahh, Fay...what you're doing...it's...it's..."

Well, look at that. A nice Polish girl had just reduced an Irish spirit/vision/something-or-other to a stuttering lump of lust. At least she hoped it was lust. And she *really* hoped he was real this time.

He unsnapped the fastening at the top of his jeans with a grimace.

Yep. Lust all right.

"My turn," he said. "Or something terrible is going to happen to me."

"Oh we can't have that," grinned Fay.

She sat back on her heels, managing to flash him a quite deliciously obscene amount of naked pussy as she did so. She relished the shiver that ran through him and jiggled the bed.

She motioned with her hands. "Come along then. Your turn. And slowly, now, remember?"

Where was this coming from? Ireland was said to be a land of magic, so she must have been possessed by the Porn-Queen devil. She wondered if she'd ever dare drink Irish Mist again, and then immediately dismissed the thought. If a little liqueur could produce a night like this, she'd buy the whole damn distillery.

With a great deal of caution, Aidan slid his zipper down, the rasping of the teeth loud in the quiet room.

Oh my. Apparently spirits didn't worry about boxers or briefs. There was *nothing* between him and his Calvins.

She sighed with pleasure at the sight of one extremely hard and handsome cock forcing its way between the fly of his jeans.

As if this sight wasn't enough to make her mouth water, he was now raising the hem of his T-shirt and stripping it quickly off over his head.

So much for going slow.

Fay's heart stopped as he lay back on the pillows, and she wished she had her camera handy to preserve this image for a lifetime. It was a hell of a Kodak moment.

Dark hair tumbled to Aidan's shoulders and his eyes were shining green fire from beneath his long eyelashes.

A firmly-muscled chest lay spread out before her, hairs dusting the very nicely defined dips and planes of his pecs and his abs, or whatever those lovely mouthwatering things were called.

Right now, they could have been called Beethoven's Fifth. Her pulse was doing a very respectable *dum-dum-dum-daaaa*, and all she wanted to do was taste him. Lick him, run her tongue around his little nipples, and trace the line of his breastbone down…down…

Fay sighed. "Oh Aidan. God. You're something else."

He grinned. "Me? You think so?"

"Oh yeaaahhhh." The inner slut surfaced again. "But let me help you here…" Fay reached for his jeans and carefully eased them down his thighs, her pulse pounding as Aidan raised his hips to free the fabric from his butt.

His butt. She mustn't forget to check that out, too.

Horrified at the direction her thoughts were taking, but enjoying every single one, a very conflicted Fay tossed up mental hands and gave in.

The jeans were thrown somewhere, and Aidan was now quite naked in front of her appreciative eyes.

Oh sweet lord.

"So, love, you think we'll do?"

Fay swallowed. Aidan had reached down for his cock and was idly running his fingers up and down its length.

"Very nicely," she murmured. "Very nicely indeed."

Aidan continued his stroking, almost mesmerizing her with his even movements. "And what do you think we should do, darlin'? Maybe this lad could feel a little of your soft skin perhaps?"

"Anything the *lad* wants," breathed Fay.

She moved nearer, between Aidan's legs, and leaned forward, just brushing the tip of his cock between her breasts. *Oh so fine.*

Shivers of fire rushed to her clit, intensifying as her nipples dappled over his hardness.

"Let me taste you, Fay," groaned Aidan. "Once, before you kill me. Let me suckle you, sweetheart. Please…"

Fay moved even further up the bed, carefully straddling him and sighing as her aching mound came to rest on his belly.

"Help me, love. I can't quite reach them…" Aidan's voice was liquid sex. Much like her pussy right at this moment.

Knowing what he wanted, she once again raised a hand to her breast and cradled it, leaning forward towards his face. "Aidan, taste me." It was a demand that Fay couldn't have imagined would ever come from her lips—but it had.

And he did.

His head closed in on her breast and his hot mouth pulled her nipple deep inside.

Bolts of lightning shot to her cunt as his tongue swirled around her, and she found herself lost in a sensual void where colors blurred, sounds dimmed, and her body focused on his.

She moaned aloud, the sound echoed by a murmur from Aidan as he reached for her other breast and played with it.

Her hips were moving, slowly grinding her clit into his hardness, and rubbing against his cock with each movement.

Aidan gently released her nipple and moved to the other breast. "Sweet," he murmured. "Sweet as life itself."

Another emotion flooded Fay. She wanted to cradle his head to her body, to hold him tighter than tight. To tell him all the wonderful things he made her feel with his sensuality, his sexuality and his gentleness. That they weren't fucking, they were making love.

That with a few well-chosen words, he'd let the woman inside her come to life. That this short time they'd spent together had done more for her heart and her life than all the years that had gone before.

She wanted him to know that she...that she was falling in love with him.

* * * * *

Aidan's heart pounded as he released her breast with a soft lick and moved to the other one.

They were food for the starving, sweetness to break the sour taste of his imprisonment, and just about the most perfect damn breasts he'd ever seen. Or touched. Or loved.

Her body caressed his in all sorts of delightful places, and his cock reminded him that there was someplace hot and wet it wanted to be. *Really* badly.

He was charmed by her innocent need, the way she offered herself so willingly to his mouth and had stripped herself bare for him. He was charmed by the light that burned behind her eyes as they turned stormy with desire, and the colors that flooded her creamy skin as he found some more tasty places and treated them to a hearty dose of Irish tongue.

He was just plain charmed. And that charm was going right past his cock, his balls, his raging lust to sink himself deep inside her, and heading for someplace else.

Someplace he thought he'd lost over the eons. His heart.

With a quick flex of his hips, Aidan rolled them, ending up with Fay beneath him.

A smile flashed over her face, followed by a moan as he pressed his hips to hers and settled between her legs. They opened for him as she settled herself to his body, letting the fiery heat of her pussy burn him and her moisture slick over his cock.

He rubbed himself against her, making hoarse cries escape from her throat.

Aidan smiled.

This was more like it. *This* made the long wait worthwhile. This woman, her sounds, her scent, her creamy skin flushing with her arousal, all of these things he had been waiting for. And he hadn't known it until now.

He reached for her arms and lifted them, stretching them out to either side of her and holding her still as he eased his full weight onto her.

Touching from breast to thigh, he paused, letting the feel of her seep into the cold places within him that had lain dormant for so long. Her warmth flooded him, her passion rocked him, and as she opened her eyes and met his gaze, his world shifted on its axis.

He knew he was finally free.

"Aidan," she whispered.

"I'm here, love."

"Oh God, I know," sighed Fay. "Do I *ever* know." Her hips moved in a demanding shiver.

An answering shudder lifted the hairs on the back of Aidan's neck as he let himself feel joy for the first time he could remember. The joy of a woman, a special woman, offering everything she had, everything she was, to him.

Like a rose unfurling, Aidan's heart opened, tears stinging the back of his eyes as he watched Fay's breathing quicken and her lips part on a sigh.

Damn, she was beautiful. A creature from his dreams come to life, waiting for him to claim her, to make her his.

And so he would. With every fiber of his body, every thought he possessed, every skill he'd ever had. And maybe a few he hadn't known about.

Slowly, he slid downwards, drawing his nails lightly along the sensitive flesh under her arms.

He grinned as she moaned, and then ran his tongue around her navel, dipping, licking and nipping the soft skin of her belly.

Her honey left a moist trail on his chest as he lowered himself downwards, and it was that honey that he sought with a hunger that boiled within him.

"Aidan, I..."

The murmur was nearly lost on Aidan. He'd reached his goal, and her pussy was open to him, her thighs spread and kept apart by the width of his shoulders.

"What, Fay-love?"

"I...you...what..."

Aidan grinned. "You've a beautiful pussy, lass. All roses and dew. And one little pearl..." He swiped her clit with his tongue, bringing a cry of pleasure to her throat. "And I like that it's bare. I can see all of you, Fay."

"I know," she groaned. "It's...it's...embarrassing, Aidan."

Aidan blinked. "Why?"

"Why?" Fay lifted up her head, cheeks flushing brilliant red as she stared at him looking up from between her legs.

"Well, you're...you're...*looking* at me. In all kinds of places where nobody's ever looked before." She thought for a moment. "Except for my gynecologist."

"Your who?"

Fay sighed. "Never mind."

"Another man has looked at you here?" For some reason, Aidan's mind fogged at the possibility.

"I'm not a virgin, Aidan, if that's what you're asking. But no, only my doctor has...has *seen* me down there. No one else ever seemed interested."

Aidan's heart eased. "Then your men have been fools, Fay. You have a rare beauty here, hidden deep and flowering just for me."

"He was a fool indeed, Aidan. And he ceased to exist the first time I saw you."

Aidan glanced at Fay and saw the honesty shining in her eyes. A jubilant song began somewhere in the recesses of his brain. Truly this woman was his.

He bent his head to her mound.

* * * * *

At the first touch of his tongue against her soaking folds, Fay went berserk. His heat matched her own, and as he learned every little nook and cranny that hid her most private depths she flew off into another dimension.

Good lord, if kissing the Blarney Stone gave a man the gift of gab, what the hell had Aidan kissed? The Wizard O'Tongue Stone?

He prodded and laved and dug deep into her flesh, finding all her special spots and even creating a few of his own with flickers and swipes.

Damn. What a musician he'd have made. Any wind instrument would have melted into a lump of useless minerals once his tongue went to work.

She lay there, writhing and sobbing as he brought her to the brink time and time again. He seemed to sense when she needed just one more touch, one more suckle to tip her off the edge of the world, and he backed off.

If he did it again, she'd kill him and put him out of her agony.

She was drenched now, her juices pouring from her like water from an Irish spring.

No wait, that was soap.

Oh what the hell...who cared? Why didn't he just let her *come*?

Her thoughts splintered as his tongue went low, very low, finding her cunt and following the folds even lower to...to...*ohmigod*.

"Even your arse is beautiful, Fay," he sighed.

Holy shit.

A lifetime of taboos reared its head and screamed within Fay's brain as Aidan's tongue found true virgin territory.

Dear God.

He ran his tongue around...around...places he shouldn't, and hot damn...it felt *incredible*.

Now something else touched her. His fingers.

He'd slathered her juices around her cleft, and stroked them soothingly into her tight ring of anal muscles.

Fireworks exploded in her brain.

Jesus God. Who knew?

"Relax, darlin'. It's all right. I'm loving you. Everywhere."

Fay tried to do as she was bid, but figured her ass was clenched tighter than a clam right about now, regardless of what Aidan was doing.

It appeared she was wrong.

With effortless coordination, Aidan found her clit with one hand and teased it, pressing up from beneath and making her gasp with pleasure. And as he did so, he slid a finger deep into her darkest places, past her inhibitions and sending her into a paroxysm of sensation.

"Aidan..." she screeched. "Aidan..."

She was coming. Nothing in the world could stop the orgasm now. It was like a freight train, building a rumbling intensity deep in her buttocks and fueled by the twin assault of his hands.

He buried his mouth in her pussy as she hit the peak.

Fay's mind exploded along with her body.

Sparks shot bursts of fireworks behind her eyelids and every single cell disintegrated into a million volts of electricity, zinging her and taking away her ability to think or breathe or do anything but ride the whirlwind.

Her cunt spasmed violently, sending shudders of heat and cold across her flesh as the rest of her struggled to keep up with the vortex of pleasure she was lost within.

She nearly blacked out, losing track of everything but the touch of his fingers and the pressure of his mouth. She could feel his touch so deep inside her, pushing her, encouraging her to heights she could never have imagined in her wildest fantasies.

And her fantasies had been pretty tame, since nothing like *this* had ever been involved.

Slowly she spun back to earth, as Aidan withdrew his hands and his mouth.

Little tremors still rocked her and she drew in a ragged breath, trying to figure out if all her parts were still in working order.

She opened her eyes and met a brilliant green gaze. Her heart lurched. Yep. That was still in working order.

"You are so lovely when you come, Fay," he said, voice husky.

Once again, Fay felt her cheeks flood with color. Was there nothing this man wouldn't say to her? She'd never ever thought a man would compliment her on her orgasm.

Sheesh.

"Let's do it again," he smiled.

Fay blinked. *Again*? He had to be kidding, right?

Wrong.

Chapter Nine

Aidan watched an expression of amazement fly over Fay's face.

She thought that was *it*?

He pulled himself up and over her, taking his weight on his hands and bending down to brush his lips against hers.

"That's your taste, Fay. That sweet taste. Better than the finest Irish whiskey and ten times as addictive."

She cautiously slid her tongue over her mouth and glanced shyly up at him.

"Aidan, you…I don't know what to say…this is all so new…"

His grin must have spread to his earlobes. A joyful heat stole through him as little tremors still flickered over Fay's body.

"Don't say anything, love," he whispered. "Just feel…"

He reached down and grasped his cock, sliding it around her drenched pussy and carefully brushing her sensitive clit.

She gasped aloud, reaching for his arms and digging her fingernails into his skin. "Aidan…that's…that's almost painful."

"How about this, Fay? Does *this* hurt you?"

Gently, he pressed his length into her, slowly penetrating between the slick folds.

Goddess, she was hot. Fire danced along his cock as he drove deeper inside Fay, and the heat of her body clutched at him, boiling his blood and sending his pulse pounding into his throat.

He battled the urge to ram himself into her up to his shamrocks, and his biceps knotted with the strain.

Sweat dropped from his forehead onto her body, and he wouldn't have been surprised if it had hissed and sizzled when it got there.

The woman was burning him up.

"No…aaah Aidan…no, it doesn't hurt," moaned Fay, tipping her head back and her hips up to welcome him deeper.

With a final move, Aidan locked their bodies together. Mortise to tenon. Tongue to groove.

They fit.

As he'd known they would from the first moment she'd stolen into his dreams.

She gloved him, swallowed him, surrounded him with living silk that caressed him and aroused him to fever pitch. He drew back a little and plunged again, even deeper, loving her sighs as he stroked himself within her.

Their bodies met as he continued his strokes, faster now, feeling his balls slap against her buttocks with each thrust.

She moved beneath him, rising to meet him as he buried himself inside her. He could feel her tension build around him, her walls tightening on his cock each time he plundered her sweetness and claimed it as his own.

"Jesus," she gasped.

"Goddess," he swore.

Aidan's mind swirled as he took Fay's body and made it his. At last he'd been freed from his eternal prison—freed to love this woman, this moment…this way.

He could have sworn for a second he heard the harp thrum as they raced towards the climax of their loving, but then the roaring of his pulse drowned out all other sounds.

His buttocks began to tingle at the base of his spine and his balls hardened to granite.

He couldn't help it. He threw his head back and roared.

"Fay!"

Her scream echoed his as he let the orgasm take him.

Powerful shudders rolled over Aidan from his toes to his eyebrows and he filled Fay's enveloping cunt with mighty jets of hot come. Each spurt wracked him with blinding pleasure, draining him, dazzling him, and urging him on to do it all over again.

His spasms were so strong he felt like he spent hours emptying himself into her. She might even have his soul right about now, since he didn't know what else was left within him to give. Just when he thought it was over, his cock jumped and pulsed once more, responding to the clinging folds that were even now caressing more and more of his come from somewhere around his kneecaps.

It was earth-shattering, mind-bending, and worth spending a couple of thousand years under a spell to experience.

Finally, when his cock relaxed at last and his balls surrendered to exhaustion, Aidan dragged in a breath to his starving lungs and loosened his arms, letting himself rest on Fay.

She took his weight easily, tucking her legs around his and clasping her arms to his back, running her hands gently up and down his spine in a soothing stroke. Her cunt still held his softening cock, cradling it with moist warmth and tenderness.

He was content. More content than he could ever remember being in his life. What little of it he could remember.

As his thought processes untangled themselves from his cock, he began to wonder if he would be allowed to stay. To finally live, to exist as a real human person, not just a shadowy presence. To love Fay. Again and again, for the rest of their lives.

He shivered.

"Aidan, you're chilled," murmured Fay.

He chuckled. "I've never been hotter in my life, love."

She wriggled, and he eased himself off her, slipping to her side and cradling her against him. His heart warmed as she pulled the quilt up and over their naked bodies, cocooning them in its fluffy folds.

"Well, goodness, Aidan." Fay's voice held a mix of astonishment and pleasure.

"Yes, indeed. Goodness. Much more goodness like that and I'll be limp as a slug in next to no time."

"And you're still here. Next to me. Warm, sweaty, sticky, your heart's pounding like a bass drum, and you're *here*."

Fay turned her head and dropped a light kiss on his chest, making him growl with satisfaction.

He tightened his arms. "And I plan to stay, too. Nothing could drag me away from you now I've found you. Now I've claimed you. You were the magic that set me free, Fay."

"And you've set me free, too, Aidan, although not in quite the same way."

* * * * *

As she spoke the words, Fay realized the truth of them.

A previously untapped well of emotions had erupted within her since the first moment she'd touched the harp earlier that night.

The music had freed her spirit and Aidan had freed her soul.

"How so, sweetheart?" Aidan's question was soft, his voice loving.

She slid a sticky thigh over his. It felt warm, slightly hairy, and she sighed with pleasure. He wasn't a man to run off to the bathroom the minute they were finished. Another good thing in favor of Irish ghosts. Or whatever he was.

She sighed. "It's hard to explain. You see, my life has always been my music. I play the piano."

Aidan's head turned as he looked down at her. "You do? I'll just bet you do it very well, too. You've got a great natural rhythm."

She blushed. "Well, that's neither here nor there. What I meant was that I've been sort of imprisoned inside my life as a musician. It's very rigidly structured, you know, after a certain point. I had to practice, rehearse, practice and rehearse again. It sort of takes over one's every waking moment."

"Doesn't sound like it leaves much room for fun."

"Playing *is* fun. Or at least it should be. But you're right. There wasn't room for much fun, not lately, anyway. And the only person I thought might be able to give me some of that fun turned out to be a real jerk. And...and..."

"And what, love?"

"And after tonight, after you...I just realized I had no idea what *fun* could be."

She felt Aidan's chest rise and fall as he chuckled. "You had fun, then, did you?"

Fay snorted. "Fun doesn't even come close. I'm...I'm overwhelmed. Stunned. *Ecstatic*. Bunches of words like that. I'm drained, exhausted, sticky and spent. And I couldn't be happier than I am right at this moment."

She sighed. It was all true. Every damn word. But questions were still plaguing her.

"Aidan, who *are* you? How come you're here? What kind of magic is this all about? I don't even believe in this sort of stuff, but you're *real*. You were in my dreams and now you're in my bed."

"And a few other places."

Fay giggled, snuggling against him. "That too."

Aidan sighed with pleasure, running his hand along her arm. "Ah, sweetheart, there are no simple answers to your questions."

"I don't want simple. Just tell me the truth."

* * * * *

The truth.

Aidan grimaced into the darkness. How to explain it when he wasn't sure he believed it himself?

He knew he was alive at last. He had an armful of the most delightfully warm and cuddly woman, and a cock that was exhausted and sticky from her loving.

That was real.

The rest of it? Where on earth to start?

"It's all because I was a young fool, Fay. An idiot with no more sense than the pigs my aunt and uncle raised."

"Go on." Her lips breathed the words over his chest.

"A very long time ago, some friends and I got into a lot of trouble. We used to drink far too much on a regular basis. It was supposed to be fun. Then one night…"

He could swear the harp was humming slightly as his story unfolded, as if it listened to his words.

"One night?"

He drew a deep breath. "One night we stole things that didn't belong to us."

"Aidan."

"I know. Stupid of us, but there you have it. The folly of youth and stupidity fueled by way too much liquor."

He closed his eyes, trying to trap the vague memories and sort them into some kind of order. Some things he knew, some he felt, and others were just half-remembered images drifting at the back of his mind.

"Anyway, we ended up with a few little souvenirs of our night of thievery. Small things, stuff we never imagined anyone would miss."

"And I'm guessing here that the owner was pissed off?"

Aidan's mind eased as he laughed. "That's a way of putting it, love, yes. She was mighty *pissed off*."

He tugged Fay even closer. "Trouble was, her name was Cailleach, Cailleach the Crone. A harsh, powerful and unforgiving woman with her own set of troubles. She didn't take kindly to our pranks."

"Well…"

"Oh I know. We deserved every single bit of punishment she meted out. But for me, it was the worst. You see, that harp was one of the few things that had made her life bearable. She'd had it made by a special craftsman, and there was much magic in it. Magic that had brought music into her life. She screamed at me that I'd stolen her music."

A chill passed over Aidan's skin. One thing that was crystal clear in his mind was that terrible screaming voice condemning him.

"What about your family?"

"I had no one but my aunt and uncle, and my uncle disappeared the morning my crime was discovered. It seems…I think he'd not deserted me…I can recall hearing his voice, knowing he was close, taking a certain measure of comfort from that. But it's hard to say, love. From that point on, my memories are blurry."

"What did she do to you? This Cailleach person?"

Aidan swallowed. "She told me I'd be nothing until her music was returned to her. And nothing is pretty much what I've been."

Fay thought for a moment. "How long, Aidan?"

"I don't know, sweetheart. I really don't know. I slept, I woke, I felt neither hunger nor thirst. I knew that the world still existed, and I found my clothing would change. And then I started dreaming."

His hand slipped to Fay's hair and he stroked his fingers through her tangled curls. "I dreamed of you."

"Me? You dreamed of me? How? Why? I'm not even from around here."

Aidan shrugged. "That I don't know, love. But it was definitely you. A bit vague at first, like you were just a spirit or something, but soon I could see you, see those eyes shining at me, and then I could touch you, hold you...almost kiss you."

Fay sighed. "Tell me about it. You were in my dreams too. Damn fine ones they were, but extremely unsatisfying."

Remembering the extraordinary hardness of his cock upon awakening from a dream of Fay, Aidan chuckled. "That I have to agree with, love. The real thing is much better."

Fay stirred a little next to him. "So somehow or other, I brought the music back?"

"It was the harp, sweetheart. Cailleach's harp. You played it, played her music, and here I am. Free to be with you and love you the way I was meant to."

"Funny thing is, I can't play the harp."

Aidan blinked. "You did though."

"Yeah, I know. But I'm not sure it was me. I just sat down tonight and couldn't stop myself from trying again." She raised herself up on one elbow and peeked at Aidan. "I have to be very honest here. The first time I touched the thing it was so awful every cat within a three-mile radius howled in terror."

"And tonight?"

"Tonight?" Fay paused. "It was like...like someone else's fingers took over mine. I knew the fingering. I knew the melody, the harmony and the chord progression. I knew where to hold my hands and how to strike the strings. It was...it was *really* weird."

Aidan thought about that, but the warmth of Fay's body and the soft gleam in her eyes distracted him.

"There's much magic in music, Fay. And in our wild country."

"And...in this," she whispered.

Soft lips lowered to his, and they shared a kiss full of promise and heat and all the things Aidan had yearned for over the ages.

He pulled back. "This is the real magic, Fay. The magic that is happening between us. The spells you cast with one glance of your eyes. One touch of your hand..." The hand that was presently straying down his chest and finding all sorts of nice places to caress.

He gulped.

"Oh, *this* kind of magic," she grinned.

Her hand slipped lower, and he groaned as his cock reminded him that he wasn't dead but very much alive, and wouldn't mind having another go at it, thank you.

She moved over him and their flesh peeled apart as skin brushed sticky skin.

"I think we should hit the shower," murmured Fay. "If you'd care to clean up a bit, that is..." She blushed. "Umm...I didn't mean to sound forward or anything..."

Aidan grinned. "I love 'forward'. Be as forward as you want. I have a lot of catching up to do, and yes, I'd love to be clean while I do it. Although it doesn't matter. I'll be happy with you any way at all, clean or dirty, inside, outside, in a field or a bed. Just as long as I'm with you, Fay-love."

As long as I'm with you.

He wondered just how long that would be, as Fay led him from the bed into the small bathroom and let him absorb the wonders of modern plumbing.

Part of him was dazzled by the magnificent array of chrome and porcelain and the instant hot water that cascaded from a spigot high on the wall. The other part was simply dazzled by Fay.

He let her draw him under the warm spray and lather him with some sweet-smelling stuff, smiling as she used her hands to work it into a froth of bubbles.

Now *this* was fun.

He took the container from her and returned the favor, slipping his hands over her sweet skin in a slick of warm gel.

Her breasts beckoned and he brushed them with his hands, smiling at the immediate response of her dusky nipples, and the quick indrawn breath she took as he covered them with his hands.

"Keep that up and we'll be sticky again before we know it," she growled, turning him around and away from her.

"Do you mind?"

"Hell no. But when it comes to showering, fair is fair, and I want my turn too, you know."

He felt her slide the lather over his buttocks. She seemed to like what she found, since she spent quite a bit of time scrubbing them, rubbing them and kneading them.

"Um…Fay? Was I that grubby then?"

"What?"

She sounded distracted.

"You're rubbing the skin off my bum, love."

"Oh. Sorry." Her hands withdrew and she sighed. "I'm going to say something I never imagined saying to a man in my entire life…you've got the most beautiful ass, Aidan."

His laugh rang out over the sound of the shower. "And nicer words I've never heard, sweetheart. Thank you." He turned back to her. "May I return the favor?"

Fay colored, but nodded, sliding around in front of him and lifting her hair off the back of her neck.

Such a delicious neck, too.

Aidan nipped it, and she moaned.

He ran his soap-covered palms down her spine, managing to contain himself at the slippery and hot sensations his movements were creating. He was hard as a rock again, desperately wanting to take Fay over and over, in any and every way he could think of.

His hands filled with her buttocks. Round and firm, they were shaped just right for his touch, full like a woman's backside should be, and covered with skin like fresh cream.

"Fay, darlin', grant me a wish." His voice was getting hoarser by the second as his fingers played and stroked and loved the warm flesh.

"Anything, Aidan."

Now *that* was a moan. A definite moan.

Aidan grinned. "Lean over the side, love. Rest your hands on that bit there..."

He pointed to a low shelf that held some bottles.

"Okay."

Her voice was breathy, a little anxious and a great deal interested, and she followed his instructions to the letter.

Sweet Goddess. She was so beautiful.

Chapter Ten

Dear God. He's looking at my ugly fat ass.

Fay closed her eyes as she followed Aidan's directions, wondering if some kind of Irish madness had come over her. Of course, an Irish spirit had come in her, but that wasn't the point.

For a second or two, Fay's mind crawled with the realization that he'd not used any kind of protection. Then she comforted herself with the thought that apparently he hadn't had sex in uncounted centuries. If anyone should be safe, it should be him.

His only worry would be rust or something.

And she hadn't noticed any creaking or joints that needed oiling. No sirree. Everything seemed to have weathered the ages in fine working order.

His hands slipped around her backside, spreading the silky shower gel as they went.

She sighed. She was on the pill, he was available, and she was not going to worry about it. It might be mad, wild and downright irresponsible, but hell. Those words described her state of mind right now.

His touch was making her extremely wild, her thoughts were downright irresponsible, and she was mad for him.

He slid his fingers down her cleft, making her gasp.

"Such a lovely arse, Fay. You're beautiful everywhere, darlin'."

"Uh...I..." Damn. She was going to say something, but what he was doing drove the thoughts from her head.

He found the tight muscles of her anal ring and circled them with his fingertips, stroking and caressing and making her cunt ache all over again.

She was a mass of screaming nerve endings and she almost came right there and then when he found her clit and slithered soapy fingers across it.

His cock was hard against her, hot and ready for her.

And she was more than ready for it.

"Aidan..." Her hips moved towards him of their own volition, inviting him, telling him without words of her need for him.

"Yes, love," he whispered. "Yes."

His skin touched hers as the head of his cock found its way into her swollen pussy. He nudged himself inside, and she heard him sigh as he slid deep into her cunt, filling her again. Completing her.

Oh yeah. Bring on the stickies.

She was so ready for him. Ready to accept the smooth deep strokes of that lovely piece of the male anatomy that had been designed just for her. For this.

Her odd angle made it easier for him to touch new places, new sensitive spots high up inside her body, spots that made her tremble as he rubbed them with the head of his cock in a regular rhythm.

She shifted slightly, and sucked in a breath as he hit one particular spot.

Holy Cosmo.

He'd found it. That mythical place that magazines raved about and women secretly dismissed as the ravings of sex experts looking for something new to talk about.

He was touching her G-spot.

It had to be. It was way deep inside her, and each caress of his hardness against it sent a shudder through her that made her want to scream, come, and possibly pee.

Her organs twisted themselves into knots as they responded to the stimulation, and the breath left her lungs as he slid a hand around and fluttered soft little touches against her clit.

He was moving faster now, his thrusts going so deep her eyeballs rolled. She gripped the shelf with both hands and hung on, surrendering to the wild sensations that wracked her body.

Holy shit.

She was coming. She could feel it, and this one was the orgasm to end all orgasms.

Her leg muscles tensed, her buttocks lumped into solid bunches and her spinal chord twanged. Her heart rate must have been doing the fastest polka ever recorded and she couldn't breathe.

She could only hang there, waiting, as the world disappeared and something inside her responded in the most primitive of ways to this mating.

Aidan pounded into her, his balls slapping against her, his breath harsh and echoing off the shower walls.

He moaned with pleasure.

Her body was doing pretty much the same thing.

Little sounds were forced from her throat, cries and whimpers that mirrored his thrusts.

And finally, with a shout, Aidan buried himself in her, hitting that all-important spot one more time and sending Fay over the edge.

This was it. She was never going to survive.

It was certain death.

And what a way to go.

Fay's eyes closed as she drowned in a total-body orgasm that rocked her universe.

Welling from her core, ripples of sensation picked her up off her feet, shook her, turned her inside out and upside down, and then shook her some more. She vaguely knew she was screaming, but her ears couldn't hear it. Blinded by flashes of light and weak from the tremors that held her tightly in their grip, she hung on, surfing wave after wave of explosive pleasure.

It took a huge effort to expand her lungs enough to suck in air.

She felt dizzy and disoriented, and when she opened her eyes the shock of seeing an ordinary bottle of herbal shampoo two inches from her nose nearly finished her off.

As her hearing cleared and her body's reaction eased, her brain vainly attempted to pick itself up and put itself back together.

"Fay..."

She heard Aidan's moan through the fog that still persisted in muffling her.

"Darlin'..."

She managed a grunt.

"You can let go of my cock now."

Slowly, his words registered, and Fay realized her body had seized his in a fierce clamp and was holding him tight.

Gritting her teeth, she forced her stomach muscles and everything within three feet of her clit to relax.

It wasn't easy.

Fortunately, the shower water was turning cold now, and the chill droplets were dancing along her bare skin.

With a gusty sigh she pulled herself upright and let Aidan's cock slide from her. Damn, she was no better than a bitch in heat.

Her legs still shook and she leaned against the tiles as Aidan reached past and shut off the shower. A soft towel surrounded her, and strong arms lifted her clean off her feet.

It was lovely, romantic, damp and blissful. And when Fay had a moment she'd appreciate it. Right now, however, she was about as close to a corpse as anyone with a heartbeat could be, and she just wanted to sleep.

With Aidan, of course.

* * * * *

The first light of morning dappled the sky outside the small Ballyreath hotel and the few leftover nighttime clouds were turning a wispy pinkish-gold outside Aidan's window.

He hadn't slept a wink. He'd spent the night cocooned with Fay, snuggled on a soft bed beneath an even softer quilt, and watching her as she rested beside him.

His cock had stirred at regular intervals whenever she did something that aroused him—like breathe. Or snore a little. Even the soft pop that made him smile as she farted in her sleep had gotten him hard.

All these things told him that she was real.

It would seem that someone, somewhere had decided he'd been punished enough, and had freed him to find the joy of living again. And the extraordinary passion of loving again.

His lips curved into a grin as she turned on her pillow and let her hand rest on his shoulder. She reached for him even in her dreams, it would seem.

Just as he had sought her for so long. He wondered how it was that she should be the one to set him loose from his enchantment—what magic she possessed that had accomplished the deed where others had clearly failed.

"It's in her heart, Aodhan Mac Murchadha."

Aidan jumped a little as a voice sounded in his head. He glanced around the room. He was alone.

No—wait. A shimmering form was taking shape next to the bed. Long golden hair, a curvy body...a pair of very long legs topped by brief pink shorts that stopped far too low for his peace of mind.

Some kind of soft glittery shirt hung to just beneath a pair of magnificent breasts, and what looked like a piece of metal was sticking out above a well-defined navel.

Good Goddess. It *was* the Goddess.

But she wasn't wearing anything that he'd ever seen in any of her images.

"It's cool, don't you think?"

That was the one thing Aidan couldn't do right at this moment. *Think*. He could only stare at the vision before him, and drop his jaw.

She was magnificent.

"Why thank you, lad," she grinned.

He could hear her words in his mind, although she hadn't spoken aloud. Well, so be it. He was either insane or had died sometime during this wonderful night.

"No, Aodhan. You're alive. As alive as that girl in your bed."

Huh? Whaaa…

The Goddess giggled in his head. Yes, that was definitely a giggle. Stunned, Aidan realized he never knew Goddesses giggled.

"Oh you'd be surprised at what we do. And you might even learn a thing or two." She tipped her head a little and raised one perfect eyebrow. "Although you did pretty well on your own last night, lad."

Aidan simply couldn't prevent the color from rising to his cheeks. Had she been watching them last night? In the damn shower?

That delightful giggle made his ears ring. "I'm not a perv, Aodhan. I'd rather play than watch."

Now his cheeks were on fire. This was certainly a weird mental conversation to be having with a Goddess. And what the hell had happened to her anyway?

"You've a lot of catching up to do, Aodhan. I'd suggest you might want to start with that…" She nodded at a small box that was sitting on a table at the foot of the bed. "Try the MTV channel. The clothes…oooh, Mother McCree." She licked her lips.

Aidan blinked.

"But never mind that. I just popped in to let you know that you're officially free now. Sort of confirm things, set your mind at rest...all that stuff. And they're going to show the newest David Bowie music video tonight. Didn't want to miss that."

Umm...er...Aidan's mind went back to stuttering.

The Goddess sighed. "Aodhan, your enchantment has come to an end. You must now learn to live in this time, and this place. If you choose to, that is. Your uncle is waiting for you at the end of the street, and I think you'll recognize the cottage."

She smiled at him, letting the full force of her beauty hit him like a blast from the noonday sun. "You've done well to survive, lad. Now it's time for you to claim your reward. Go to Bantry. Now. Don't wake the girl, just go. Let events work themselves out as they were destined to do. Trust me..."

The vision faded, and Aidan's mind emptied, the last words lingering somewhere around the nape of his neck.

Trust me.

Right. Trust a Goddess who giggled, wore clothing that showed every single nook and cranny, and talked about some man called David Bowie.

"I mean it, Aodhan. Go to Bantry. He'll help you set things to rights."

Fuck. She was still there.

"I'm gone, babe. I'm the wind. Have a nice life."

She was the wind? No she wasn't, that was someone else, another God. What the fuck was she on about? Had he imagined the whole thing? What was a "channel"? What was MTV?

He sighed. She'd been right about one thing. He had a hell of a lot of catching up to do.

But damn it all, he hated to leave Fay sleeping.

He'd hoped to wake her with some fine Irish loving, sliding his cock into her sleepy body and feeling it wake beneath his.

He'd hoped to watch her eyes turn all kinds of hot as he roused her to that peak again and gently pushed her over into mindlessness. Damn, she was *so* beautiful when she came for him.

But orders were orders. He'd spent too long in his confinement to risk pissing off *another* Goddess.

Gently, Aidan slipped from Fay's side and gathered the clothing that littered the room.

His pants were one place, his shirt another, and sometime during the night a stout pair of boots had appeared which looked like they'd fit him.

Quietly he dressed, always aware of the woman sleeping soundly in the bed, her chest rising and falling with her even breaths.

His heart turned over. She was his woman. His life, his soul and his future. He just prayed that the Goddess was right and that he'd "catch up" as she put it in time to bind Fay to him.

Life without her would be worse than all the centuries he'd spent in the harp.

Life without Fay would be death for him.

Silently, he slipped from the room and out into the Ballyreath dawn. His future awaited him.

Chapter Eleven

Fay yawned, stretched, and let her muscles loosen into total relaxation. She felt wonderful.

There were aches and cramps in a few odd places this morning, but she was contented, sated, and happy just to lie there next to Aidan.

She smiled and turned over, reaching for the warmth that had snuggled next to her through the night.

Her hand met cool sheets.

Oh God *no*.

A surge of adrenaline brought her heart into her throat and she jerked upright in the bed.

She was alone.

She couldn't believe it. Couldn't accept it. Couldn't get her mind around the fact that he wasn't there.

She leaped from the bed and rushed to check the bathroom. It was empty, the towels still lying in disarray from their adventures in there the night before.

Fay's throat clogged.

This soooo can't be happening.

She stood in front of the fireplace, heedless of the fact she hadn't a stitch of clothing on her.

The room felt cold, and although the dent left by Aidan's head still showed in his pillow, she knew he had gone.

The harp stood silently on the floor, no sparkling glitters of green and gold flashing from it this morning.

She bent and ran her hand over the wood.

It was just wood.

Desperation welled up inside her and she sat down on the rug drawing the harp into her body. She raised her hands to the strings and started to play, but the sound was empty, hollow, and she missed several notes as the melody in her head seemed incomplete and *wrong* somehow.

Pain wracked her, the pain of loss, the pain of her emptiness and the shattering pain of her heart.

It was breaking in two, unable to survive without Aidan. She gasped as a bolt of grief shattered through her.

She rested her head on the harp and wept.

* * * * *

The next weeks passed in a combination of dream and nightmare for Fay.

Her first thought had been to check in with the front desk—perhaps there'd be a message for her.

But Maureen had shaken her head, and soon the look in her eyes had turned to sympathy for Fay as she regularly asked each morning and evening. It was the same question. *Any messages for me?*

Fay didn't care if Maureen thought she was waiting for a man. She didn't care who knew or who thought what. It took her two days to accept the fact that Aidan had disappeared from her life much as he'd appeared in it.

Mystically, magically and totally.

Then the anger set in. Anger at Aidan for making her feel such wildness and passion, and anger at herself for falling in love with him.

She snorted. Damn ghosts and spirits. Damn Ireland.

It *owed* her, and she set out to collect.

Determinedly she booked each and every tour she could get her hands on.

She took rolls of photos and made regular trips to the little gift shop to replenish her stock of film.

She spent a day wandering around the Belleek estate, trying to admire the marvels of magnificent pottery.

She oooh'd and aaah'd with the rest of the tourists as they stood in awe of the Belleek International Center Piece, a mammoth urn-like thing, magnificently ornate, full of history and the pride of the Belleek family.

It dominated the Belleek Center Museum, and would have ordinarily brought Fay's artistic nature to the fore. She loved art in all its incarnations, and this was truly an incredible work.

But as her eyes traveled up the creation, past the Irish wolfhounds supporting the base, she saw the decorations at the top.

They were Irish harps.

The pain returned and she moved away from the crowd to find solitude and her tissues. If only she could stop the damn tears from coming back every time something reminded her of Aidan.

Fay managed to find a nice little vase for Carly, along with a matching pair of candlesticks. Focusing on the task was a help since it kept her thoughts occupied. Making arrangements for the gift to be shipped overseas and dealing with the complexities involved took her mind off her miseries for all of about twenty minutes.

She ranted privately at herself for turning into a lovesick wimp.

Refusing to surrender to her pain, she spent that night down at the "Rolling Pig", accepted several offers of Guinness and barely managed to avoid throwing up when she staggered back to her room.

At least she slept that night, but the headache she woke up with the next morning was barely worth it.

All this time the harp stayed put. She couldn't bring herself to touch it, and nor could she bring herself to go back to Bantry's shop and return the bloody thing.

She spent a day in Derry, letting her thoughts roam freely as she walked between buildings older than she'd ever imagined. The Crafts Center lured her, and the charm of the old stone walls shone down on her.

The Guildhall tower soared above her like a cross between a church and something out of a gothic novel. It was stunning, beautiful and ancient, and Fay found herself wondering if it had been around when Aidan had lived.

Dammit to hell and back.

There didn't seem to be anything she could do, anyplace she could go, that didn't remind her of her Irish lover.

At the end of the first week, she'd had enough. It was time to head back to the little thatched cottage at the end of the village. She grabbed the harp and tucked it under her arm, only to hear the low rumble of thunder in the distance.

Rain spattered her window.

Shit. Now she'd get the damn thing wet and Bantry would probably refuse to accept it.

She put the harp back down and frowned at it. "Don't think I'm taking you back to the States. You got me into this mess in the first place."

The harp sat quietly, just doing what it did best. Being a harp.

Fay grunted, grabbed her slicker and headed out into the rain. She wasn't one to worry about getting wet when she had a mission. She was going to demand Bantry take it back and refund her money.

The street was soggy and puddles barred her way. The skies were a solid grey mass overhead and the rain fell like it really meant it. No Irish dew here. Just a healthy downpour.

Her sneakers were soaked by the time she reached the end of the main street, and a growl of temper burst from her as she reached the gate of The Thatched Cottage.

It was locked, and boldly sported a sign announcing that the store was "'Temporarily Closed for Business".

The shutters were drawn, and there really did seem to be no life inside.

Fay frowned. It looked quite a bit bigger than she remembered. She squinted. No—it must be a trick of the light. The second doorway into the building and the rain-slicked mullioned windows beside it had been there last time she'd visited.

As had the carved block of wood nailed to the lintel. The elegant script flowed across the dark surface—"The Thatched Cottage. Ballyreath Artisans Guild".

She paused, trying to remember how that sign had looked last time. It was funny. She couldn't quite recall it as clearly as she would have liked. She swallowed and dismissed an irritating thought that wouldn't show itself. Yep. It looked like it had last time, except for the fact that nobody was at home.

She turned away into the rain, ignoring the fact that some of the moisture on her cheeks was salty. Tears from her eyes and tears from the skies.

It was a sadly tragic moment.

Fay wondered where the playwright or the poet was who could do justice to it.

For the first time in a while, Fay itched for a piano. To be able to pour out some of her pain onto the keys and let the sounds lift her soul from the mire. It wouldn't solve her problems, but it might help.

So instead of burying herself in her hotel room and succumbing to another bout of misery washed down with a couple of glasses of Bushmills' fine whiskey, she turned towards the small parlor of the hotel.

A little piano sat inside, seldom used, but available should any guests get the urge to play.

Fay had the urge.

Like coming home to a much-loved friend, Fay lifted the lid and slid onto the well-worn piano bench. Her fingers drifted idly over the keys, testing them, feeling their particular characteristics, learning the sound they made.

She could close her eyes and let her mind wander as her hands played some of her favorite airs. The light and soothing chords carried her away from her grief for a time, comforting her and, to her surprise, attracting a crowd.

She played the final notes of "When Irish Eyes Are Smiling" and was completely taken aback by a round of applause.

"Eh, lass, you play like an angel," smiled an elderly man.

"Indeed you do, Miss Fay," added Maureen, who'd left her desk to listen.

"Well...I...I..." Fay looked at the pleasure shining from the faces that surrounded her. It wasn't the time to mention her qualifications or her experience. "Thank you."

"D'you think *I'd* ever be able to play like that?" A little girl pushed through the crowd and stared up at Fay, worship in her eyes.

Fay smiled. "Of course, sweetheart. It takes a lot of practice, but if you've got the desire *here*..." she touched the child's heart, "...then you'll find you can learn the skill *here*." Fay's hand brushed the child's soft hair and the girl smiled excitedly.

"I'm goin' to ask me Mum."

A little of the pain eased inside Fay as she watched the sturdy legs toddle away. Perhaps another famous concert pianist had just been born. It was a warming thought.

She cherished it through the last few days of her vacation, but all too soon the days dwindled, and she was left with a half-packed set of luggage, her toiletries—and the harp.

No sense in putting it off any longer.

Her flight was booked for the following day. She'd be going back to the States, back to her real life, and leaving all this pain and confusion behind.

And damn if she hadn't done the same thing three weeks before. Perhaps it was her destiny. Wherever she went, she'd end up leaving a trail of pain.

Only she knew it was going to be a lot harder to leave Ireland than it had been to leave Boston. She'd left a broken relationship behind her at Logan Airport.

This time she'd be leaving a broken and shattered heart.

She reached for the harp, tucked it under her arm and left the room. It was time to return it to its rightful owner, Mr. Bantry Murphy.

Chapter Twelve

Aidan Murphy hummed a little as he worked over his latest project.

The lathe hummed along with him as the leg of a small side table emerged beneath the blade of his chisel, curved and elegant, yet raw and unfinished.

He sighed with pleasure and glanced at the clock again. It was nearly time.

Time to set all to rights and claim his woman.

In the two weeks since he'd seen her, his heart had been full of her, but his mind had been constantly bombarded with information, plans, details, memories and so much *stuff* he'd sunk into his bed each night exhausted.

Only to dream of Fay.

But he'd not been able to touch her, to reach her, only watch as she walked across the green hills of his home.

Bantry had been thrilled to see him when he'd arrived at his uncle's door after leaving Fay's bed. Aidan had the odd feeling that he was expected, since a pot of tea was ready, and a plate of hot scones was waiting for him.

And as of that moment, his education had begun.

How to live in this time, this incredible age of technology and scientific marvels. A world that had shrunk to the size of a potato, and a small one at that.

A world that also included enough magic to create a home and a past for Aidan...one that he knew would remain firmly fixed right where it was.

It was that knowledge, that realization, which kept him sane. The long days filled with information and instruction would mark the foundation of his life with Fay. One he was determined to live to its fullest, no matter what it would bring.

"So, lad, you're ready then?"

Aidan turned off the lathe and pushed up his safety glasses. "As ready as I'll ever be, Uncle. You're sure she's coming?"

Bantry snickered. "Can't keep a woman away from a Murphy. Not once she's lain with him."

Aidan scowled. "She's taken her time. Maybe she wasn't as impressed by the Murphy technique as you'd like to think."

Bantry sighed. "We've been over this. You know damn well that you needed time to adjust. To learn what you needed to know. And the Goddess had to set everything in place for you. For both of us as a matter of fact."

"I hate the thought of losing you, Uncle Bantry." Aidan swallowed. "It's a high price to pay for mortality."

"Oh come on, lad, you'll never *lose* me. I have other things to do, is all. My job is far from done. Settling you is just the first of my tasks. The Goddess will protect me."

"Yeah," grinned Aidan. "But who's going to protect *her* in that dangerous little rock star outfit she's taken to wearing?"

Bantry shrugged. "Clothes. Seems even goddesses have a thing for them." He glanced out of the window.

"But she's done a damn fine job here in Ballyreath, I'll say that for her."

"No arguments from me."

"So you understand what will happen, Aidan? Fay will remember you, but nothing of your mysterious arrival. To her, you'll be the man who sneaked into her hotel room for a night of passion, and then disappeared. You'll have to come up with something to explain why you did it, but she'll know you as Aidan Murphy, craftsman, not Aodhan Mac Murchadha, Irish spirit."

"She'll forget all about the harp. Yep. I've got it." Aidan brushed the sawdust from his hands and pulled off his woodworker's apron. "But how much will I remember, Uncle?"

"Don't know. The Goddess was a bit vague on that. Last time we spoke she was a bit vague about everything. She'd been to some party or other and all she wanted was food. Kept demanding Twinkies of all things. Her eyes looked a bit red too..." Bantry frowned.

"Oh well. I suppose only time will tell. My immediate concern is Fay and making sure she doesn't even *think* of leaving." Aidan shivered at the thought.

"Don't worry about that, lad. We Murphys can handle the women."

Aidan raised an eyebrow. His uncle obviously still remembered the old days. One of the first things *he'd* absorbed about life in the twenty-first century was that women were a whole new kettle of fish. And the luscious salmon he'd landed wasn't about to be "handled". Well, not in *that* way at least. But in other ways...

Aidan's heart beat a bit faster and his jeans got a bit tighter as he thought about all the different ways he'd like to handle Fay.

"Keep your cock in your pants a bit longer, lad. She's coming."

Dammit. She'd better be, since just thinking about her makes me want to come too.

* * * * *

Fay walked through Ballyreath with a determined stride, feeling the sunshine warm on her head and the harp firm beneath her arm.

She nodded and smiled at the few greetings she received as she passed the shops just opening for the day, while her mind busied itself with the task that lay ahead.

Letting go of Aidan.

Letting go of the memories of one incredible night that had truly changed her life.

Saying goodbye to the magic that had awoken a song in her heart and helped her rediscover the music that had slept inside her for so long.

She sighed as she approached the path to The Thatched Cottage.

This was it.

The neatly paved walk stretched to the doorway which was open this morning, and the elegant shrubs either side were loaded down with buds about to burst into bloom. She paused, some urge making her reach for a gate.

Which wasn't there.

That was odd.

Shrugging off the feeling, Fay neared the steps and smiled at the sound of a very modern piece of music coming from inside. The Irish Rovers. In spite of everything, those lilting songs could still bring pleasure to her. They probably always would.

The open door beckoned her and she stepped inside, peering around at the large bright room, filled with crafts, quilts and beautifully made pieces of woodwork.

"Hello? Mr. Murphy? Bantry? Anyone here?"

A figure moved at the far end of the workshop, stepping into a patch of sunlight.

Fay's heart stopped dead. Then resumed its beating, double time, and jumped into her throat, threatening to strangle her on the spot.

It was Aidan.

"Hello, Fay-love."

He was speaking. She could see his lips move, but damned if she could hear a word over the ringing in her ears.

He was *there*. Casting a shadow, touching a tool, running his hand through his long dark hair and smiling at her. Walking towards her with a look in his eyes that threatened to melt her underwear.

The world rocked around her.

Bring out the straitjacket and the padded cell, because I'm surely going insane.

There was a slight movement behind him and for a fleeting second Fay swore she could see...Britney Spears?

She blinked and the hot-pink vision was gone.

Well, that's it. Better plug in an IV-drip of some antihallucinogenic drug while you're at it, girl. You're waaaay over the edge.

Then Aidan's face loomed over her, his hands reached out to cup her face and her mind emptied of everything but him.

"Fay, ah Fay," he sighed. "I'm so glad you're here."

And once again his lips touched hers, familiar and warm and all the fabulous things she'd remembered from their night together.

He teased her with his tongue, making her mouth open so that he could deepen their kiss.

Strange things started to happen to Fay, besides the customary heat in her body and the immediate production of excess moisture that promptly soaked her thong. They were a given where Aidan was concerned.

But this was different.

Little sparkles flashed behind her eyelids, and her mental processes felt like they were shifting about a foot or so to the left.

It was almost as if someone was in her mind, tidying up, putting thoughts in the proper drawers and folding her psychological socks.

She clung on to Aidan with her free hand, still clasping the harp between them with the other.

She was scared she was going to fall into some whirlpool of madness and never come out. She was safe as long as Aidan was holding her, but if she let go…

His tongue plunged deep, finding a welcome as she twirled hers around it and tried to suck it deeper still.

She moaned, and almost missed him removing the harp from her grasp, only noticing it was gone when their bodies met flush with each other and her breasts clashed hard against his chest.

His arms were around her now, pulling her even closer and molding her to him with a fierce and desperate heat.

He ground his hips against her, and she realized that if her underwear was wet, then his must be really pinching, since he'd grown a very nicely sized bulge beneath his fly.

Oh yeah. Oh very *very* yeah.

Finally, when they were both panting for air, Aidan pulled back from her lips, only to hug her close again.

"I've missed you so much, Fay," he whispered.

"You left me," she wailed. She couldn't help it. The last two weeks had knocked any emotional control out of her. Her pain flooded from her in those three little words.

"I love you."

Well, okay. There were another three little words that were likely to stop her heart all over again. "You do?"

She opened her eyes and gazed at Aidan.

He was staring at her, doing one of those "devouring her face" things that she'd read about but never imagined experiencing. Like he was committing each and every eyelash to memory.

"I do, sweetheart. Oh yes, I do."

"That's good. That's very good." Fay swallowed, trying to breathe, think, hold Aidan, and come to terms with the fact that the man of her dreams had just told her he loved her.

And not pass out.

"Come sit down, love. We have to talk."

Aidan half-carried her over to a smooth bench by the window and settled her in the sunshine, cuddling her onto his lap.

She sighed. "I'm all muddled, Aidan."

"I know, love, and it's my fault. I should never have crept into your room that night…but Fay, it's like you were my dreams come to life."

Once again, Fay's mind struggled to wrap itself around Aidan's words. He'd sneaked into her room at the hotel and loved her silly.

Yes, of course he had.

"Well, I wasn't exactly objecting, if I remember rightly," she said. God, he smelled good. Like sawdust and honey and something nice and male.

"I didn't want to wake you. You were sleeping so soundly, love, cuddled next to me. And I fully intended to come back later that day. I swear by the Goddess."

"Why didn't you? It's been miserable, Aidan…"

He sighed deeply. "I got a surprise message about a shipment of wood I'd ordered, sweetheart. I had no choice but to go to Belfast and see to things. Absolutely no choice. There was no one else to go in my place."

"You could have left a message or something." Damn it. She was whining.

"And I probably should have. But what would I have said? 'Wait for me so that I can love you silly again'? 'Fay, please don't leave because I think I'm in love with you and I want you in my bed again'? 'Oh by the way, my name is Aidan Murphy and I own the Ballyreath Artisan's

Guild. Can we please fuck some more'?" He chuckled. "I didn't have your phone number. And can you imagine Maureen's face at any of those messages?"

Fay grinned. She couldn't help it. "Well, I guess…'

"I couldn't find the words, Fay. I didn't know what to say. I just got back yesterday, and the first thought in my mind was to find you, but…but to be honest, I was scared."

"Scared? You? Of what?"

Aidan picked up her hand and played with her fingers. "Scared because of what I want to tell you. To ask you."

"What's that, Aidan?"

He lifted her hand to his lips and kissed it. "Stay with me, Fay. Don't leave Ireland. Be here with me. Build a life with me. Teach music to our kids and the other kids in Ballyreath. There's a whole little music school just going to waste next door…" He nodded at an opening in the far end of the room that Fay hadn't noticed before.

A small piano stood silently inside.

All the pieces fell into place within Fay's mind.

Aidan Murphy, master craftsman and owner of The Thatched Cottage. Founder of the Ballyreath Artisan's Guild. The man who'd seen her in the village and crept into her dreams and her room—and her bed.

Not to mention her heart and her soul.

She didn't hesitate.

"Yes."

Chapter Thirteen

Dear Carly,

This is going to come as one hell of a shock, sis, but I'm staying in Ireland. Not only that, but I'm going to marry the most wonderful man in the entire world.

Okay...so you've picked yourself up off the floor, and you're wondering how all this happened. Well, hell, so am I.

But it's real, Carly. I love him so much I can't begin to find the words to explain it, and when I look into his eyes I know he loves me the same way. It's like some kind of magic, I suppose. Almost as if he was the man of my dreams and then he became real.

He's unleashed the music in me. Silly thing to say, but something in him brings out the joy I used to feel for my career, for the concertos and the symphonies. Something I'd lost, that Aidan frees with a look, a touch...and yeah, a bunch of other stuff that would be TMI, even between sisters. (Giggle)

Let's just say that now I've got a pretty good idea why those Irish eyes are smiling.

Anyway, let me tell you about him.

His name's Aidan Murphy—yep, faith and begorrah, 'tis a fine Irish name—and he's a master craftsman here in Ballyreath. And oh, Carly, he makes such beautiful things. Got a great business going, along with a gift boutique, and guess what? A little music studio right next door which is just crying out for a music teacher. And yes, you guessed it...that would be a position about to be filled by the new Mrs. Murphy.

Ahem. That would be me…

Sorry, I'm getting ahead of myself. Let me tell you how it all started. You see, I bought this old harp and wanted to get it repaired…

* * * * *

"You did a good job, Bantry," said the golden-haired Goddess. Today she was wearing a few tiny pieces of leather, which did nothing to hide her assets. The matching boots were a major distraction.

Bantry Murphy fidgeted.

From their position on the roof of a nearby barn, both he and the Goddess could see two heads close together in the workshop of the Ballyreath Artisans Guild.

Invisible to anyone who might be looking their way, Bantry stretched his short legs out over the shingles and sighed. "Well, one down and two to go."

"You'll do it. I have no doubts on that score."

"And what about these two? They'll be all right will they? He's my kin…I can't help but worry about him."

The Goddess tossed her hair back over her shoulder and laughed. "Oh yes, sweetie. They're going to be fine. Aidan's few remaining memories will fade with the years, and Fay is already convinced he's someone she met on her vacation. They're all set."

"Um…"

"What is it, Bantry? Something bothering you?"

Bantry chewed his lip. "Well, yes…"

"Go ahead. Spit it out."

"You're a Goddess. Someone with powers the rest of us can't begin to imagine. Someone we look up to. Worship even..."

She nodded.

"So do you *have* to dress like Britney Spears?"

The End

About the author:

Sahara Kelly was transplanted from old England to New England where she now lives with her husband and teenage son. Making the transition from her historical regency novels to Romantica™ has been surprisingly easy, and now Sahara can't imagine writing anything else. She is dedicated to the premise that everybody should have fantasies.

Sahara welcomes mail from readers. You can write to her c/o Ellora's Cave Publishing at 1337 Commerce Drive, Suite 13, Stow OH 44224.

Also by Sahara Kelly:

A Kink In Her Tails
Beating Level Nine
For Research Purposes Only: All Night Video
Guardians Of Time 1: Alana's Magic Lamp
Guardians of Time 2: Finding The Zero-G Spot
Hansell and Gretty
Joshua 4.0 (*Ellora's Cavemen: Tales from the Temple I*)
Knights Elemental
Madam Charlie
Magnus Ravynne and Mistress Swann
Partners In Passion 1: Justin and Eleanor
Partners In Passion 2: No Limits
Persephone's Wings
Peta And The Wolfe
Sir Phillip Ashton's Eyes (*Mesmerized*)
Sizzle
Tales Of Beau Monde 2: Miss Beatrice's Bottom
Tales Of Beau Monde 3: Lying With Louisa
Tales Of Beau Monde 4: Pleasuring Miss Poppy
Tales Of The Beau Monde 1: Lying With Louisa
The Glass Stripper
The Gypsy Lovers
The Sun God's Woman
Visions (*Mystic Visions*)
Wingin' It

KISSING STONE

Tielle St. Clare

Chapter One

"Jess. Kit. It was fun, as always. I've got to get to class."

Kit, in mid-bite of her peanut butter and jelly sandwich, nodded as Jackson Knight, Jax to his friends, grabbed his shoulder bag and stepped away from the table.

"What time are you getting out of here?" he asked Kit.

She swallowed quickly, peanut butter clogging her throat. "I've got some kids coming in at six. I should be done by seven."

"I'll be in my office until then. Stop by on your way out. It's Wednesday. McGill's is calling my name."

Again she nodded. In the six months that they'd known each other, it had become tradition. Wednesday nights. Beer and corned beef at McGill's. Jax and Kit. It was like a bad buddy movie.

"See ya later. See ya, Jessie."

Jax turned and walked away—his pale khaki pants highlighting the exquisite male butt and long strong legs.

Kit tried to pull her eyes away, but like almost every other woman in the room, she had to look. Had to watch that deliciously curved tush walk away and think about giving it a light pat, a gentle squeeze. Still, the man was her best friend. She shouldn't be lusting after him. She took a deep breath and once more dragged her thoughts away from sex.

As he turned left out of the dining room, Kit heard Jessie whimper softly beside her.

"I know you said you two are just friends and there's nothing romantic between you—" Jessie spun in her chair and nailed Kit with her eyes. "But sometimes, don't you just want to grab him, throw him on the floor and bounce on him for hours?"

The man was as near to physical perfection as Kit ever expected to see. Tall, with sandy blond hair, a muscular chest, well-ripped arms and a tight ass. And damn it, he was a nice guy.

"Almost constantly," Kit moaned before collapsing onto the table.

"What?!"

Jessie's shriek of laughter drew the room's attention, forcing Kit to straighten and shield her eyes. Though most of the students ate at the other dining hall during lunch and the room was half-empty, Kit hated to be the center of attention.

"Keep it down," she hissed.

"I'm sorry," Jessie said between giggles. "I just wasn't expecting that. You've always professed an undying, platonic relationship. But you're secretly lusting after him. This is so great. It renews my faith in single women." Jessie, married for fifteen years, liked to believe that Kit lived a wild and crazy life—filled with wild and crazy sex. Until now, Kit had been a major disappointment.

"Very funny." Kit sipped her soda and tried to think of a way to steer Jessie off this conversation. "Are you ready? I've got some students coming in soon." In reality, no one was scheduled for an hour but Jessie didn't know that. Kit stood up. Jessie followed suit.

"So, why don't you go for it?"

"Go for what?"

"Jax. Mister Tall, Dark and Gorgeous. Not to mention Mister Rich, Nice and He Likes You."

Kit let her book bag fall to the floor. "Jessie, Jax and I are friends. I want to keep it that way. Even if I could persuade him to—" *fuck me silly* "—uh, be interested in me, it wouldn't last. I've seen the kind of women he dates and they don't look like me." She made a casual wave toward her less than voluptuous body. "And I don't want to risk our friendship for a few nights of—" *Really, really hot sex.* "—Uh, you know, romance."

"Who cares about romance? Go for the sex," Jessie said, practically reading Kit's mind.

The tinny ring of a cell phone interrupted Kit's strangled groan. She silently sent a "thank you" to the heavens when she realized it was hers.

She flipped the phone open and waved goodbye to Jessie all in the same motion. She didn't care who was on the phone. It got her out of the conversation about Jax and sex.

"Hello?"

"Kit? So glad I got a hold of you."

It took only seconds for her to run through her memory and attach a face to the feminine voice on the other end. Alison Doyle, the publicist hired to promote the book Kit had written with one of the other professors.

"Listen, we've run into a snag with the America Today Show."

Kit ignored the panic in Alison's voice. Alison surrounded herself with drama and made a production out of everything. But Kit knew that she would work through it. She usually needed a few hours to rant and rave before the perfect solution presented itself. No reason to get her own blood pressure up.

"What's wrong?" Kit asked patiently as she headed out the door and into the beautiful spring air. She took a deep breath as Alison once again reminded Kit how important it was to be on the national morning talk show, how it would provide much needed publicity for the book she and Tim Tyler had written.

"So, they've scheduled the interview for Friday. And Tim's in Greece."

Kit's co-author for "Living Myths and Legends" spent his free time traveling the world supposedly researching local myths. But since Kit had done most of the research for this book, she wasn't sure what Tim did during his travels. Not that it mattered. Tim was a great co-author. His writing style matched hers. He was clever and, best of all, Tim loved the press and the public. If it involved a crowd, Tim wanted to be in front of it.

Kit froze up in a group larger than three people.

They worked well together.

"Don't worry," Kit soothed the ruffled promoter. "Tim's scheduled to be back tomorrow morning. Plenty of time to get ready for Friday."

"No. It seems Timmy T. decided to bring home a few souvenirs that the Grecian government views as national antiquities. He's in a jail cell until they figure this out."

Kit sighed. Tim had a knack for getting himself into situations like this. He also had a knack for getting out of them. She didn't doubt he would be back in a few weeks.

"Reschedule." She shrugged even though Alison couldn't see her.

"You don't understand. We can't reschedule. No one reschedules for America Today. It's just not done."

Kit felt her own heart start to pound. This wasn't good. The panic underlying Alison's voice was coming to the forefront. And sounding decidedly real.

"So, what do we do?"

"We have to send someone else."

The silence between them was ominous. Dread the likes she hadn't felt in years crept into her stomach.

"Who?" she asked though she could predict the answer.

"Kit..."

"No, you can't be serious. You can't mean it."

"It has to be you. They want one of the authors. That's you or Tim and it's unlikely they'll give Tim a weekend pass out of a Greek dungeon." Alison's voice was starting to squeak.

"But...you don't understand."

"I do understand. I do." The sympathy in Alison's voice did nothing to calm the churning in Kit's stomach or the rapid increase in her heartbeat. "But it has to be you. There isn't anyone else. Listen, hon, I've got another call. You'll be great. We'll talk soon. Plan on being in the city at six AM on Friday. Ciao."

The connection ended before Kit had a chance to protest. Or to beg Alison to call 911 because she was going to have a heart attack. She stared at the ground a full minute—listening to her heart pound.

Her chest began to bellow. She had to hide, run, escape. Still clutching her phone, she looped her book bag over her shoulder and took off in a full-length stride. Gut-wrenching, skin-peeling fear chased her across campus. The rapid pace seemed to draw off the excess oxygen her body was consuming and her breath calmed to a normal rhythm.

She couldn't do it. Flat out. There was no way she could talk on national television. No matter how much she loved her book, this hadn't been part of the agreement. She couldn't even speak in front of a class of students. That's why she'd ended up tutoring instead of teaching. The thought of twenty-five faces staring up at her ignited panic attacks that no medicine could quell.

Turn those twenty-five students into twenty-five million viewers…

She couldn't even think about it. She concentrated on walking—putting one foot in front of the other. Distance disappeared. She was vaguely aware of leaving the campus and heading toward the business district. She found herself walking down a street, lined with gunmetal gray warehouses. The scenery was easy to ignore and her mind did so, dragging her back again and again to the reality she was trying to avoid.

It has to be you. Alison's voice haunted her, increasing her speed.

A clap of thunder stalled her turbulent thoughts, scattering them as she looked up. There wasn't a cloud in the sky. No predictions of rain. The thunder rumbled again.

And rain started to fall. First in light layers, then with growing strength. Drops splattered onto her cheeks and spilt into her eyes, stinging her skin.

Blinking the water from her lashes, she searched for shelter and spotted a little shop crammed between two warehouses. The sign swaying in a nonexistent breeze declared it The McMac Shop—Fine Irish Goods.

Kit didn't care how fine the goods were. She just needed a place to escape the rain.

The storm was at her back, almost as if the rain was driving her in that direction. She ran across the street. Water dripped from her hair, soaked through her shirt, and shivered down her back by the time she opened the door and lunged inside.

"Whoa. That was weird," she said to the empty room. Or it appeared empty until a little Irish man popped up from behind the counter. That he was Irish there was no doubt. He looked like a leprechaun. Complete with pipe, beard and mischievous eyes. Bigger than she would have expected a leprechaun to be, but still, there was no mistaking the image. *Well, the costume fits the store, that's for sure.*

"Good afternoon, lass. Welcome to the McMac Shop."

"Hi." She whipped her hair back. The chin length strands clung to her face like slimy claws.

"How can I help you today?"

"Oh, I really don't need anything." She looked around at the sweaters and silver that decorated the store. *And there's probably nothing I can afford.* "I just ducked in to escape the rain," she said, a bit sheepishly.

"Well, that's fine then, but I'm thinkin' I can interest you in something that might change your life."

That seemed like a mighty big goal for an Irish knick-knack shop but Kit smiled.

"Come in and tell Murphy what brought you here today."

"Uh, nothing. I mean I was just out walking and..." She let her voice trail away as she wandered toward the counter and the little man behind it. She tried to smile but it was a half-hearted attempt.

"Now, lass, you look like a woman with troubles. You can share them with ol' Murphy here."

Even knowing he couldn't possibly care about her troubles or that ranting about the situation wouldn't help, she found herself telling him all that had happened.

"So, what does your young man say about all of this?"

"My what?" She shook her head in confusion. "Oh, a boyfriend. I don't have a boyfriend, or anything."

Murphy stepped back and stroked his chin as he observed her. "That's odd because you have the aura of someone in love. Or on the verge of love."

Kit choked on the thought. "On the verge of love? I just want to be on the verge of not making a fool of myself on national television."

He stared at her for another long, penetrating moment.

"I think I have the perfect thing for you."

He ducked down behind the counter. Soft crashes and thuds reached her from the other side. She looked at the door. The rain had stopped. She could make a run for it before he stood up. But he had been kind enough to listen to her ramble.

"Here it is. I was afraid I'd lost it and then I'd be in a world of hurt now, wouldn't I?" He straightened. Dust covered his hat and the tip of his nose. "This will be fixin' all your troubles."

This turned out to be a piece of…rock. Green rock, appropriate for an Irish store, but still, it was just a piece of rock.

"Uh, thanks, but you know, I don't need any rocks right now."

"This is no ordinary rock." He leaned forward and his voice dropped to a whisper. Kit found herself leaning in to hear him. "This is a piece of the Blarney Stone. The real Blarney Stone, not that one tourists smooch all the time." He leveled that strangely observant gaze at her. "Do you know the legend of the Blarney Stone?"

She smiled. "I do, actually. I deal with legends every day. I believe the tale goes that a man—" She waved her hand vaguely in the air. "I can't remember his name, kissed the stone and was able to keep the queen from taking his castle."

"Not just that. He was able to *persuade her*, convince her. That's what this stone does." He held up the green rock. "You kiss it and you're given the gift of gab, persuasive eloquence." He kissed the rock and placed it on the counter. A strange glow surrounded it for a moment but when Kit blinked, the light was gone.

Great, now I'm hallucinating.

"Now, as you can imagine, I wouldn't sell this to just anyone."

Kit had to stop herself from rolling her eyes. The man was really getting into this sales pitch. Well, she wasn't having it. She didn't need any more knick-knacks cluttering up her house.

"Believe me. It's a special prize for a special person. Someone who will use it wisely. It's a powerful stone but used properly, you can find the most powerful gift."

As she listened, she couldn't help but stare at the stone. His words settled into her head. The stone was pretty and it wouldn't hurt to have it around the house. She could use it as a talisman—to give her confidence when she needed it. Like that feather they gave the elephant to convince him he could fly.

"I think it's made for you, lass. The stone itself is calling you."

She could almost feel it. Something deep inside her wanted that stone. Kit nodded. "I'll take it."

Murphy's smile contained a whiff of triumph but Kit ignored it.

"How much?" As she said the words, a soft voice reminded her that she wasn't going to buy this stone. Somehow that didn't seem to matter now.

"Fifty dollars."

For a chunk of rock he probably picked up in the street? She ignored the logical sentiment and opened her purse. Mentally slapping herself for being silly, she wrote a check for the amount and collected the stone.

"It will bring you what you most desire." He looked around, his head snapping side to side as if he was sure he was missing something but didn't know what. He clicked his fingers and disappeared behind the counter again. He popped up almost immediately and slapped his hand on the counter. "And you'd better take those."

Kit looked at the four cellophane wrappers.

"What? You give out free condoms with every purchase?" That was taking promoting "safe sex" a little too far.

"Not every purchase but this is special." He reached beneath the counter. "Take these as well." Two more condoms joined the pile.

Six condoms? Why would he think she needed one, let alone six? "Uh, I haven't used six condoms total in the past two years."

He winked at her. "I have a feelin' that'll be changin'."

Not sure what else to do, she gathered the condoms and slipped them into her purse along with the rock. Her *fifty-dollar* rock. "Well, thanks." She walked to the store window. The rain was gone. The sun dominated the sky again. *Weird storm, weird man, weird day.*

She replayed the encounter as she walked back to campus. And each time she came to the same conclusion.

"He scammed me." She grimaced as she entered the tutoring lab and took her place behind the desk.

She had four hours to go. As she opened the lab, students began to wander in searching for help on every subject from English (her specialty) to math (not her specialty). She did her best to help and logged the questions that required answers. It was a busy afternoon with midterms only a week away. Every time she had a break, her thoughts went back to Alison's phone call and the terror of potentially being on television. Kit looked at her watch. Another hour and she was done. Then she could meet up with Jax. He would know how to get her out of this.

* * * * *

"I don't think you can get out of it." Jax shrugged and took a sip of his beer. "Your publicist is right. It's a major deal to get on America Today."

He would know. He'd spent years working for promoters and public affairs groups around the country. He'd taken the job teaching Communications at the University because he was ready to leave the fast lane but he knew the ins and outs of publicity.

"I know it's a major deal, but there has to be a way that someone else, anyone else, could do it."

"Kit, it's you or Tim and it doesn't sound like Tim's going to make it back in time."

"And I'm going to kill him when he does."

Jax chuckled and picked up his corned beef sandwich. "I'll call him and tell him he's safer in a Grecian jail."

"Do that." She picked up her own sandwich and munched down. "It's just that—don't they realize this won't help? Having *me* on that show won't make people rush out and buy the book. In fact, it will make the people who have bought it, return it."

"Kit, you're going to be fine."

"Are you nuts? In a crowd of more than two people, I lose all ability to speak."

"Kit, you've got a secret weapon."

She put down her sandwich and waited for him to finish.

"Me. You've got me."

Kit casually scanned the room then leaned closer to Jax. "How is that going to help?"

"This is what I do. What I've done for years. I train people to talk to the media," he explained. He reached across the small circular table and covered her hand with his. "I can help you."

It was difficult to tell which was stronger. The comforting thought that Jax would help her. Or the lust that spun through her stomach as he touched her. She stared at their hands for a long moment and decided to ignore the lust. As she had done many, many times before.

"Don't worry, Kit. I've handled much more difficult cases than you."

Kit raised her eyebrows in mock surprise.

"Okay, well, that might be a bit of an exaggeration, but I think we can do it. I see it as a personal challenge." He lifted his beer.

Resigned, Kit raised hers and tapped his glass. In unison, they tilted their heads back and drained what was left of their pints.

"Kit, Stone, you want another round?" McGill called from behind the bar.

Kit shook her head. Jax did the same.

Kit set her glass on the table. "Why does he call you Stone?" she asked. She'd been curious about that for a while. The hint of a blush on Jax's cheeks made her even more curious.

"It's a stupid high school nickname."

Kit could only think of one reason to call a kid "Stone"—if he was always hard. The idea made her insides all hot and gooey.

"Uh, what brought it on?" she asked, hoping her voice didn't shake with unrequited lust.

"Oh, you know kids. My name was Jackson. We studied Stonewall Jackson and people started calling me that. Eventually, it got shortened to Stone. I told you it was a stupid nickname."

Kit stared for a moment then nodded in agreement. She liked her explanation better—that he was always hard.

"I'm going to run to the ladies room," she announced, standing quickly. "You going to wait?"

"Have I ever let you walk home alone?"

"Uh, no."

Jax smiled and waved his hands toward the bathroom.

Kit grabbed her bag and left the table. She finished in the stall and stepped into the open area, facing the mirror. Her plain brown hair stood out at odd angles, highlighting the sharp, spiky ends. *I look like the wicked witch. Great.*

She opened her purse, there had to be a comb somewhere in her bag. Now that she knew what she looked like, she couldn't go back outside looking like this. What would Jax think?

She stared in the mirror. Her plain face—sprinkled with pale freckles and dominated by large green eyes—reflected back. Why would Jax care?

He was her friend. Tall, gorgeous and sweet. But still her friend. Even if he wasn't her friend, there was little chance he would look at her at all.

Still, vanity prevailed and she dug to the bottom of her purse. Her hand closed around the rock she'd purchased. Pulling it out, she held it in her palm. The stone warmed her skin and for a moment she thought she saw the eerie green glow she'd seen in the store.

"Fifty dollars for a rock. I'd better have my head examined." She was about to drop it in her bag when Murphy's voice came back to her.

It will bring you what you most desire.

Jax.

Yeah, right. Kissing this rock would make Jax drag her off to bed.

She tossed the stone in her hand but didn't put it away. She looked in the mirror once more. Was it possible to feel any sillier? It had to be the beer but it didn't matter. She was going to do it. She held the stone to her lips and planted a kiss on the smooth surface.

The rock turned hot. Like a lightning strike, her lips began to tingle. The shiver skittered from her lips through her body, stopping to make her nipples rock-hard and speeding down into her sex. The tiny tingle exploded into a sharp ache. Kit slapped her hand low on her stomach, trying to contain the shock. She stared into the mirror, watching her cheeks redden and her chest expand in a long, deep breath.

She held the rock up to the light. *This is supposed to give me the gift of gab, not make me orgasm in the bathroom.*

With a dazed shake of her head, she dropped the stone back into her purse and fluffed her hair. The boring brown color seemed to capture some of the light giving it a hint of gold. And the ends didn't look scary now—they looked wild but sexy. As if a man's hands had been running through her hair. During sex. Tousled.

I've got sex on the brain, she decided as she left the bathroom.

Jax waited for her at the front door. He smiled as she approached and Kit felt another tingle deep in her sex. She felt empty inside. Empty and waiting to be filled.

She couldn't shake free of the sensation. Where normally she was able to push the desire aside, it lingered, building with each step. She stopped inches in front of him. The pulsing between her legs made it difficult to concentrate.

"Ready?" Jax asked with the same friendly smile he always gave her.

"Oh yes." The simple response came out of her mouth soft and breathy. And alluring. She blinked and stared at Jax to see if he'd noticed. His eyes widened for a moment, then the corner of his mouth kicked up in a half-smile. Good. He thought she was teasing. She could still get out of this without embarrassing herself. "I have an early session." Almost as if it was beyond her control, she took a step closer, until she was inches away from Jax's body. Suddenly, those inches were too much distance. She wanted to be right up against him, rubbing her breasts against his chest. She leaned even closer and stared at his mouth. "I think it's time for us to go to bed, don't you?" The strange, husky, "come fuck me" voice was something she hadn't known she possessed.

Jax's eyes narrowed. "Kit, are you okay?"

"I'm great," she sighed, breathing deeply and inhaling his masculine scent. The smell settled into her chest. The words landed on her tongue, screaming for release. "Mmmm. You smell so good. Like wild sex and warm breakfast muffins." She couldn't believe those words were coming out of her mouth but she also couldn't stop them. "Like hot bodies on cool clean sheets."

What are you saying?

The mental reprimand and the surprised look on Jax's face were enough to stifle her suddenly loose tongue.

She stepped away.

"We should probably go," she mumbled as she reached for the door, and stalked outside, silently cursing herself. What was she thinking? She'd just plastered herself against one of her best friends and practically begged him to take her to bed.

It wasn't like her. She didn't behave like this. She was saying things that…well, to be honest, she'd thought about for a long time but never expected to say aloud. Seducing Jax was not on her agenda. Not that she had to worry. He hadn't exactly grabbed her and thrown her to the ground when the invitation had tumbled out of her mouth.

Jax shook his head and followed Kit more slowly out the door. Was his imagination fucking with him? What was going on with her? Comfortable, quiet Kit was exuding some strange pheromones that made him want to throw her onto the grass and mount her like a bull in rut. She'd come back from the bathroom looking wild and sexy, her nipples pressing hard against her shirt as if she'd been pinching them. He licked his lips. He could spend days worshiping her nipples, loving them, biting them. Sucking them deep into his mouth.

He pressed his lips together and concealed a groan. Too bad the hard-on he was rapidly developing wasn't as easily hidden.

The sensation wasn't new. He'd had similar thoughts about Kit for months. Almost since they'd met. But Kit had made it clear she wasn't interested in anything more than friendship and he could accept those boundaries.

Until she started lowering her voice and standing close to him. Practically rubbing her nipples against his chest. This wasn't the Kit he knew so well.

He wouldn't mind knowing this version of Kit better. He'd always suspected there was fire buried beneath the sweet, shy English tutor. The way she ate gave it away. She ate with passion, savoring each bite like it was the first exquisite taste. It made him hard every time he watched her. But tonight was different. Tonight, when she'd returned, the fire hadn't been hidden. It had been humming across the surface of her skin.

He sighed. It didn't make sense. If she had been bent on seducing him—why the hell did she run away just as it got interesting? He'd probably imagined it all—the sexy whisper, the full lower lip pushed slightly forward, just begging for his teeth. All the late night fantasy sessions were causing him to be sleep deprived. That, along with being sex-deprived, was probably making her voice sound deeper and her eyes hotter than reality.

"Kit, wait up. This isn't a race." He hurried along the street.

She slowed her steps. "Sorry. I just needed some air."

Though it was dark outside, he knew she blushed. He could hear it in her voice.

"I know the feeling." He took a deep breath, filling his lungs with cooling, calming oxygen.

Kit did the same. Unable to stop himself, his gaze dropped to her chest, watching those still tight peaks rise and fall. It wasn't cold outside but it looked like she'd been rubbing her nipples with ice cubes.

Damn, when had her nipples become so fascinating to him? He'd thought about them before, but never like this.

"Let's walk," he said, spinning her around and setting off at a rapid pace. The walk would do them both good. It would get his mind off fucking Kit and get her mind off...well, whatever, whoever she was thinking about.

"So, what's your schedule for tomorrow?" he asked focusing on her upcoming interview. It would get his mind off sex.

"Huh?"

"What's your schedule? We need some time to work before Friday. That only leaves tomorrow."

"Jax, I really appreciate it." Her tired chuckle was so familiar, so Kit, that his erection—while it didn't begin to fade—maintained a consistent level. Now he just needed it to go down before she noticed it. "But there is no way you can train me, in just under thirty-six hours to be coherent, much less interesting on national television. I'm a researcher. I spend my days reading old legends and hiding in library stacks. That's what I'm good at and that's what I like." They turned down the street where they both lived. Kit's house two from the corner. Jax's three beyond that. "It's not that I'm not thrilled with your offer but it won't make a difference."

"You don't seem to understand who you're dealing with, Kit. I'm a master at media training. I've trained politicians and CEO's of major corporations. I've trained people who were incredibly bright but couldn't put a decent sentence together if they were given a dictionary."

"Yeah, but—"

"I've trained oil company execs to the point that they've been standing on an oiled beach and the press still declared them heroes. I can help you."

They turned up Kit's stone walkway. It was tradition, like their Wednesday night dinner—he waited at the end of the sidewalk until she was safely inside. He turned and took her hands in his, holding them gently but firmly. Kit looked at their connected hands and then slowly raised her eyes to his.

An unfamiliar heat glowed in the green depths—unfamiliar but similar to the one he felt burning in his own chest. The fire was back, bright within her.

"You're pretty persuasive." She reached up and brushed the tip of her middle finger across his lower lip. "Can you do anything else with that silver tongue?"

Chapter Two

As the words left her mouth, she blinked, looking almost as surprised as he was. But the seductive taunting was already creating images in his mind — of sliding his tongue into her mouth, her cunt. Tasting her. Licking her. And he knew he had to do it.

Before she had a chance to retract it, to decide this wasn't a good idea, Jax took the opportunity presented to him. Praying to God he didn't screw up their friendship, he placed his hands on her waist and pulled her the final step to him. And kissed her.

The first touch of their lips exploded in a ball of sensation and fire that landed in his gut. Kit gasped and Jax captured that sound. He wanted it all. This was no light, hesitant first kiss. He took her mouth, and she accepted him. He drove his tongue deep inside the hot moist cavern, absorbing her flavor and locking it into his senses.

Her body slammed against his as she wrapped her arms around his neck. One thought kept spinning through his mind. She wasn't running, she wasn't resisting, she was, oh God, sucking on his tongue like she wanted to swallow him whole. He slid his hands down her hips until his palms rested on the upper curve of her ass. She didn't need any more encouragement. She pressed forward, stretching up and cuddling his erection between her legs. He moaned as the warmth from her pussy flowed through their clothes and into his cock. She shifted against him and he could feel her opening, relaxing and preparing for his penetration. His cock hardened—readying itself to slide into her body.

Kit was desperate for a breath but she didn't want to pull her mouth away. She couldn't believe this was happening. It was Jax and her. And they were practically having sex in her front yard. Surprisingly, that thought didn't freak her out the way she knew it should. Instead, she rubbed against him, massaging his thickening cock between her legs, loving the groans he fed into her mouth along with the hot, mind-melting kisses. A car with a bad exhaust system backfired as it chugged by—jerking her back to reality. They were standing on the sidewalk in front of her house—necking. Kit searched for the strength to pull back. It was difficult, almost impossible. Jax's cock was hard and pressed up against the peak of her thighs, his hands warm on her butt. It was so tempting to hike up her skirt and let him plunge inside. And his mouth...her pussy wept with the need to feel his lips and tongue.

She suppressed a groan and did what she knew she had to do.

It was hard—and God, so was he—but she had to do it. She had to pull back so they could discuss this in a logical fashion. Determined to do the right thing, she peeled her lips away from his and almost whimpered at the loss. With one part of her body disconnected, she forced her hands to his shoulders, easing her breasts from his hard chest muscles. She could practically hear her nipples cry in protest. One more section left. She had to convince her pussy to release the promise of his cock.

"Listen, I think we should..." *Slow down. Back away. Think this through.* All good sentiments. She stared into his eyes and they flew from her head like bats at dusk. "We should go into my house and fuck like wild bunny rabbits."

His cock pulsed against her crotch. She choked, unable to believe those words had come from her mouth.

"I mean..." She tried to make her mind function normally but it was as if she wasn't controlling her own speech. "I want to feel your mouth on my skin." She stroked his cheek, drawing a line to the edge of his lips. "I want you to go down on me and let me feel that sweet, silver tongue deep inside my pussy." She heard herself speaking. Her voice—and she was sure it was hers because it was saying things she'd thought a million times in the past—sounded nothing like her. It was deep and husky. Mellow. A complete opposite to the fire spiraling through her body.

"I want to feel you lick and kiss my cunt until I come and then I want your cock—hot and hard inside me, driving so deep I can feel you in my throat. So hard I feel like you'll drill through me."

She backed toward her door. The protesting voice in her head was silent as she stepped up onto the porch. Jax didn't say anything. He opened his mouth against her neck, nipping her skin with stinging bites that tightened the delicious pressure in her sex.

"You have such a great mouth," she whispered. "Do you like to eat pussy?"

She couldn't believe she'd asked that question but here, now, it seemed appropriate.

And his answer was perfect.

"I would love to eat your pussy." His deep voice rumbled in her ear. There had to be a connection between her ear and her cunt because she swore she almost climaxed at his sexy growl.

"Good. Because my dreams are filled with your mouth on my skin—" She dragged the words out, feeling their sensuous tone flow through her sex. "Feeling you lick me, taste me."

He opened the collar of her shirt and kissed her collarbone.

"And your cock. I want to feel it inside me, hard and deep. I want you on top of me. I want to watch you come."

"Yes," he hissed against her skin.

Her uncoordinated fingers fumbled behind her back trying to find the knob. The door finally swung open and they stumbled through. Kit kept herself upright by holding onto Jax, opening her legs and letting his thigh settle between them.

He kicked the front door shut and pulled her against him, shifting her hips until her clit rubbed against his growing cock. She groaned and grabbed his head, dragging his mouth back to hers. A desperate internal hunger billowed up from her sex. She needed him. Needed to feel him inside her.

"Thank God you live alone," he muttered as he trailed kisses along her jaw and he sucked her earlobe between his lips.

"Why?"

"Because no one's going to scream if I fuck you right here in the entryway."

She tossed her head back, pulling slightly away so she could stare at his lips. "No one but me," she purred. "And I definitely want to scream."

She wrapped her arms around his neck feeling triumphant at the hunger reflected in his eyes. She licked his upper lip, teasing him, tempting him to come into her mouth. Jax wound his hand into her hair, holding her in place as he took her up on her offer of temptation. He seized control of the kiss. And Kit let him. He conquered her mouth, plunging his tongue inside. The power with which he entered her mouth was a promising sign to his entering her cunt with equal force and strength. The thought made her shiver and press harder against him. Her nipples rubbed against his chest, heating the already blazing need low in her stomach.

She captured his groan and wrapped her tongue around his, wanting more of the delicious sound and fury.

Deep in the farthest corner of her mind she heard a voice saying that this wasn't right—that it was strange that Jax would be so willing to fuck her in her living room. But despite the nagging voice, there was no way she was stopping this. It felt too good. She might regret it tomorrow but she was going to enjoy the sin before the repentance.

Needing more, needing him closer, she tried to lift her left leg and wrap it around his waist, but the tight line of her skirt restricted the movement. She growled in frustration.

"Jax, please." The breathless sound of her own voice sent flutters through her sex. Jax lifted his gaze to hers. "I want your mouth on me. I want your mouth on my pussy."

Jax would have sworn he couldn't get any harder, but the fierce glint in Kit's eyes and soft whisper of her request made his cock ready to burst. But first, he would give her what she asked for.

He nudged her back against the door and sank to his knees. His fantasies had always remained decidedly vanilla where Kit was concerned — simple, hot sex. But now with Kit begging for his mouth and his cock, a whole world of wild fucks came to his mind. Shy, quiet Kit was a sex goddess.

She looked down at him and he felt like a supplicant kneeling at the foot of that goddess, prepared to worship. He sat back on his ankles, waiting to see where she would take this. Her fingers gripped the soft material of her skirt. He took a shallow breath anticipating the sight. She hesitated and he knew it was to tempt him. He raised his eyes and nearly groaned. Kit had never stared at him with such power. The confidence radiating from her body was unbearably sexy. She was in control and, damn it, she knew it. And she would use him as she saw fit.

After long drawn out seconds, she continued pulling her skirt up, baring inch by tantalizing inch of soft, rounded thigh. Jax watched her slow teasing. The urge to pull her down and drive his cock into her almost overwhelmed him. But this was her show. And there was time for that later. For now, at her request, he had a pussy to eat. He licked his lips.

The skirt slid up. He placed his hands just above her knees, keeping his touch light, making brief forays higher as more skin appeared. She'd asked for his mouth. He would give it to her, in his own way. He leaned forward and licked the inside of her thigh, flashing his tongue across her flesh and feeling her quiver.

"Jax," Kit said with a throaty warning. "You're supposed to save your appetite for my cunt."

The teasing reprimand slammed into his gut, fueling the fire that was keeping his cock hard and ready.

"Just having a little appetizer," he said against her skin. "But it's made me hungry for more." He kissed her thigh, licked again. "Starving."

Again, she laughed. It was a sound he'd never heard come from Kit's throat—sexy and taunting. Tempting him to be man enough to turn that chuckle into a sigh, a scream.

"Well then." She drew her skirt above her hips. "I wouldn't want to keep a starving man waiting."

A vibrant blue strip covered her pussy. The shiny material glowed against her pale skin.

She placed her hand along his cheek, tilting his face until he looked into her eyes.

"I want you to remove my panties." It wasn't a direct command but Jax knew better than to disobey. "With your teeth."

Kit was no longer surprised at the words coming from her mouth. Wherever she'd found them, they were working. She'd just ordered Jackson Knight to remove her underwear with his teeth. And from the light in his eyes—he liked the idea.

Jax's lips pressed against her hip. His teeth scraped against her skin as he bit down on the thin material of her panties. A steady tug pulled the leg of her underwear to the side, teasing her clit. As if he knew what the pressure was doing to her, he tugged again. She grabbed her lower lip with her teeth, trying to hold back the whimper. Sharp tendrils of heat spiraled from her clit, making her cunt even wetter. She let her head fall back against the door and savored the slow slide as he dragged her panties to the ground.

She forced oxygen into tight lungs. Thoughts flew through her head, barely stopping before evaporating in the lusty haze Jax was creating.

He lifted her foot—freeing her from her underwear. She looked down. Jax sat on his heels. It could have been a submissive pose but the light in his eyes told her he was anything but. He looked at her sex, his large hands resting at the top of her thighs.

"Spread your legs for me." His hot breath teased her skin. She took a step, widening her stance. But Jax didn't let her stop there. He slipped his hand behind her knee and lifted her leg over his shoulder.

Cool air kissed her wet pussy. Then fire took its place. Jax pushed up on his knees and placed the softest kiss just above her clit. It teased and tempted but did nothing to satisfy. She tensed for a moment as he traced his tongue down the inside folds of her sex—slow, gentle licks—as if he wanted to learn her flesh. The heat from his mouth melted her, extracting the strength from her legs. The lazy exploration started a slow build of urgency in her sex. She rolled her hips, trying to guide his mouth to the center where she needed his touch.

He ignored her silent direction and licked down, away from her clit, slipping the tip of his tongue into her cunt. He wiggled the end, flicking it against her sensitive walls. A shallow squeal burst from her throat and filled the silent room. She didn't move. Couldn't move. He kept on, licking and tasting—avoiding her clit but coming viciously close until Kit thought she would scream.

More moisture flowed down her sex, drenching her thigh. Jax lapped at the cream. Then, with long, luxurious strokes of his tongue, he moved until he hovered over her clit. Kit waited, panting, holding back the pleas. Just when she thought she'd go insane, his lips closed over the tight bundle of nerves and he began to suck. Kit yelped and dug her heel into his back.

"Oh my God, Jax!"

He pulled back. "Too much?" He followed the question up with a lick along her slit.

"No! It's perfect. Perfect." The sexy, confident demands were gone, replaced by breathless sighs that couldn't form real words. She could only moan as he continued to lick and suck her cunt. Each stroke of his tongue sent her up, until she was at high altitudes and couldn't get enough oxygen. She leaned against the door and let the wild, wet sensations flow through her body. It had been so long since anyone had licked her pussy and Jax was so damn good at it, with a few more deep tongue kisses, she was close to coming. She sighed—relieved when he returned to her clit, his touch alternately light and hard. The rhythm was perfect and she cried out as the orgasm slammed into her pussy and shattered her control. Her right leg weakened and she sagged against the door, grabbing the handle with one hand and Jax's head with the other.

"Don't worry, baby, I'm not going anywhere."

Before she could find the breath to speak, he began again, licking and sucking, re-igniting the fire he'd created. He tilted her hips even farther forward and once again slipped the tip of his tongue between her sensitive lips. The light flutter teased her flesh and sent another ripple of pleasure.

"Damn, Jax, please. I need you."

"You've got me, baby. I'm here."

She shook her head, feeling her hair fall down around her face. "No, I need you inside me. Please."

"Soon."

"Now!"

He ignored her command. Up to this point, he'd let her have control—now he was going to enjoy her as he saw fit. He opened his mouth against her clit. Knowing she had to be sensitive, he kept his touch light, tasting her, feeling her squirm against him. He held her ass firmly in one hand and used the other to spread her sex open. Displayed before him, he let his lips and tongue wander across her wet flesh, exploring her, lapping up her flavor. And absorbing the groans and pleas as she continued to grip his head.

He pushed her, driving toward another orgasm, loving the taste of her, the feel as she moved against him. She was so responsive. And verbal.

She curled her hips forward. He slowly pushed two fingers into her. The hot, wet walls closed around him. He heard his own groan this time. She would be so tight around his cock. He pumped his fingers into her pussy, while he continued licking her clit. Her cries filled his ears and drove him on, desperate to please her, make her scream for him.

The high-pitched squeak was close enough, as if she couldn't believe what was happening to her body.

He lifted his head, pulling back from between her legs. Her thighs were quivering. Jax couldn't stop his smile. He'd made her knees weak. It was a powerful thing for a man.

Kit rolled her head slowly to the side until it fell forward. Her hair hung down around her face, wild and free.

Finally, she opened her eyes. Blatant desire poured from her gaze as she stared down. The sensual confidence remained as well.

"I was right." She rubbed her tongue across the edge of her teeth. "You have an incredible mouth—it's made for eating pussy." She glanced down to his crotch. His cock pressed against his pants as if it was rising to the call of her eyes. "Are you as equally talented with your cock? Because after a really..." She released a sound that was a blend of a groan and a chuckle, and it wrapped around his dick like a fist. "...*really* good session of having my pussy eaten, there's nothing I like better than hot, hard fu—"

He didn't let her finish. He lunged upward, plastering her to the door. His mouth covered, conquered and commanded hers as he plunged his tongue between her lips. He dominated the kiss, wrapping his tongue around hers, biting not-so-gently on her lower lip. She tasted the musky flavor of her own sex. And the hot masculine flavor of Jax.

Exultation flooded her already sated body. Another need came upon her, another desire. She wanted to shatter his control the way he'd taken hers.

He bent down and jerked her blouse open, giving little consideration to the buttons. Kit didn't care. She'd never been with a man so hungry for her that he'd ripped buttons off to get to her. Jax peeled away her bra. Hot hands encompassed her breasts. There was no time to worry that she was too small, not curvaceous enough. His pleasured groan eliminated her insecurities.

He massaged her breasts—lingering on her tight nipples. She leaned against the door, putting inches between their bodies. She felt wild and decadent—topless and fucking in her living room. Jax followed her, leaning down and capturing one nipple between his lips. He began to suck, circling his tongue around the tight peak. His teeth bit down, gently with just a touch of sting. Kit relished the hard touch and groaned her approval. He kissed and licked his way across the valley of her breasts and gave the same attention to her other nipple.

Kit reached between their bodies and gently squeezed his erection. He groaned and pushed into her palm but didn't release her mouth. Her head was spinning but she knew she wanted to touch him—wanted to feel her hands wrapped around his shaft. She opened the button and slipped her hand inside. The warm brush of his soft briefs made her stop and linger, rubbing her hand up and down his shaft.

"I'm going to come if you keep doing that." He gave the warning and then kissed her again. His lips wandered, trailing kisses along her jaw, her neck.

It was tempting to let him control the action but she wanted him—wanted to feel him inside her.

The long downward slide of his zipper was a sensuous experience for her—the quiet buzz as the teeth released, the soft sigh from Jax as she pushed his pants and briefs aside. His shaft bounced free, pushing against her stomach. She wrapped her hand around his cock. It was Kit's turn to groan. Her fingers didn't quite reach around. She'd never had a man this thick before, but oh, she wanted to try.

"Ooh, you're so thick and long." The deep seductive voice returned. She took him in both hands and stroked him. Tension vibrated through him as if his nerves were shuddering with joy. Her words and her hands were getting to him. "You'll feel so good inside me."

"We need to fuck. Now."

As if to prove his point, he pushed his hand between her legs, sliding two fingers back into her pussy. Kit released his cock and grabbed his shoulders as he fingerfucked her. Her knees, already failing her, sagged again and she had to use Jax as support.

"Damn, you're so tight." He growled the words softly, almost to himself but Kit felt them in her pussy. His desperation became hers and she needed him inside her.

She wrapped her leg up and around his back, opening herself to him. The blunt head of his cock pressed against her opening. She tilted her hips forward, preparing for the heavy penetration.

"Damn."

The soft curse shook Kit. More than the curse, the fact that he stopped and even pulled back sent panic through her core. He couldn't stop now. He couldn't. She gripped his hips, refusing to release him without protest. "What's wrong?"

"Condom?"

"Damn."

She hesitated for a second. She hadn't needed condoms for a while. And wasn't there an expiration date on those things? The little man in the store...

"Wait. My purse." Without releasing her hold on Jax, she scanned the room and found her purse hanging on the doorknob. She pulled out one of the packets and ripped it open. Jax reached for it but Kit pulled it out of his grasp.

"Mine." Jax placed his hands on the wall next to her shoulders, giving them inches between their bodies. And revealing his cock to her for the first time. It was beautiful. Long and thick and hard. Very hard. She couldn't resist running her palm down its length.

"Kit." The warning in his voice told her she didn't have long to play. She placed the condom over the head and began to roll it down, sliding her hands along his hard flesh, caressing him as she inched downward. She looked up and saw Jax—teeth clenched, eyes closed, struggling for control.

In her wildest fantasies, she'd never imagined that she could push him this close to the edge.

With the condom securely in place, she reached around and gave his ass a caress and a squeeze. She wrapped her leg around his waist.

"Fuck me, Jax."

He opened his eyes. The heat and desire was incredible. His gaze held hers while he cupped her thigh, holding her steady as he guided his cock between her legs. Pressure built as he pushed the full head into her sex. The soft sexy words that had flowed off her tongue disappeared. She couldn't think of anything but the long lovely slide of his cock into her body. Bracing herself against the door, she canted her hips forward and felt each delicious inch slide into her, savoring this first time. He moved slowly, giving her time to adjust, but he kept on, gently rocking forward, going a little deeper until there was so much of him inside her, she couldn't hide the feminine whimper.

She was stuffed, full, she was sure. Jax held himself still, then took a deep breath. She knew from the taut line of his arms as he braced himself against the wall, he was holding back. She deliberately relaxed around him, shifting her hips and drawing him deeper.

"Just a little bit more," he promised. "You're so tight. Can you take more?" He followed the soft request with a kiss below her ear and another shallow thrust.

"Yes." Another fraction of an inch slid into her pussy. With one more gentle push, he was in, pressed deep against her mound, rock solid inside her.

He brushed the hair away from her face. Tenderness and concern hovered behind the lust in his gaze. And she could see his silent question—he wanted her permission to continue. She checked her body. Though his cock stretched her, the slight pain was a pleasurable thing. She nodded and slowly he pulled back.

With methodical, steady motions, he began long thrusts into her body. It was strange after the urgency to get inside her, he seemed to be moving so carefully, almost delicately, as if he was afraid she'd break.

"Please, Jax, you can go slow next time. I need you harder. Harder."

Her husky plea snapped his thin control and he plunged inside her. The fear that he might hurt her—she was so tight and tiny—was eased when she groaned, "Oh yes. Just like that."

So he gave her more—driving deep, loving the tight grip of her cunt as he pulled almost free. Her body clung to his, begging for his return and he pushed back in, penetrating her again and again, sliding easily into her wet passage.

He held her ass in his hand, holding her for his heavy thrusts. She pressed her shoulders against the door, giving her more leverage, and pushed against him. She definitely craved a hard fuck.

Damn, she was sexy. He could feel his climax rising and wanted her with him, wanted to feel her come around his cock. Her gasps became pleas and then cries as he pounded into her. She was close. He reached between their bodies, finding her clit with his finger and teasing it lightly.

She shivered in his arms. "Jax!" He couldn't hold back, not after the sweet seduction of her orgasm. Her cunt contracted around his cock and he thrust into her one final time.

He leaned into her, his weight pinning her against the door as they both struggled for breath. He didn't know how long they stood there before Kit lifted her head and smiled at him.

"Wow. A talented mouth and a talented cock. You are one hell of a package."

The lazy, satiated drawl of her voice made his cock, still buried inside her, twitch, like it was thinking about hardening but hadn't quite decided. She must have felt it too because her eyes widened for just a moment.

"Hmmm. That makes me think there's more." She opened her mouth against his in a long, hungry kiss.

"There's definitely more." He eased his hips back, sliding out of her sex. The sweet grip as he pulled free of her body combined with her hot whisper, making his cock harden. He straightened his clothes, closing the waistband of his pants but not zipping them. "I want you naked this time." He backed away and took her hand, ready to lead her down the hall to her bedroom.

"Wait." She tugged on his hand and for a moment he thought she was going to send him home. "My purse. I have more condoms in my purse." She slipped her hand into the open fly of his pants. "And we're going to need more."

He grabbed the handbag and walked down the hall, holding Kit in one hand and her purse in the other.

Chapter Three

Kit's hands trembled as she attempted to froth the milk for her homemade latte'. It was a treat usually saved for the weekend but this morning she needed the extra hit of caffeine, needed it to deal with the realization that she'd had sex with Jackson Knight.

No, to be accurate, she'd fucked Jackson Knight. And he'd returned the favor. A number of times. She stared up at the cabinets. Just how many orgasms had she had last night? It had to be a personal record. In fact, she knew it was, because one and a half had been her previous standard. They'd beaten that before they'd gotten naked. And then...there had been the time in bed, then another in the shower and...

She jammed her hands onto the kitchen counter to keep herself upright as the memories shot into her sex and drained the strength from her knees. Damn, just the thought of the man made her horny. It always had. Now she had reality to contend with as well as fantasy.

But she'd managed for six months to keep the raging hormones controlled. Until last night.

Something happened—something changed. Dramatically.

Her milk gurgled and sloshed dangerously close to the edge. Moving by rote, she pulled the pitcher away and poured it into her cup. She took a sip, remembering as it burnt her tongue that she hadn't added the coffee yet. She dumped the coffee in and stared blindly at her cup.

Her mind, blurry from sex and no caffeine, struggled to pinpoint the moment when last night had gone from a typical dinner with Jax to door-banging sex.

All had been normal until she'd come out of the bathroom and then she'd started saying things. Unbelievable things.

Nothing special had happened in the bathroom. She'd peed, washed, fluffed...and kissed that stone.

Her chest tightened. She'd kissed that stone and suddenly she was the slut goddess from hell fucking her best friend.

It couldn't be that. Could it?

The old man had said it was a piece of the Blarney Stone.

And he'd given her condoms—which had been put to good use—almost as if he'd known what would happen. But that was impossible, ridiculous.

Kit gulped hot coffee and hurried to her office. It was really a second bedroom but she'd set it up as an office-slash-library. Reference books lined the walls. She moved directly to the shelf she needed and grabbed a book of Celtic fairy tales and legends.

It took her only seconds to find the page and the legend of the Blarney Stone. Queen Elizabeth I demanded Cormac MacDermot MacCarthy, Lord of Blarney, take the tenure of his lands from the Crown. Cormac set out to plead to the Queen for his traditional rights. Because he was not well spoken, he despaired of furthering his cause. Along the way, he met an old woman who asked why he was so downhearted. He told her his woeful tale and she replied, "Beneath Castle Blarney there is a stone, which, if you can kiss it, will give you the power of persuasive eloquence." He returned to his castle, kissed the stone and went to visit the Queen where he was able to persuade her to allow him to keep his rights to his lands. Since then, many have traveled to Blarney Castle to kiss the stone and receive the gift of gab.

Several other versions of the legend were scattered about the pages but they all ended with one thing. The power of persuasion. Persuasive Eloquence.

Oh my God. I persuaded Jax to sleep with me. Suddenly, the band for her bra seemed too tight. All the sexy, explicit words she'd said—as if she'd known precisely what to say to seduce him. But if that were true, then the rock she'd bought for fifty dollars really *was* a piece of the Blarney Stone. It was impossible. She walked through the kitchen, gulped more scalding coffee, and went into her bedroom to find her purse. It lay dumped out beside the bed. Three empty condom wrappers were scattered around it. She ignored them and the rumpled bed sheets and grabbed the purse and the stone.

She turned the rock over in her hand as she walked back to the kitchen. Maybe there was something on the stone, something that made her hallucinate. Made her horny.

Okay, it didn't take a rock to do that. Just Jax.

She examined the green rock by the kitchen window. In the morning light, it was a deep green. No supernatural glow. No strange heat. Maybe there *was* something on the stone. She turned on the faucet, stuck the rock under the hot water and scrubbed it with dish soap. After five minutes of washing, she held the wet stone up. If there had been anything weird on the stone, it was gone now.

She put it on the counter and sipped her coffee. The smartest thing to do would be to get rid of it. There was no reason to keep it.

Except, what if it was true? What if it truly was the Blarney Stone?

Even telling herself it was silly, she picked it up and put it back in her purse. She needed to test it with something that didn't involve sex. She had to meet with the dean about the tutoring center budget. That was about as far from sexually interesting as she could get. She would kiss it before the meeting. She paused. Maybe that wasn't a good idea. What if the rock was focused on sex and she asked the dean to go down on her. Like she had Jax.

And he'd done it. And done it again. An ache blossomed in her sex, a sharp stab of pleasure in response to the memory of his mouth between her legs. God, that man had a mouth made to eat pussy.

She released a long, pent up breath, and willed away the sensation. Brushing back her hair, she straightened and mentally prepared herself. Just because she'd finally had incredible sex with her best friend, she wouldn't let it mess up her day. It was a day just like any other.

By noon she realized how wrong she was. Her body didn't want to let go of the memories of Jax, the feel of him inside her, pumping deep into her sex, his hot mouth on her skin, sucking on her nipples. Kit fanned her hand in front of her face. The slightest reference to Jax or sex or pretty much anything, made her almost double over with need.

When she was able to divert her thoughts from him, her mind turned to the upcoming television show.

A strange mix of lust and terror battled for control of her body and mind.

A call from her agent confirmed Alison's command and Kit's appearance on America Today. None of her pleading, begging, and—she hated to admit—whining, did any good. She'd agreed to participate in promoting the book when they'd signed the contract. And she was expected to follow through. Kit didn't reply that *she'd* expected promotion to be uncomfortable book signings and hanging posters around town. Not embarrassing herself on national television.

But there appeared to be no way out of it. That left Jax. He'd said he could help. She would have to take him up on it.

If she could keep her hands off him.

She'd managed for six months. Surely she could do it again. For one night.

She fingered the stone, which she'd taken out of her purse and shoved into her pants pocket. There was something comforting about the smooth sides and rounded edges. She rolled it over in her hand, using it as a talisman against the nerves that rumbled in her stomach. Squeezing the stone, she wished for calm and strength. She opened her hand and saw the indentation of the rock in her palm, but felt no calmer.

Kiss the stone.

Yeah, she thought, then maybe I can persuade *myself* that I didn't screw up a perfectly good friendship by seducing Jax.

She skipped lunch. She couldn't face Jax. She had to figure out what she was going to say—how she was going to explain jumping him in her front yard last night.

Besides, her hormones were on the very thin edge of controlled. If she had any hope of making it through the afternoon, she couldn't take another injection of desire. Instead, she called his office and left a message asking for a time for tonight. And then decided to be a true coward and turned off her phone before he could call back.

She spent her lunch going over her presentation for Dean Greerson. She hated these meetings. The dean was always threatening to close the tutoring lab, saying that the money could be used in other areas. Kit had been diligent in keeping her budget steady for the past three years but now she needed new computer terminals and she needed help. More and more students were coming to the lab for assistance and she wasn't able to help them all.

By one o'clock, she was impatiently pacing outside the dean's office.

"Kit, Dean Greerson will see you now."

Kit nodded at the assistant's announcement. The stone was cool in her hand. What could it hurt? It was doubtful that she would start spouting sexual innuendoes to the Dean of Liberal Arts. Deciding to test the stone and the little old man who'd sold it to her, she surreptitiously raised the rock to her lips and kissed it.

The rock didn't warm. No shocking spark went off in her clit. Her nipples didn't tighten the way they had last night. She shook her head. She was standing outside the dean's office, making him wait—while she kissed a rock.

She would get rid of it. As soon as the meeting was done.

Pasting on her best professional smile, Kit pushed her shoulders back and walked inside.

"Dean Greerson, it's good to see you."

Thirty-minutes later, Kit, not bothering to hide the stunned look on her face, left the office.

"Oh my God, are you all right?"

She looked up. Jessie waited outside the dean's office.

"He didn't eliminate the lab completely, did he?"

Kit shook her head—not really sure what just happened.

"Did he totally axe your budget? Do you still have a job? I'll protest if they try to get rid of you. You've done so much for the students here. We—" Jessie finally stopped. "Kit, what's wrong?"

"I got it all."

"Got what all?"

"All that I asked for." She looked up in a daze, still amazed at the result.

The Dean had begun with his usual, "Kit, we just don't have the money to keep the lab open..." And when it came time for her to speak—for once she'd found the words. She'd pled her arguments, eloquently, she thought, and at the end of the discussion, the dean was nodding when she did and promising to sign the requisition forms later today. "I asked for four new workstations, a part-time assistant and extending the lab's hours, and he agreed." Her voice resonated with wonder and amazement. She still couldn't believe he'd agreed to everything. She rubbed the stone and shook her head. It couldn't be the stone. That defied all reason, all logic. Every sensible thought she'd ever had rejected it. But still...

"And why is this a bad thing? You don't sound pleased."

"It's just weird."

"It's been a day for it."

Something in Jessie's tone slowed Kit's racing thoughts. "What happened? And don't you have a class?" Kit looked at her watch.

"The professor can be late by ten minutes, right?" She grabbed Kit's elbow and pulled her down the hall toward her classroom. "So, what's going on?"

"What do you mean?"

"I mean you didn't come to lunch."

"That's no big deal. I was busy and I have missed lunch before. I mean there's no reason to read anything into it." She realized she was rambling. "Or anything."

"Right." Jessie's lips squeezed tight together in disbelief. "You skip lunch and Jax is edgy and snapping and asking me if I've seen you and are you okay and why would he think you weren't okay?" Jessie stopped walking. "*Are* you okay?"

Kit shrugged. I might have a magic stone that convinced Jax to have sex with me but besides that..."I'm fine."

"So what's wrong with Jax?"

"He's fine. Or he was..." She stared at Jessie for a long moment. She had to tell someone. Had to get advice from somewhere. And Jessie at least wouldn't think she was too crazy. "He was when he left my house at five this morning."

It was a slow realization that moved across Jessie's expressive face, widening her eyes and dropping her mouth open. "Oh my God, you did it. You slept with Jax!"

The squealed whisper echoed down the almost empty hall.

"Jessie, hush."

"What happened? Yesterday you were buddies for life and now you're doing the nasty? When did all this occur?"

"Last night. At McGill's and it's kind of hard to explain. You have class." Kit couldn't decide if she was pleased or not about that. She could use a sympathetic ear and a voice of logic. Jessie could at least provide the former.

"It's okay. It's Intro to British Lit." Jessie opened the classroom door and stepped inside. "How many of you finished the book?" Though Kit couldn't see the students, she didn't hear much movement. "Just as I thought. Class is cancelled. I suggest you take the time to finish Pride and Prejudice because there will be a test on Tuesday." She held open the door and waited as twenty confused freshmen cycled out. Kit gripped her book bag and hesitated, briefly contemplating walking away with the class.

If she stayed, she would have to explain it all to Jessie. And she couldn't even explain it to herself.

Jessie must have read her thoughts and grabbed her hand, pulling her into the room after the class filed out. With the door closed, Jessie swung her butt up on to the teacher's desk and clapped her hands eagerly, like a five-year-old waiting for a bedtime story.

"I'm not really sure what happened. Or how it happened," Kit began.

"But you had sex with Jax?"

"Yes."

"Good sex?"

"Oh yes."

"So, tell me everything. I need to live vicariously."

"You have a great sex life."

Jessie giggled. "I know, but I want to hear details anyway. In case I can learn anything new. So, you went to McGill's and what? They had love potions on sale?"

"Not exactly. It was more of a magic rock."

"What?"

"I bought this rock." She pulled it out of her pocket and held it out to Jessie. "From this little Irish shop down on twentieth, near those warehouses."

Jessie tilted her head and stared at the rock and then up at Kit. Her eyes tightened and she scrunched up one side of her mouth. "I don't think there is a shop on twentieth."

"It must be new because I've never seen it before either, but I bought this rock and the guy told me it was a piece of the Blarney Stone." She kept talking, not wanting to give Jessie a chance to interrupt. "And last night, at McGill's I kissed it and then next thing you know, I'm seducing Jax. Persuading him to have sex with me."

"I bet he didn't need that much persuading."

Kit ignored Jessie's muttering and kept on. "I don't know what happened. One minute everything was normal and the next, I was saying these things that never come out of my mouth."

"And you think it's because of this rock." Jessie held out her hand and Kit placed the stone in her palm. Jessie fingered it, much the same way Kit had been doing.

"Does it feel warm to you?"

Jessie shook her head. "No, it feels like a rock. I know you do a lot of research into legends, but this is just a pretty green rock."

"You don't understand. I felt something when I kissed it. Something happened."

Jessie inspected the rock. Though Kit knew her friend didn't believe her, Jessie was at least humoring her while she explained.

"Maybe you should go back to that shop and see if they know anything more about it," Jessie suggested.

"Good idea." Kit snatched the stone from Jessie's hand and grabbed her bag. "I've got enough time before my next group comes in." She ran out the door before Jessie could stop her.

Speed walking helped burn off some of the energy she'd been suppressing all morning. It also helped stretch out the tired and worn muscles unused to the rigorous activity from the night before.

She strode down the street until she reached the area where the storm had struck yesterday. Her steps slowed. An empty space stood between the two buildings. She looked up and down the street. This was the right road. The right location. She remembered the clothing warehouse on the right side.

But the McMac Shop was gone.

The entire building was gone. Still not believing that the whole building could have disappeared, she ran across the street and stood between the two warehouses.

Nothing.

Kit hiked up and down the street, even popping over to the next road, to see if she had missed the location but there was nothing resembling the little store. Or the shopkeeper who'd sold her the rock.

Finally, she turned around and walked back to campus. The next group of students came into the lab and she was able, for a few hours to lose herself in instructing. When memories of the night before tried to weasel their way into her thoughts, she abruptly pushed them aside. She did the same with the panic about the book appearance and her questions about the green rock in her pocket.

By the time she got home, there were two things she could no longer avoid. Jax and the TV show. She needed Jax's expertise. She'd resigned herself to appearing on America Today. Now, she needed some help so she didn't look like an idiot in front of millions of TV viewers. She didn't bother to hope for looking good. She just didn't want to be mortified.

He'd left a message on her cell phone, in response to her message, telling her to come by at six and they'd get to work.

Jax had also recommended she wear the outfit she was planning for the show to his house to get used to sitting in it.

Kit went to her closet and pulled out a long, loose skirt. She wanted to be comfortable when she made a fool of herself. The material swirled around her legs, brushing lightly against her calves. The neat, long-sleeved blouse she wore matched the skirt and made her look—she stared into the mirror—classic and conservative.

Deciding she liked the outfit, Kit fiddled with her makeup then made herself more coffee, watching the time pass. It was just past six. She should be at his house but was stalling. What if the rock had cast some sort of spell? It might very well have worn off. What would she do if he stared at her with an "oh-my-God-how-could-I-have-slept-with-her" look on his face?

There was no way to know until she actually stood before him and looked into his eyes. Those warm brown eyes that had stared into hers that first time, when he'd slid so deep inside her.

The phone rang startling her out of her thoughts. She recognized Jax's number on the caller ID box.

She picked up the handset. "Hi, Jax."

"Kit, you comin'?"

She felt the question deep inside her sex, tightening her cunt. If he'd asked the same question last night, she would have responded with a seductive, sexy answer. Now, any words she might have said died in her throat.

"Kit?" he prompted.

"Uh, I'll be right there."

The walk to his house was over too quickly. When he opened the door her own false smile dimmed. There was something different in the way he looked at her—as if he was cautious and careful not to get too close. Damn, he probably thought she was going to jump him again.

"Hi." He greeted her with a short nod but didn't smile.

"Uh, hi."

"Missed you at lunch." There was a silent prompt in his statement. And maybe a touch of hurt.

"I was avoiding you," she answered honestly. "I didn't know what to say, you know, about last night."

Though she'd had plenty to say last night. It had been her mouth that had gotten them into this situation. But that same persuasive tongue was missing tonight. She thought about the stone, once again in her purse. She could kiss it and see if it would help explain to Jax why they'd ended up naked and horizontal in her entryway.

Actually, her mind corrected, it had been clothed and vertical in her entryway. Naked and horizontal had been in the bedroom.

"What about now?" Jax asked.

Kit grimaced. "I'm hoping we can not talk about it until later, you know, after I've embarrassed myself on national TV."

Jax leaned against the doorframe as he considered the idea. "I never thought you'd be the kind of woman who would avoid these sorts of discussions."

She winced like he'd poked her with a stick. Jax watched in amazement. It was fascinating—the change from last night.

She looked cute standing on his porch, sucking the corner of her lower lip into her mouth, unsure of herself— very much like the Kit he'd connected with over beer and corned beef. Last night, she'd been bold and aggressive and sexy. The words she'd said had cranked him up higher and harder than anyone before. And then when he'd finally gotten inside her—it had been incredible. The tight grip of her cunt around his erection had kept him hard last night and the memory of it had put him on the verge all day today.

Here she was, looking cute and nervous, and he wanted to pull her into his arms and make love to her, slide back into that delicious, wet passage that had held him so close. His cock hardened. He wondered how Kit would respond if he started to repeat back the words she'd said to him last night—the sexy, risqué words that had freed the desire inside him. The pale blush on her cheeks warned him she wasn't ready for that.

And tempted though he was, he knew she needed to rehearse for her interview. Work before sex.

Damn.

He nodded and stepped back. "Okay, come on in."

He led her to his studio downstairs. He'd set it up for the consulting side of his business. Using ancient TV cameras and tape machines, he was able to simulate most television situations and tape the results. He'd moved the furnishings into a typical morning show set—anchor chair and couch. He waved to Kit toward the set and followed behind her. She slipped her purse off her shoulder and set it on the ground next to the couch.

He reached out to touch her, to guide her forward, but he stopped himself. They had work to do and he wasn't entirely sure if he touched her now, they wouldn't end up naked. Work before sex, he thought again.

"Okay, it will look something like this." He began to run through the studio set up. For people like Kit, it helped to have an idea as to what the studio would look like. Feel like. She didn't like surprises. Knowing the layout ahead of time would give her some confidence.

He led her through the process of sitting down, making sure her clothes were properly straightened, and how to clip on the lapel microphone.

"When you sit down, look directly at the interviewer. You don't have to talk to anyone else. Just think of it as a conversation with one person."

"But there will be millions of people watching." The panic rose again in her voice.

"You don't have to worry about them. Just focus on him."

She bit her lip and nodded. The slight nervous shine in her eyes was flashing like a beacon.

"You're going to be fine," he assured her.

Kit gave an imitation of a smile.

Jax left her alone for a few minutes while he went to the back room to start the tape machines rolling.

He returned and sat down in the anchor chair, giving her a charming smile. She didn't return it.

Kit—intelligent, beautiful and sexy as all hell—was terrified.

"Let's get started. We'll do a quick run through just to see how you do and then we'll know where we need to work."

Chapter Four

Two hours later, Jax stood up. "I'm going to go change tapes. I'll be right back," he said, his smile strained but still supportive. Kit sagged back into the deep couch cushions and watched him leave. She was going to screw this up. She was going to go on this show and look like an idiot. And worse, she would fail Jax. She knew he would feel as bad about this as she did.

She puffed up her cheeks and then blew the air out in a heavy sigh. No, she told herself. She wouldn't let him down. She would do this. She could do this. Using the last bits of energy lingering in her body, she grabbed the arm of the couch and dragged herself to sitting. She just had to focus. Remember everything he'd taught her. *Concentrate on your message. Give full answers but don't ramble. Don't fidget.* There was so much to think about.

She closed her eyes and tried to run down the list of instructions. She rolled her hips trying to make herself more comfortable. Her foot bumped her purse.

She reached down to move it out of the way. And stopped. The stone was in her purse.

The meeting with the dean came back to her in a flash. She'd said all the right things. She hated to fail Jax. He was trying so hard. It wasn't his fault she was a hopeless case.

Still, it didn't seem right. If this was the Blarney Stone—and she hadn't quite convinced herself of that—

should she really use it for something like a TV interview? Shouldn't she be persuading world leaders to give peace a chance? Still the little man in the store had told her it would bring her what she most desired.

She thought about Jax, naked in her bed, fucking her against her front door. Those items had been at the top of her wish list.

And right now her greatest desire—besides a repeat of last night—was to make it through this interview.

She would do it. Once more. Just to get the confidence that she could succeed.

Hoping Jax didn't return before she finished, she dug the rock out of the bottom of her purse, held it to her lips, and placed a single, simple kiss against it.

Heat once again jumped into her mouth and zinged through her body. Like last night, her nipples popped out and her sex began to relax. She didn't have time to enjoy the sensation because Jax walked back into the room.

"Ready to try it again?"

"Oh, definitely," she answered, remembering several things from last night she wanted to try again. And again. Then they could explore some new options. Then mix and match.

Jax stepped in front of her to get to his chair. She gripped her hands together to keep from reaching out and patting his butt as he walked by. He sat down. Though she was vaguely aware of him rolling his shoulders back, she was focused a little farther down his body.

The chairs were close enough together that she wouldn't have to stretch far to put her hand on his cock. Slide her fingers around his thick shaft. Her pussy melted, preparing and urging her to action. He'd felt so good last night—thick and hard. And strong. He'd ridden her deep and long—not stopping until she'd begged to come.

She squeezed her legs together to try to contain the sensations. It only made the slight pulses worse. Damn, it was happening again. Something about that rock and Jax made her think of nothing but sex. Okay, well, Jax did that on his own but as soon as she kissed the rock, the fantasies became sharp clear images in her mind. And the words began to circle in her brain. *Fuck me, Jax. Let me feel your mouth on my skin.*

Kit gulped.

"Ready? Let's go again and remember you know this information. Just focus on talking to me." Jax's tone was all business. Kit slowly raised her eyes up from his crotch. Jax tilted his head in silent question.

She offered a half-smile while trying to drag her own thoughts back to what she needed to do.

"I'm ready whenever you are," she said. And then some. She rolled her hips settling herself comfortably on the couch, and felt a soft flutter in her sex. *Careful.* She sent the mental warning to her mind and body since neither seemed ready to listen to common sense. *Just answer his questions before you end up stripping off your clothes and dragging him down on top of you.*

And that's a bad idea, why?

Kit was saved from answering her own question when Jax cleared his throat, sat up in the chair and looked intently into her eyes.

"Katherine, tell me about why legends and myths are so important to our world today?"

There was nothing sexual about his question but his voice flowed from his mouth like melted chocolate. Kit leaned forward wanting to get closer to those lips that spoke so sweetly. With a furtive gesture, she undid the top button of her blouse, letting the neck gape just a little.

"Well, Jax, our legends and myths are part of our culture." Her low voice took on an exotic rhythm—one designed to catch the listener's attention. "They connect us to the past. And they help us frame the future."

Jax blinked in surprise and gave a shallow nod as if acknowledging that she'd done it right. He asked the next question and the next. And each time the answers flowed out of mouth with precision and clarity.

"Give me an example of some myths that impact our daily life."

She felt her lips curl into a seductive smile. And she could see Jax's reaction to it. His eyes heated and he shifted in his seat. Knowing she had his attention skimmed her tongue along the edge of her upper lip before answering.

"Well, there is the persistent myth that size *does* matter with a man's erection."

She could tell she'd shocked him but after a momentary hesitation, he cleared his throat. "And you're saying size doesn't matter?" There was a twinkle in his eye and a teasing flip to his question.

Kit slid one leg up and draped it over the opposite knee. It didn't reveal any skin but the motion was slow and sensual and she watched Jax's eyes widen for a moment. "I wouldn't say it was size that was of interest. More the intensity. Because sometimes..." Her voice naturally dropped and her head tipped to the side. It was easy to remember how inventive Jax was. He had it all— creativity and a big cock. "Sometimes a woman just wants to be stuffed full with her man's cock." Jax shifted again in his chair but didn't otherwise react. "A thick...hard...shaft driving into her. You see, what a woman really wants is to feel desired. As if her lover needs her desperately. As if he needs to come inside *her* more than anything else. That her pussy is the one, and the only one, he wants to fuck. That's what a woman wants. She wants to be spread beneath her lover."

Though surprised by the words she spoke, she didn't attempt to stop them. Her pussy was practically begging to be filled and Jax was definitely responding to her verbal seduction. She spread her legs apart—the loose skirt gave her plenty of room—and slid her hand down her stomach between her thighs. Knowing he watched her hand, she rubbed her palm lightly over her mound. "To lie beneath him and feel him inside her. Feel that hard shaft over and over again." She couldn't stop the groan that slipped from her throat. She continued the slow steady massage, imagining it was Jax's hand touching her.

"Just thinking about it makes me wet," she whispered as she looked at him. His eyes flared—the same wild heat from last night. She moved without thinking, letting her words guide her actions. "I get like this whenever I think about your cock inside me." She leaned back, keeping one hand touching her sex and reaching the other up to release the clip that held her hair. The soft brown strands fell down around her face and she smiled, letting the memories from the night before fill her words. "You fit inside me so perfectly—filling me—stretching me."

She could feel Jax watching her, his hot gaze following her hands.

"You were so hard inside my pussy. It made me wonder what you'd feel like in my mouth, with my tongue licking up and down. Hmmm." She allowed a moan to escape and twisted on the soft cushions. Her words were having the correct impact—but on her, not on Jax. Damn, she wanted him.

She opened her eyes. He sat on the edge of his chair, his hands propped forcefully on his knees as if he were holding himself back. She rolled to her side and slid off the couch, slowly crawling toward him until she knelt between his legs. He adjusted to give her room. She placed her hands on his strong thighs then smoothed them upward until her fingertips touched the hard line of his erection. The soft denim teased her palms as she touched him, but the jeans would have to go. She wanted him in her hands.

She kept every movement leisurely, knowing it would torment him and she wanted this to last.

She placed both thumbs on his cock. With gentle pressure, she ran her thumbs up his erection and then back down. She continued the dreamy massage as she looked up into his eyes. "You've spent the last two hours teaching me to…use my mouth effectively." She released a sultry chuckle. "I think I should show you what I've learned. Show you just how well my mouth works. How it feels with your cock sliding in and out."

His fingers dug into his knees. "God, Kit, you're killing me."

She clicked her tongue. "We can't have that." She pulled herself up high on her knees until she could reach his mouth with a light kiss. She moved back when he tried to deepen it. Her hands skimmed across his thighs. "I need you very much alive. I have plans for you. Plans that involve your delicious cock and your very talented mouth."

She reached up and opened the top button of his jeans. The button fly gave her a sensual feast. Her fingers lingered on each button, stroking him through the sturdy denim and then through his briefs. Silently she worked, pulling his jeans open and down a little. Kit sighed with pleasure as his cock popped out, as if thrilled to be free from constraints.

"Hmmm. Is that all for me?" She wrapped her hand around the base of his shaft and squeezed gently. She didn't give him a chance to answer before bending down and licking the flat of her tongue up the underside of his cock. His thighs trembled. She sucked the head into her mouth. She heard his groan and let the sound guide her.

He stared down at her—watching his cock slide between her lips. She pulled back and began to taste him—long heavy licks interspersed with delicate flickers of her tongue. Jax thought his brain was going to explode. He knew his balls were about to. He'd thought every fantasy had been fulfilled last night but here she was, creating new ones. And satisfying them.

He slid his hands into her hair, needing to hold her while she moved her mouth against his shaft. She kept the pace dangerously slow, lavishing attention on the sensitive underside and adding pressure, just enough.

"Kit, please, honey."

She straightened and Jax almost snarled as she pulled back.

"Please what?" Her pink tongue appeared at the edge of her lip. "Please let you come in my mouth?" The smile on her lips warned him she knew precisely what she was saying and how powerful the effect would be. "I'd like that."

Her words drove a shaft of fire into his cock. Damn, where had she learned sex talk like this? He didn't care. It was hot. He was hot.

"Yes."

"Hmm. Soon." She leaned down and swirled her tongue quickly around the crest of his cock. Jax pumped his hips up, aching for her to take him back inside. Instead, his temptress pulled away. "It's a little warm in here, don't you think? Maybe I should take this off." She fingered the buttons on her prim white blouse. She didn't wait for his agreement, just began to undo the buttons and slip the garment over her shoulders. A white lace bra cupped her small, firm breasts. "And this." She reached between her breasts and undid the front clasp. Jax followed the movement of her hands. The slow revealing of her breast, the hint of skin before it was bared made his mouth water. She pulled the cups back. Her nipples were small and tight. And delicious. Her hands floated across her skin, brushing across her breasts down to her waist, until she reached the waistband of her skirt. She hooked her thumbs into the elastic waistband and pulled her skirt and panties down in one swift movement.

She tossed the skirt away and pushed up high on her knees. The dark brown hair that protected her pussy teased him—creating tempting shadows he wanted to explore with his tongue. He licked his lips remembering how she'd responded to his mouth.

It would be so easy to pull her down, spread her legs and taste her cunt once again. He considered the idea but she seemed to have other plans in mind. She held her hands away from her body, inched her knees apart so she was open before him, and presented herself to him—as if waiting for his command to continue.

She raised her eyes to his and blinked. A hint of innocence sparkled in her gaze but he knew that was part of her act. The Sex Goddess had returned.

"Do I meet with your approval?" she asked in the same, husky tone that curled around his cock like warm tendrils of fire.

"You're amazing." He'd always thought of Kit as cute and sweet but kneeling before him—she was exotic and sexy.

She dropped her gaze as if shyness took over. Then she looked up. It wasn't shyness or modesty in her eyes. It was fire and lust.

"I'm glad you like what you see." She reached out and put her hands on his knees, using him for balance as she crawled forward. "Do I have your permission to continue?" She trailed two fingertips up the underside of his cock.

He wanted to speak but couldn't say a simple yes, so he nodded.

"Now, where was I? Oh yes. I was licking this tasty cock." She sucked the head into her mouth, and then pulled back. "Do you like the feel of my tongue on you?" As she spoke, her breath teased his sensitive flesh. The light brush pushed him closer than he wanted to be. He wanted to extend the experience. But her words and her actions weren't going to let him.

"Take me inside your mouth."

"Soon," she promised again and Jax knew he was in for a long torment before she let him come.

She bent down and repeated the caress—running the flat of her tongue up the full length of his cock. Then she returned along the side, licking and flicking her tongue, hot wet strokes along his shaft. He grabbed the arms of the chair, holding onto it and resisting the temptation to grab the back of her head and push his cock inside her mouth. The urge was hard to fight. She looked so seductive, teasing him with hot licks of her tongue, easing her hand between his legs and cupping his balls. She used her other hand on his shaft, massaging its length.

Finally, she sucked the end of his cock into her mouth. He struggled not to thrust, letting her move on him. With each pull back, she turned her head slightly, twisting like a corkscrew. The motion massaged his cock, covering every inch in sensation. He felt his eyes roll to the back of his head. He wasn't going to last much longer—not with the delicious motion of her mouth. She picked up speed. Not quite fucking speed but a steady sink and withdrawal. She sucked in her cheeks as she pulled out. Jax groaned and ground his teeth together. He was so close. Just a little more...

Her jaw was beginning to ache but she kept on. If his groans were any indication, he liked what she was doing. And she loved doing it to him. She felt already tight muscles bunch even more and knew he was close to coming.

"Please, baby, I'm about to come."

She didn't know if that was a plea to stop, pull back or keep going. She decided to keep going. She wanted his release—wanted to feel him lose control inside her. She widened her mouth just a little as she sank back down on him, accepting as much of his length as possible. He hit against the back of her throat. She sucked as she pulled back. His fingertips tightened on her head and he exploded in her mouth.

She swallowed him all, letting him come deeply down her throat. She licked her tongue across the crown one final time then pulled back. Jax fell back into the chair, his eyes staring blankly at the ceiling, his chest rising and falling in long, heavy breaths. He looked wasted—completely blown away. Kit couldn't hold back her smile. Well, he had been.

He groaned and pulled his gaze back to her. The lust in his eyes hadn't faded. If anything, he looked even more hungry than before.

She pushed back on her heels and stood up. Without breaking eye contact with him, she returned to the couch behind her and sat down. And spread her legs. She leaned into the cushions, naked, bare and open to him. Knowing he watched, she placed her hand daintily over her pussy and sighed.

"I thought I was wet before," she whispered. "I guess sucking you off excited me just a little." Two fingers disappeared, sinking into her cunt. He watched as she used her own fingers, moving them slowly in and out. She wasn't fucking herself hard—enough to pleasure but not to come.

Her other hand reached up and pinched her nipples, moving from one tight peak to the other.

"I lay in my bed at night, and I think about you...and I touch myself. I imagine it's your fingers inside my cunt, your mouth on my breasts. And then I long for your cock—thick and hard. Now—" She groaned. "I know what it feels like. It's better than my dreams."

Though he'd just come, he was returning to the state she described—thick and hard. She had the ability to do that. With a few words. A look.

He stood, kicked his jeans aside and with one step was kneeling between her thighs, one knee on the couch, the other foot on the floor. She looked incredible, open before him. He watched for a moment, unable to pull his gaze away from her seductive movements, the way her body twisted as she let fantasy take her. Her fingers still pumped inside her pussy. That was where he wanted to be. He let her continue as he opened the buttons of his shirt.

Kit watched as he stripped his shirt off. She loved his chest—tight and muscular. And those defined abs and well-cut arms. She drove her fingers deeper, needing a little more. Jax dropped his shirt and stood before her naked.

"I think this is my pussy to fuck tonight," he said pulling her hand away from her cunt. He lifted her fingers to his mouth and sucked them inside, licking her juices from her skin.

His mouth skimmed across her flesh collecting the cream. Kit shivered, feeling each lick between her legs. He closed his eyes for one brief moment as if he was savoring her taste.

"You're delicious and I might get around to licking your tight cunt but for now—I want to fuck." A gentle kiss on her palm was the complete opposite to the rough sound of his voice. He scraped his teeth across the heel of her hand, biting lightly before releasing her. "Turn over. I want your ass in the air."

Kit felt her eyes widen. She'd never heard such a commanding tone to Jax's voice. It sent a flood of moisture to her pussy and inspired a touch of defiance. Not that she planned to disobey.

She lifted her chin and stared into his eyes. The blatant dare she saw there forced her to move. She curled her leg up, baring more of her cunt and her ass before swinging her leg between them. She kept her movements deliberate and as sexual as she could, rolling over until she was kneeling on the couch.

"Were you looking for something like this?" she asked in a deep husky voice.

She knelt there, blind for long moments, waiting. He didn't move, didn't touch her—but she knew he watched. Just being in this position made her pussy flutter with anticipation. Finally, his warm hands slid down her hips to her butt. He cupped her rounded cheeks giving them a gentle squeeze.

"You've got a very nice ass." One finger ran up the back of her leg, up the sensitive crack of her backside. "Probably from all that walking around campus." He seduced her with his words and the light stroke of his fingers across her skin. "Now, whenever I see you walk across campus, I'm going to think about how sexy you look kneeling on my couch."

"Jax," Kit moaned. She wanted him inside her. "Please."

"Spread your legs for me, honey."

She did, subconsciously arching her back and pushing her backside out. He signaled his approval by sliding his hand forward and tickling her lower lips. He took her moisture and seemed to spread it around.

"Very nice. Now, be a good girl and tell me you brought condoms with you." He pushed two fingers into her sex.

Kit squeezed her lips together to smother her groan. He felt so much better than her own fingers, thicker, stronger, and with the promise of his cock. "My-my purse."

She felt him move but the stroking inside her pussy continued. He pushed deep, then curled his fingers, as if tickling the inside of her cunt. Shivers exploded from inside her. She arched her back and he repeated the motion.

"Oh, damn, Jax, fuck me."

Her mind was rapidly losing the ability to think, much less form words. It was like the previous night. Once he was close to entering her, her sexy words disappeared.

She heard the soft tear of cellophane as he ripped the package open. His hands left her for a moment but the memory of his touch remained. Her pussy still felt the luscious slide of his fingers. And a second later she felt the thick nudge of his cock at her entrance. He slipped the tip inside but gave her no more, pumping shallow thrusts just into the very edge of her cunt.

Kit dug her fingernails into the couch and squeezed her eyes shut. The pressure was incredible. The slow steady pulsing sent waves of heat into her pussy. She groaned and dropped her head down, pushing her ass farther up in the air. It was wonderful but not enough for her to come. He wasn't giving her enough.

"Please, Jax. Put it inside me. I want to feel you." The final words came out as a moan.

"Soon, baby, soon. Hmmm. You're going to feel so tight when I enter you." He smoothed his hands down her hips, her legs, rubbing her everywhere like he would pet a cat—and she purred beneath his touch. She rolled into each caress, instinctively seeking his warmth.

"That's it. Now, you're ready for me, aren't you?"

"Yes, Jax, oh please." She didn't know how she would survive if he didn't come into her soon. Her body was tight, on the edge of coming but his touch only increased the devilish anticipation.

His hands tightened on her hips. Kit grabbed the cushion beneath her hand and held on. She knew, this wouldn't be a gentle fuck.

He started to push in. At first he moved slowly, then with more pressure, and with one strong thrust, he slammed into her. Kit gasped at the sudden shock of feeling his thick length inside her. It was incredible. Her body opened to welcome him, clinging to him. He hesitated and held himself still. But she needed him to move. She needed him hard and deep, pounding into her.

She pressed back on her knees, shoving him farther into her.

"More. Oh, Jax, you're so thick, give me more."

Her cry must have worked. He began long hard strokes into her slick passage. There was nothing teasing or tempting. He was fucking her. Hard.

Just as she'd described in the final interview. Filling her with his cock, letting her know hers was the pussy he wanted to fuck. She dropped down to her elbows and braced herself, pushing back against each thrust. He growled, a sound so animal-like she thought he might howl next. The tiny sting of his teeth against her neck only increased her pleasure.

"Give me your hand," he said, his command barely audible beneath his ragged breath.

His hand collected hers and guided it down to the wet, hot flesh of her sex. He pressed her fingers against her slit. She could feel him moving inside her. "Can you feel that? I love being inside you." He threaded his fingers through hers and touched her clit. "I love riding this tight little cunt." His words added fire. She was close, close to coming. She couldn't stop herself. She had to come.

She spread her fingers to the sides of her clit and began to rub.

"That's it, baby, show me how you do it." His hand left hers and he gripped her hips, pushing harder and deeper into her. "Touch yourself, Kit, come for me, baby, while I fuck your sweet pussy."

She did—rubbing hard, until she couldn't stand it any more and the pleasure was on her. She screamed, burying her face in the couch, her mind gone—lost somewhere in a completely sensual place. Vaguely aware, she felt Jax pound into her three more times. His groan followed quickly on the heels of hers as he tensed, holding himself inside her for a long moment.

They collapsed on to the couch, their bodies bound together.

Kit opened her eyes and saw nothing but burgundy upholstery. She'd done it again. Moments after kissing that stone, she'd seduced Jax. She didn't know if she should feel guilty about it—she was sure the guilt would find her later—but now, she was too exhausted, too worn out to worry about it.

Jax moved, his cock sliding out of her passage. She tried to hide the soft hiss but it escaped. She was going to be sore tomorrow, but she couldn't seem to let go of Jax. She sensed him walk away and heard him go into the bathroom. She turned over and looked up when he returned. His cock was soft and hanging long between his legs. She'd worn him out. For now.

She looked at it and then made her way up to his face. "You are one delicious fuck," she said in a sultry voice. She followed the comment with a visible shiver. "It makes me want more."

She dared him with her eyes. He just smiled in return.

"And that's what you're going to get."

Chapter Five

Kit squirmed beneath the blankets, readjusting until she rediscovered that precise position where she could drift back into her dreamless sleep. The bed moved with her, fitting to her form until it was perfect. She smiled as she snuggled deeper. Her bed was warm and toasty this morning. And furry.

Furry?

Her eyes popped open and stared at the soft hair covering Jax's chest.

It came back to her in an instant. Sex with Jax for the second time in two days. And sex with Jax had led to sleeping practically on top of Jax.

She pushed herself up, trying to ease her body away from his without waking him. She'd successfully avoided their "relationship" discussion last night. She wasn't prepared to start that conversation at—she peeked at the clock—five in the morning.

She had a lot going on this morning and didn't have time for—*five o'clock?!*

"Oh shit!" She launched herself off Jax's chest and leapt from the bed. She took off in a dead run. Her clothes. She needed her clothes. She'd been wearing them when she'd arrived last night but had no idea where they ended up. The circumstances under which they'd been removed were clear in her memory. And that when Jax had carried her to bed both of them had been naked.

"Kit, honey? What's going on?" Jax's bed-warmed voice slowed her steps for a moment and the sexy way he called her honey was almost enough to draw her back to the bedroom. "Oh shit!" Jax shouted. He'd obviously seen the time. "We've got to leave in fifteen minutes."

Kit skidded to a stop in the living room. She looked at the unfamiliar furniture for a moment. She remembered deep burgundy upholstery. She'd had to dig it out from underneath her fingernails at one point. The forest green that covered this sofa didn't fit the one in her memory.

Wait, we weren't on this couch. We were downstairs. With my clothes. She raced down the steps to the studio. The room looked like it had last night when she'd entered. Except for her blouse and Jax's pants thrown haphazardly across the floor. A deep heated flush reminded her of those moments when she'd opened those same trousers and the delicious licking she'd given Jax. Unconsciously, she licked her lips. The tactile sensation sent off residual shocks to her pussy.

Trying to block the images from her head, she found her skirt and dragged the wrinkled mess over her hips. She was stuffing her arms into her shirtsleeves when Jax came down the stairs. His hair stood on end, and the dark shadow of his beard gave him a dangerous appearance she wasn't prepared for. He looked rugged and tough...and weird "mountain man rescuing innocent virgin" fantasies sprung full grown from her head.

The lust and desire had been bad before she'd slept with him, now it was ten, twenty times worse.

"Okay, run home," he said, his mind obviously not in the sexual gutter that hers was. "Shower, change. You've twenty minutes."

"I can't be ready in twenty minutes." She protested walking up the stairs.

"You can do your makeup in the car while I'm driving."

She stopped at the front door. "You're coming with me?"

The tender light in his eyes soothed the lust in her chest and started a different, much more complicated kind of emotion. "You didn't think I'd let you face the wolves alone, did you?" He turned her toward the door and patted her butt. "Now go. I'll be right behind you."

"Thanks." She opened the door and was ready to step outside but stopped. Something just felt wrong. She was forgetting something. Besides her panties and bra. It took a moment to figure out what it was. She couldn't leave like this. She turned around and kissed him.

It wasn't a passionate, tongue-locking kiss like those from the past two nights, but a "good-bye, have a good day" kind of kiss. One that lovers gave when they expected to see each other soon.

He was smiling when she backed away.

"Go, honey. I'll see you in a few minutes."

Her stomach ached with the sweetness in his voice. She ran across the three lawns separating their houses, raced inside and straight to the shower. Her thoughts were jumbled together as she stood beneath the hot water. The speed with which she had to get ready didn't allow her time to focus either on the fact that she'd spent a second night having sex with Jax or that in less than two hours she was going on national television. There was only room in her brain for the actual process of dressing, drying her hair and pulling on clothes. She chose a slim blue skirt and a crisp, high-necked blouse that closed at the top with a matching rose at the collar. She pulled her hair back into an efficient clip in the back of her head.

Taking a bracing breath, she stared into the mirror. Amazing. After being rushed, she looked prim and precise. Controlled. Considering the turmoil inside her body, mind and spirit—it was a pretty good illusion. A knock on the door was followed almost immediately by Jax's call.

"Kit, you ready?"

Smoothing her shirt one final time, she shoved her makeup into a bag, and ran to the living room. A pair of pumps sat by her front door and she slipped into them, pushing her bag into Jax's hands and locking the door.

"How do I look?" she asked breathlessly.

He scanned down her with cool observation. She looked fantastic but that had more to do with the lingering sex in her eyes and the breathless glow in her cheeks.

"You look great. Let's go." Truthfully, she looked a little conservative in the outfit. That was fine with him. He was thrilled that he was the only person who knew she was pure temptation under those clothes.

He glanced at her as they drove off. *You would never know to look at her.* She kept her fire concealed, but when it burned it was scorching. He could still remember the feel of her mouth on his skin. And the seductive groans erupting from her throat. As if she'd loved feeling his cock moving in her mouth.

Kit pulled down the mirror in front of her seat and began applying her makeup. Knowing she had enough to focus on, trying to put on makeup and think about the interview ahead, he kept quiet. They needed to talk about their future. If they had a future. Two nights of great sex did not a relationship make. He knew that. He'd had enough good sex to know that it didn't necessarily lead to anything more meaningful. But with Kit it was different.

For one thing the sex wasn't just good—it was great. Phenomenal. And he liked her. Really liked her. They'd been friends for six months, now they'd just taken it to another level. But where did they go from here? A few months of fucking? Or was it something long-term?

He watched Kit line her lips. Now was probably not a good time to ask that question.

She hadn't wanted to talk last night and he'd been willing to go along with that. They'd had serious work to do. And now, she had to concentrate on getting ready. Running late wasn't going to help her maintain her composure at all. Of course, it wouldn't give her time to get stressed out either.

He drove silently, speeding twenty miles above the limit to get them into the city on time. Kit didn't seem to notice. She applied and then adjusted her makeup. The way she kept fussing, Jax decided she was avoiding him.

He would let it go for now, but soon, they were going to have a conversation.

He pulled into the parking garage and slid into a spot. Kit dragged her makeup bag over her shoulder and joined Jax in running across the parking garage to the studio entrance.

"Things like this don't happen to me," she said as they hit the door.

"You'll be fine."

They signed in and got a visual reprimand from the assistant who met them. With tightly pursed lips, the woman directed them down the hall to the last door on the right. Jax watched Kit closely, checking for any signs of true panic. That final time last night, she'd been relaxed and comfortable in front of the camera. And damn sexy. He hoped she could find that same attitude today—toning down the sex just a little bit.

Her hand quivered as she smoothed her hair. She was starting to think and that would lead to worry. He considered offering soothing words but knew Kit wouldn't want to hear platitudes at this point. He would get her alone for a few minutes before the interview and go through the points one final time, help her focus on what she knew. She would get it. She would be fine.

"Stone! Oh my gosh, what are you doing here?"

He stopped and turned at the feminine cry and was immediately wrapped in a close embrace. The platinum blonde hair bouncing against his cheek revealed the identity faster than her face, which was currently hidden against his neck.

"Jennifer, how are you?" he asked, disengaging himself from her grip. A quick glance at the cool glare in Kit's eyes warned he hadn't pulled back soon enough.

"I'm so good. Are you back in the business? Who are you working for?"

He shook his head and smiled. "I'm still at the university. Still teaching. Jennifer, this is Katharine Bauman. Kit, this is Jennifer Thompson."

Kit tensed, expecting a distinct chill when the woman looked her way. After the way she'd hugged him—more of a full body wrap than a hug—they had to have been more than friends. Instead, Jennifer smiled and offered her hand.

"Of course, you're the author. Nice to have you here." Before Kit could do more than nod, Jennifer rattled off the obviously rehearsed instructions. Kit listened closely, focusing on the mechanics of what to expect so she could ignore the fact that she'd forgotten absolutely everything Jax had taught her last night.

With a perky smile to Kit and a seductive wink to Jax, Jennifer turned away and led them down a short hall to a tiny room. One wall was a huge mirror surrounded in light bulbs. A shallow counter stuck out from the wall.

"Just have a seat," she waved to two cushion chairs in the corner. "And I'll come get you in about—" Jennifer looked at her watch. "Seven minutes." With that she pulled the door shut, isolating them from the busy hallway.

Kit was too wound up to sit so she began to pace. The room was only five feet wide and part of that was counter. It didn't leave her much room before she ran into Jax. She stopped seconds before bumping into him. She couldn't bear to face him. She'd done it again—she'd kissed the stone and ended up dragging Jax off to bed. He was going to ask her about it. She could see that in his eyes.

And within moments, her worse fears were going to be realized. She was going to go into the interview, embarrass herself, and Jax would feel horrible because he hadn't been able to help. It was too much to deal with.

When she bumped into him the second time, she found the courage to look at him.

"Kit, you're going to be fine," he assured her. "Better than fine. You'll be great."

She nodded absently. He had to say those things. He was her friend, her teacher, and her lover. All three relationships required that he be supportive even when they both knew she was going to make a fool of herself in front of millions of people.

Kit smoothed her skirt for the forty-seventh time, then dug her fingers into her thighs, crushing the material in her palms. Her stomach began the flip-flops she knew so well. The panic started to build. Knowing she couldn't let it control her, she reached for her purse. She would kiss the stone. It would give her that boost of confidence she needed. Logic told her there was no way that kissing a rock would allow her to speak better, but logic didn't matter in situations like this.

She dealt with legends and superstitions every day. She knew how they impacted daily life. None of it mattered as she stood there, with minutes to go before she made a fool of herself.

She needed that damn rock. She looked around.

"Where's my purse?"

Jax shrugged. "I don't think you brought it. You didn't have anything with you except your makeup bag when you got in the car."

"What?" The tiny flutters of panic burst forth into waves. "But I have to have my purse."

"Don't worry. I've got money if you need anything."

"No." She grabbed Jax by the collars and pulled him to her face. "I need my purse."

He placed his hands over hers and squeezed gently. "Kit, what is it?"

She opened her mouth to answer, then looked into his clear, intelligent eyes. She couldn't tell him. How did she confess what she'd done? That she'd seduced him by kissing a piece of rock. "Uh—I...I just..."

Jax looked at the door, as if to insure it was closed, then he turned back. There was concern in his eyes.

"Kit, what's wrong?" The serious undertone of his voice wrenched something deep inside her.

She couldn't lie to him.

"You'll think I'm crazy, but I have a piece of rock in my purse. And I need it."

"What? To hold?"

"Uh, no. To kiss." The deep, long blink of his eyes told her Jax was trying to comprehend her statement.

"Huh?"

"You really will think I'm crazy but the other day..." She proceeded to tell him about the little store and the salesman and the piece of rock.

"And you believe this rock is a piece of the Blarney Stone?"

She dropped her hands and spun away. "I told you it was crazy but it worked."

"What worked?"

"The stone. I kissed it and I convinced the dean to increase the budget in the tutoring lab. And last night I kissed it before that last time and you have to admit I did better."

"Kit, you had practiced all evening, that's why you improved, and I'm sure you were well prepared for your meeting with the dean. Neither of those is proof that this rock is a piece of the Blarney Stone."

"There's you." Her voice was soft and sad.

"What?"

"You."

"Now you've lost me."

She sighed and leaned her hip against the makeup counter. "You. Me. Sex. It's all because of that stone. I kissed the rock, Wednesday night. At McGill's. Didn't you notice anything different? I came out of the bathroom and suddenly I'm a…a…I don't know what I was."

"A sex goddess. That's kind of how I pictured you," he said with a teasing smile. Kit wasn't laughing. Her stomach rolled over and she rushed on with her confession.

"See, you did notice it. I kissed that stone and suddenly, I'm saying all these things and dragging you off to bed. Don't you see? That wasn't me. It wasn't you. I seduced you. That's what the Blarney Stone does. It gives you the power to persuade people and I persuaded you to have sex with me."

"Wait." Jax held up his hands and shook his head. "You think that by kissing this stone you were able to convince me to go to bed with you."

"Jax, you never showed any interest in anything more than friendship with me until I kissed that stone. Then, within minutes, you're going down on me in my living room and fucking me against my front door." Her voice naturally dropped to a frantic whisper. "Don't you find that a little suspicious? It was the same thing last night. I kissed the stone and suddenly, we're having sex again." She felt her shoulders droop. "I'm really sorry. I didn't mean to do it. Not really."

"Kit…"

"Well, I mean I did," she corrected, "because I wanted to do all those things but—"

His lips pulled up in an openly reluctant smile.

"Kit," he said again, taking her shoulders in his hands and forcing her to look up at him. "Listen. You didn't seduce me. All those things you said the other night, and last night, yes, they turned me on, but they weren't what persuaded me to sleep with you." She tried to look away but he leaned down until her eyes met his. "To be absolutely honest, if you wanted to fuck me, all you had to do was grunt and crook your finger. I'd have come running."

She couldn't believe what she was hearing.

"But...you never..."

"I've been trying to figure out how to get you into bed for six months, but you seemed so determined to keep us 'just friends', I didn't think I had a chance."

"I didn't seduce you?" A strange combination of disappointment and relief filled her chest.

"No, you seduced me, but it was you. Not some stone you kissed."

She leaned forward, her head falling against his shoulder. His arms wrapped comfortingly around her back.

"I guess that's good."

"Very good."

"But I'm just not sure if I can do this without that rock. It really seemed to help me."

Jax stepped away, forcing her to straighten or fall on her face. She blinked in confusion as she looked up.

"I'll be your Blarney Stone."

That was sweet. She kissed him lightly on the lips. It was nice and for one brief moment it settled the fighting butterflies in her stomach. Then they were back—battling and raging until she was sure she would be sick.

"Thanks." She tried to smile but it didn't work.

"No. We can do this." He placed his hands on the sides of her head. "Close your eyes." His voice was so soothing, she complied and let her eyelids droop down. Without his command, she took a deep breath and felt some of the tension slip from her shoulders. "That's good." He was closer to her. Then she felt the first brush of his mouth against hers. It was light and then more, harder. His hands cupped her hips, pulling her forward until she could almost feel him, sense him just out of reach.

He teased her lips with his tongue and she opened to him. She would take this moment and enjoy it before she went out there and made a fool of herself. With the mental reminder, she pulled back. Jax didn't let her go far.

"No, stay with me. Kiss me." It was the same bedroom voice she'd discovered after hours in his bed. A voice that could lead her into destruction—and she'd be smiling as she went.

She opened her mouth at his silent request and accepted his tongue. Then let herself fall into his kiss, wrapping her arms around his neck and holding on. His hands sank into her hair and the strong massage of his fingers soothed more of her tension. She leaned into him, loving his strength and the hard press of his muscles against her breasts. She ached to feel his mouth on her skin, sucking and licking her nipples the way he'd done the past two nights.

Their hips connected—his growing erection positioned against the apex of her thighs. He rubbed against her, as if searching for the perfect connection. Sexual instincts that had been so well satisfied over the past two days urged her to respond—to ignore the fact that someone could walk in on them—and bring him inside her. She shimmied until he pressed against her clit.

"That's it, baby. Think about how it feels to have my cock inside you."

And she was. Imagining it, dreaming it, almost feeling it.

He leaned farther down, placing hot kisses along her neck, underneath her ear. She turned her head, giving him more access. She forgot where they were or even why they were there. There was no way she could think beyond his kisses. They were too important, too vital. His mouth was hot against her skin, burning her from the inside out. He kissed and licked his way down her throat, his touch light and seductive, drawing her deeper into his spell.

She rolled her head back and let him trail his mouth along her collarbone. His hand gently squeezed her breast. The peaked nipple tingled as it brushed against his palm. If his goal was distracting her, it was definitely working. It was also draining the strength from her legs. In fact, she couldn't quite remember why she'd been so tense in the first place. All that mattered was Jax and his mouth. And those wicked hands.

His kisses wandered across her skin, dipping down deep into her cleavage and licking the warm valley between her breasts. She rubbed against him, wanting a harder touch—on her breast and between her legs. One hand captured her backside and pulled her forward, giving her the pressure she needed.

He straightened and pressed his lips against her ear as he began a slow steady pulse of his cock against her clit.

"When you walk out there…you'll be the confident, sexy woman I know you are." His deep melodious voice sank into her bones, into her flesh. She could almost feel it move through her body. "There is no room in your head for worry. All you'll think about is me. Every time you say the word 'legend'—" he pumped against her, sending a quick tightening into her pussy. "You'll think about my mouth on your cunt, licking you, sucking on your tight little clit. Because when I get you alone, I'm going to lick your cunt, sip all that luscious juice. You're wet, aren't you? Already wet for me."

And she was. She opened her mouth and tried to breathe but it was as if there wasn't enough oxygen.

"You're so delicious." He continued the erotic whisper. "I want more. I'll spend hours with my mouth between your legs, loving you, tasting you, slipping my tongue into your pretty little cunt." She groaned, feeling his words like a million tiny fingers tickling her pussy. "Every time you say the word legend, you'll think of me and what I can do to you. You'll remember how it feels to come against my mouth."

The memory struck her right between the legs.

But his words didn't stop, his voice didn't change. The hypnotic rhythm lulled her. "You'll know that as soon as you're done, I'll take you somewhere and fuck you hard, sliding my cock deep inside you. Hard—just like you like it. You like a deep hard fuck, don't you?" She nodded, trying to gasp out her agreement but unable to find the breath. "After I make you scream, coming around my cock, I'll have you slowly. Riding you deep and long. But we won't stop there. I'll spend hours loving you until you can't scream—you can barely breathe."

The steady rubbing from Jax's erection against her clit increased the pressure until she thought she'd explode.

"Jax, please." *Fuck me.* She didn't speak the words but she knew Jax heard her. Knew he understood her silent plea.

The seductive whisper continued as if she'd never spoken. "Whenever you say the word 'legend', you'll think of me licking your pussy, tongue fucking you, and then fucking you with my cock. You'll feel me deep inside you for days, you'll always remember what it feels like to have my cock inside you." He strung his words together until she couldn't tell where they stopped and started.

He reached between their bodies and placed his fingertip right against her clit.

She gripped his shoulders and held on as every bit of pleasure that had gathered slowly between her legs, exploded and spread through her body.

The door snapped open. "Katherine? Are you ready to go?" Jennifer, the overly friendly stage manager, smiled.

Kit blinked. What was the woman talking about?

She felt Jax's hand on her lower back, gently pushing her toward the door. Unable to focus on anything but the orgasm that released a little more pleasure with each step, she went where he led her.

The bright lights momentarily blinded her as she reached the edge of the set. She stopped and stared blankly at the scene before her. What was she doing here? She wanted to go back inside that room—back to fucking Jax.

He wrapped his arm around her waist and pulled her back against him. The hard press of his erection rubbed against her ass. He held her for a moment as if wanting to insure she felt all of him.

"You'll do great. And remember what I said," he whispered. He gave her hip a gentle squeeze. "Legend."

Kit gasped. Everything Jax had promised came back to her in a flash.

"Let's go," Jennifer said with another smile.

Kit stumbled behind her, following Jennifer's feet across the floor. Halfway across the room, Kit looked up and caught a glimpse of herself in the TV.

Air left her body in a rush. She looked nothing like herself. The confident, professional image she'd left her house with was gone and a sexual creature had taken her place.

Her hair was wild and loose. Three buttons on her blouse were undone and the rose decoration was long gone, lost under Jax's skillful hands. But the material changes were nothing to the blush in her cheeks and the sensual glow in her eyes. Jax had done this to her.

Following blindly, she sat down on the couch as directed. The set reminded her of Jax's living room, and that quickly led to the memory of what had happened on his couch. Her hands shook as she clipped the lapel microphone to her collar and smiled at Nick Bradley, the male anchor for the show. Rampaging nerves exploded in her stomach as Nick looked at her, glanced at the pictures on the book jacket and then back at her. Confusion and curiosity marked his face before he shrugged and flashed her a million wattage smile.

"Stand by," an invisible voice called. "We're back in five, four, three…"

Nick smiled toward a camera in the middle of the room.

"We're here today talking with Katherine Bauman, Co-Author of Living Myths and Legends…"

The word "legend" drove a spike of need into her sex. She placed her hand against her stomach, trying to soothe the ache.

"So, Katherine, how are legends impacting our lives today?"

Legends. I'm going to lick your cunt, sip all that luscious juice.

Her cheeks warmed and she cleared her throat. She wouldn't think about Jax's comments. She quickly processed Nick's question. "Well, we operate so much of our lives out of…" She couldn't say legends. She'd orgasm right there. "Uh, myths. Some of them are common superstitions and some are folk tales but we pass them along whether we know it or not…"

The words she'd practiced last night with Jax seemed to flow from her tongue. *Focus on the message. Make your point. Stop talking.*

Nick nodded with what appeared to be real interest.

"So what sort of legends do we see in our day to day lives? Give me an example of a legend we might run into."

Damn. There was that word again.

I'll take you somewhere and fuck you hard, sliding my cock deep inside you. Hard—just like you like it. You like a deep hard fuck, don't you?

"Yes," she sighed then she laughed. Nick's bright white smile flashed in response. "Well, for instance, getting worms from cookie dough. It's a myth passed down from my mother. When you think about it, there isn't anything in raw cookie dough to give you worms."

"So, it's just a tale to stop kids from eating raw cookie dough before it gets baked?"

Kit chuckled. The sound was raw and husky. "Not necessarily. It has a purpose. Raw eggs can be dangerous, so yes, you can get sick. That's one of the basic legends…" *I'll spend hours with my mouth between your legs, loving you, tasting you, slipping my tongue into your pretty little pussy.* She swallowed and tried to continue her sentence. "…that infiltrates our daily life but probably had some basis in necessity."

"Tell me about some urban legends. Those seem to be the ones that terrify us."

"Yes, we see a lot of those particularly in the days of the Internet."

Kit let the words flow out of her mouth. She knew she was speaking and was pleased to hear she sounded like she was making sense. But it seemed so distant to what was happening in her body—in her thoughts. Everything Jax had described appeared in her head.

Jax, moving inside her. Long deep thrusts. His mouth sucking on her nipples and licking her sex. The warm caress of his voice across her skin. She needed him. Soon.

"Well, Katherine, we're out of time but I want to thank you for coming here today. The book is called

"Living Myths and Legends" and if the book is half as entertaining as its author, it should be a very interesting read indeed. We'll be back right after this."

The room froze for one moment in time. Then the voice cried, "Clear!" from the corner. "Three minutes in break."

Nick leaned forward. "Katherine, that was a delightful interview." His eyes flickered downward to her breasts and Kit knew her nipples were pressing against her shirt. "It was a *pleasure* to meet you." It was supposed to be a seductive tease but Kit just nodded. She had to find Jax.

Jennifer returned to collect her and led her back across the set. Jax stood just off to the side. When Kit saw him there she didn't know whether to deck him—or jump him. He took the decision from her when he pulled her into his arms.

"You were great." He hugged her close, giving her a quick, friendly squeeze before stepping back. "Excellent."

"Katherine, you did very well." Jennifer waved as she walked by. "Stone, it was great to see you again. Just follow the blue hallway and you'll find your way out."

Energy pumped through her veins as she followed Jax out of the building. Success built on the lust that Jax had inspired until Kit felt incandescent with all the power flowing through her. They walked into the parking garage and Kit decided she couldn't stand it any more. She stepped in front of Jax, wrapped her arms around his neck and slammed her mouth into his.

His energy seemed to match hers. He grabbed her and pulled her body to his, positioning himself hard against the apex of her thighs. They stood, locked in long, hot kisses. Finally, Kit dragged her head back.

"How fast can you get us home?" she asked.

Jax laughed and grabbed her hand pulling her the rest of the way to the car.

While he'd gone twenty miles over the speed limit to get there, he went almost thirty on the return. The trip was silent. Kit couldn't find the words. She was almost afraid to speak. She didn't have the stone so she didn't have the sexy words and despite what he'd said, she knew that played a huge part in their getting together.

He pulled into his driveway and they both scrambled out. The drive back hadn't killed her ardor. It had only increased.

Jax held the door open and indicated she should enter first. She expected him to drag her upstairs. Instead, they stopped inside the entryway and Jax took her hands in his and held them between their bodies. He seemed so serious that Kit started to worry.

"Jax, what is it?"

He hesitated then finally spoke. "You said you kissed that stone both nights before we made love."

She nodded.

"So, do you think the stone made you want to make love with me?"

"You don't believe in the stone," she said, shaking her head.

"No, but you do. Do you think this stone is some kind of magic rock that makes you want to sleep with me?"

"What? How could you think that?"

"The same reasons you thought you'd seduced me. You've never indicated any interest in sleeping with me or changing our relationship from just friends, and then you kiss this rock, and the next thing I know, you're all over me. So, did that rock somehow make you horny?"

Her mouth fell open as she looked at him. "Jax, I didn't think you'd have any interest in sleeping with me." Her upper lip curled upward. "I'm still not really sure why you are." He started to speak and she held up a hand to stop him. "No, let me say this. I've been attracted to you, *lusting* after you, since day one. I think kissing the stone just gave me confidence to say and do all the things I've wanted to before."

She waited, not sure what his reaction would be.

Finally, he nodded. "Well, I just want to make sure you're not going to need to pull out that rock every time we want to have sex."

Her smile turned into a grin and then a laugh. "Oh, don't worry. I don't need any inspiration besides you."

His lips squeezed together like he was pondering that concept. If she hadn't seen a hint of laughter in his eyes, she would have worried. But he seemed resolved with the stone issue. Now, he was just messing with her. Finally he nodded. "I see. Well, why don't we test it?"

"Test what?"

"Test whether you need that stone to want me." He opened his arms wide. "I'm here." The taunting glint in his eyes made her step forward. "Show me you'll seduce me without that stone."

There was a dare in his eyes and no way was she going to let him get away with that. Jax had said the stone hadn't seduced him—now was her chance to prove it. For both of them.

With a confidence she hadn't expected to find in herself, she grabbed the edges of her blouse and gave it a quick tug. The buttons snapped off and flung far and wide, clicking as they struck the walls.

"Remember what you said to me before I went on the air?" She took a step forward, reaching for the placket of his shirt. She gave it a sharp tug and snapped the buttons off as well. Jax just smiled, daring her to continue. "It worked. Every time I said the word 'legend' I thought about you. Fucking me. Loving me." She reached up and cupped her breasts, thinly protected by her lace bra. "I thought about your mouth on my skin, licking me." She placed her hands on his chest and skimmed them downward, not stopping until she cupped his growing cock in her palms. "I thought about how thick you feel inside me and that slow, steady thrust." She massaged his cock and watched the pleasure reflected in his eyes. Her pussy contracted in response. She was wet and aching, hungry for this man. "The deep, hard penetration." She groaned at the memory and reached up, slipping one hand inside her open blouse to caress her nipple. She needed him. It had been hours since she'd held him inside her and it was way too long.

She pushed him up against the wall and placed her mouth on his. He instantly took control of the kiss. Kit allowed it for a few seconds before she pulled back and stepped away, her blouse fluttering around her arms.

"Do you want me?"

Jax nodded. She took one step up the stairs.

"You want to fuck me?"

Again, he nodded and this time he followed as she moved up one more stair.

"How badly?" she teased, taking another step away. "How badly do you want to be inside my pussy?" She lured him up the stairs and into the bedroom, almost making it to the bed before his control broke and he dragged her to the floor, stripped off the remainder of her clothes, and drove his cock into her.

After the verbal foreplay and mental seduction of the morning, Kit was ready to explode. She came almost immediately. Jax followed with a groan moments later.

Kit loved the feel of his heavy weight on top of her and she hated to disturb him but reality and hope for their future forced her to move.

"We have to go downstairs."

Jax raised his head and squinted at her like she'd gone insane. "Now?" Though he asked it with a disgruntled tone, he was already rolling off her.

"Yes, now."

He stalled a few seconds to clean up and pull on some clothes before Kit could convince him to come with her.

"Come on, I want to show you this rock. See what you think of it."

"Kit, it's not important."

"I want you to see how this stone works."

She practically dragged him down the stairs to his mock set. Her bra and panties still lay on the floor. She ignored them and picked up her purse. After long moments of digging in the bag, she growled in frustration.

"It's gone."

"The rock?"

"Yes. It was here in my bag. Last night. And now it's gone."

"Kit, don't worry." He spun her around until she looked into his eyes. "You don't need that piece of rock. Trust me, if you want hot sex..." He waited for a beat, then smiled. "You've just got to keep kissing Stone."

About the author:

Tielle (pronounced "teal") St. Clare has had life-long love of romance novels. She began reading romances in the 7th grade when she discovered Victoria Holt novels and began writing romances at the age of 16 (during Trigonometry, if the truth be told). During her senior year in high school, the class dressed up as what they would be in twenty years—Tielle dressed as a romance writer.

When not writing romances, Tielle has worked in public relations and video production for the past 20 years. She moved to Alaska when she was seven years old in 1972 when her father was transferred with the military. Tielle believes romances should be hot and sexy with a great story and fun characters.

Tielle welcomes mail from readers. You can write to her c/o Ellora's Cave Publishing at 1337 Commerce Drive, Suite 13, Stow OH 44224.

Also by Tielle St. Clare

Simon's Bliss

Shadow of the Dragon: Dragon's Kiss

Just One Night

Close Quarters

Ellora's Cavemen: Tales from the Temple II

Shadow of the Dragon: Dragon's Fire

Shadow of the Dragon: Dragon's Rise

Why an electronic book?

We live in the Information Age—an exciting time in the history of human civilization in which technology rules supreme and continues to progress in leaps and bounds every minute of every hour of every day. For a multitude of reasons, more and more avid literary fans are opting to purchase e-books instead of paperbacks. The question to those not yet initiated to the world of electronic reading is simply: *why?*

1. *Price.* An electronic title at Ellora's Cave Publishing runs anywhere from 40-75% less than the cover price of the <u>exact same title</u> in paperback format. Why? Cold mathematics. It is less expensive to publish an e-book than it is to publish a paperback, so the savings are passed along to the consumer.
2. *Space.* Running out of room to house your paperback books? That is one worry you will never have with electronic novels. For a low one-time cost, you can purchase a handheld computer designed specifically for e-reading purposes. Many e-readers are larger than the average handheld, giving you plenty of screen room. Better yet, hundreds of titles can be stored within your new library—a single microchip. (Please note that Ellora's Cave does not endorse any specific brands. You can check our website at www.ellorascave.com for customer recommendations we make available to new consumers.)

3. *Mobility.* Because your new library now consists of only a microchip, your entire cache of books can be taken with you wherever you go.
4. *Personal preferences are accounted for.* Are the words you are currently reading too small? Too large? Too...**ANNOYING**? Paperback books cannot be modified according to personal preferences, but e-books can.
5. *Innovation.* The way you read a book is not the only advancement the Information Age has gifted the literary community with. There is also the factor of what you can read. Ellora's Cave Publishing will be introducing a new line of interactive titles that are available in e-book format only.
6. *Instant gratification.* Is it the middle of the night and all the bookstores are closed? Are you tired of waiting days—sometimes weeks—for online and offline bookstores to ship the novels you bought? Ellora's Cave Publishing sells instantaneous downloads 24 hours a day, 7 days a week, 365 days a year. Our e-book delivery system is 100% automated, meaning your order is filled as soon as you pay for it.

Those are a few of the top reasons why electronic novels are displacing paperbacks for many an avid reader. As always, Ellora's Cave Publishing welcomes your questions and comments. We invite you to email us at service@ellorascave.com or write to us directly at: 1337 Commerce Drive, Suite 13, Stow OH 44224.

Discover for yourself why readers can't get enough of the multiple award-winning publisher Ellora's Cave. Whether you prefer e-books or paperbacks, be sure to visit EC on the web at www.ellorascave.com for an erotic reading experience that will leave you breathless.

WWW.ELLORASCAVE.COM

Printed in the United States
30771LVS00001B/46-489